LEMON DROP
DEAD

LEMON DROP DEAD

Amanda Flower

KENSINGTON
PUBLISHING CORP.

www.kensingtonbooks.com

KENSINGTON BOOKS are published by

Kensington Publishing Corp.
119 West 40th Street
New York, NY 10018

All Kensington titles, imprints, and distributed lines are available at special quantity discounts for bulk purchases for sales promotion, premiums, fund-raising, educational, or institutional use.

Special book excerpts or customized printings can also be created to fit specific needs. For details, write or phone the office of the Kensington Sales Manager: Attn.: Sales Department. Kensington Publishing Corp., 119 West 40th Street, New York, NY 10018. Phone: 1-800-221-2647.

The K logo is a trademark of Kensington Publishing Corp.

First Printing: May 2021
ISBN-13: 978-1-4967-2204-1
ISBN-10: 1-4967-2204-3

ISBN-13: 978-1-4967-2207-2 (ebook)
ISBN-10: 1-4967-2207-8 (ebook)

10 9 8 7 6 5 4 3 2 1

Printed in the United States of America

For Kimra Bell

ACKNOWLEDGMENTS

I am always grateful to return to Harvest. And even more grateful for you, Dear Readers, who want to travel there with me. Whether you read the Amish Candy Shop series, the Amish Matchmaker series, or both, thank you. Readers are the ones who keep series alive.

Thanks as always to my super agent Nicole Resciniti and my awesome editor Alicia Condon. I'm so grateful to be working with the two of you for so long.

Thanks, too, to Kimra Bell for her help with my manuscripts and to my guy, David Seymour, who hears every version of the plot from the ridiculous to the fully formed. And to my amazing friends who cheer me on.

Love to my family, and always, gratitude to my Lord in heaven for allowing me to make a living off what I love to do most.

CHAPTER ONE

The front door of Swissmen Sweets swung inward, causing the large shop window to rattle in its frame and the shelves holding jars of jelly beans, caramels, and gumdrops to shake. The noise made me jump. It was late afternoon, and I stood alone, sweeping under the three café tables at the front of the shop where customers could rest while waiting for their candy orders or visit with friends and neighbors while enjoying one of our sweet treats.

The shop would close soon. I looked forward to locking up for the night. My boyfriend, Aiden Brody, had promised me a date night that evening. They were hard to come by for us. We both had crazy work schedules. He was a deputy at the Sheriff's Department, and I was constantly juggling my duties at Swissmen Sweets, the Amish candy shop I ran with my grandmother in Harvest,

Ohio, with the responsibilities of my cable television show, *Bailey's Amish Sweets,* which filmed in New York City. It was rare that neither of us had an obligation. Sadly, I had a feeling my night off was about to disappear when Aiden's mother walked through the door.

I stepped behind the domed-glass counter. "Good afternoon, Juliet. What can I do for you?"

Juliet Brook stood on the other side of the counter beaming from ear to ear. From past experience, I took the giant smile as a bad sign.

On this mild May evening, she wore a green and blue polka-dotted blouse over black trousers and black-and-white high heels. Her blond hair was smoothed back into a French twist. Polka dots were her style statement, from her clothes to the black-and-white, polka-dotted potbellied pig she held under her arm. Jethro stared at me in bewilderment as if to ask how he had gotten there and what on earth was happening. Granted, the little bacon bundle had that expression on his pudgy face ninety percent of the time. Until recently, Juliet had toted Jethro, who was roughly the size of a toaster, just about everywhere she went.

But in the last several months since she had married Reverend Brook, the pastor of the large white church on the other side of the village square, she had been carrying Jethro around a lot less often. At least when it came to church functions where she was working in her capacity as pastor's wife. Those times when she needed to concentrate on her church duties and could not focus on making sure Jethro wasn't knocking over the church altar, she dropped Jethro off with her favorite pig sitter . . . *me.*

Now, I didn't ask for or want the title of go-to pig sitter for Jethro or any other pig, but Juliet had got it in her head that I was the person for the job ever since I had saved the little pig from an untimely death a couple of years back. Because of that, she believed that Jethro and I had a special bond. I wasn't nearly as convinced. So, when she waltzed into Swissmen Sweets late that afternoon, I had every reason to believe that Jethro was being pawned off on me again.

"Bailey! Bailey! Is it true? Is it true?" Juliet cried in a breathless voice.

I placed the stack of receipts I was checking against my accounts on the counter. "Is what true, Juliet?"

"Emily!" she cried.

"What about Emily?"

"Oh, for goodness' sake, Bailey, you know what I mean. Emily is having a baby! A baby! Can you believe it! It's a miracle. I love babies so much." She gave me a quick glance. "You know I have great dreams of being a grandmother. Can you imagine me as a grandma? I would be the very best." She held Jethro up above the counter so that I had a better view of his face. "Think of how well I treat Jethro."

I wasn't sure how I felt about Juliet comparing a future grandchild to her comfort pig.

When Jethro grunted, she lowered the pig. "Jethro is a good support to me as I wait for that happy day, if it ever comes." She stared at me from under her lashes.

It took all my willpower not to grunt back in frustration. Over the last several years, Juliet had made it no secret that she would love to see her only child, Aiden, settled down with a wife and family. Because I was Aiden's girlfriend, I was certain that she saw me as part of the holdup.

Juliet seemed to ignore the fact that Aiden and I weren't

married, and we had only been officially dating for a year and a half. I thought our relationship was moving along nicely. Juliet begged to differ and, despite the lack of proposal or ring, considered us engaged. She had great and outspoken hopes for a summer wedding this year, but seeing how it was May and we weren't yet engaged, those hopes would go unfulfilled.

Both Aiden and I wanted to get married, and we'd been talking about it privately with more and more frequency, but our schedules made it difficult to even fathom a wedding. I just didn't know how I would plan a wedding with all of my other responsibilities for Swissmen Sweets' expanding business and *Bailey's Amish Sweets*. The show had me flying to New York to do promotion or filming every three months. And my calendar wasn't the only problem. Aiden worked long hours as a sheriff's deputy. As the second in command to a grumpy and disengaged sheriff, he had to shoulder much of the workload and administrative duties required to keep the department running smoothly.

A little part of me—okay, a *giant* part—wanted to elope, but I knew Juliet would never forgive us if we did that. Aiden was her only son and her golden boy. She wanted to be there for the wedding. I was pretty sure she wanted Jethro to walk me down the aisle, too.

"Yes, I know Emily's expecting," I said. "The baby is due next month. It's not been a secret. Everyone at Swissmen Sweets is so happy for her."

Emily Keim was one of my shop assistants. She was a young Amish wife who'd married Christmas tree farmer Daniel Keim a year ago. The young couple was expecting their first child in July. Actually, it would be Daniel's first child, but not Emily's. I was certain Juliet knew nothing about Emily's history as a mother, and I planned to keep it that way.

"I can't believe I'm just hearing about the baby. I know I've been very caught up in the church. You would not believe all the responsibilities I have as the pastor's wife, but I'm determined to be the very best and make Reverend Brook proud."

I smiled. There was something endearing and old-fashioned about the fact that Juliet still called her husband Reverend Brook even though they were married. "No one would doubt for a second that you are the perfect pastor's wife."

She blushed, and then asked, "What are you going to do about Emily's baby?"

"What am *I* going to do about it?" I asked. As far as I knew, there was nothing I could or should do about Emily's baby.

"Aren't you going to have a baby shower? She needs a baby shower! You have to host a baby shower."

I held up my hand to stop her. I thought if she said "baby shower" one more time, my head might explode.

Juliet didn't take the hint. "You're the perfect person to put it on. You're so organized and do such a good job planning events. Why, we can't think of a better person."

I thought Juliet was laying the compliments on a little thick. And for her, that was saying something. "*We*?"

"Well, the village of course. But mostly Margot and me. We were discussing it this afternoon when we were tending the church garden. Springtime does mean flowers, don't you know."

I did know.

"The shower will be a great way to build relations between the church, the English community, and the Amish in Harvest. As the pastor's wife, I see community relations as an essential part of my work." She smiled.

She set Jethro on the floor. As soon as she did, the shop's orange cat, Nutmeg, crawled out from under the candy shelves next to the café tables in the front of the shop. It was his favorite place to hide when he needed a little alone time. The pig and cat touched noses and then started to walk around the front room like the old friends they were.

"So are you going to do it?" Juliet asked. "You have to recognize that this is an opportunity for the whole village to come together and celebrate Emily's baby, as well as the community we all share."

"Juliet, I'm pretty sure the Amish don't have baby showers. At least not the kind you're imagining. I'd have to ask my grandmother for sure. Emily and the Keim family wouldn't want to do anything that was against Amish customs. That would hurt English-Amish relations, not help them."

"How could a baby shower be against Amish customs?"

It was a fair question, but since moving to Ohio's Amish Country I had learned that not all the Plain People's rules made sense. At least they didn't make sense to a New Yorker's mind.

"This is the twenty-first century." Juliet waved her arms. "Even the Amish have changed with the times. Goodness, do you know how many Amish have cell phones nowadays or know how to use a computer? Surely Bishop Yoder would be open to Emily's having a baby shower. I mean, it only seems right to me. There's no harm in it."

"The Amish who have access to those pieces of technology are allowed to use them because it's necessary for their work. It'd be very difficult for them to run their businesses without access to a cell phone or a computer. That's just what it takes to run a business in the English world. We can't make the claim that a baby shower is work-related."

She put her hands on her hips. "We have to do something for Emily. Goodness knows, her sister won't do anything."

I winced at this comment, mostly because it was all too true. Emily and her older sister, Esther, hadn't spoken to each other since Emily got married and stopped working at the family's pretzel shop last year. Yet they saw each other almost every day, which made it especially awkward. Emily worked part-time for me at the candy shop, which just happened to be next door to her family's shop, Esh Family Pretzels, where Esther worked as the sole employee and spent every waking moment of her day.

Jethro put his snout to the floor and followed a scent until he found my large white rabbit, Puff, curled up asleep in the corner of the front room. He snuffled the rabbit, and Nutmeg swatted him away. Puff yawned and scooted over, making room for the small pig, which wasn't that much bigger than the rabbit. It seemed to me that I would have to put Puff on a diet. Who knew a bunny could grow so plump just eating vegetables.

"Honestly, Juliet, I do like your idea. I had even toyed with the possibility of throwing Emily a small shower myself. We want to celebrate her baby at Swissmen Sweets, but I stopped myself because I wasn't sure it was what Emily would want. She is a very shy person. I'm not sure she would like all the attention. It's really up to Emily to decide if she'd like a party. I don't want to do anything that might embarrass her in front of her Amish district."

"It could be a surprise." Juliet's eyes were bright.

I wrinkled my nose. I knew from experience Emily wasn't one for surprises. "Let me ask her, and then we can take it from there."

"Ask her now!" She clasped her hands in front of her chest. There was nothing Juliet loved more than a party. She had hoped to celebrate a wedding this year, and maybe this baby shower would fill the void. I also knew that she was sincere in wanting to improve Amish and English relations in her capacity as pastor's wife. If anyone could do it, it was Juliet with her positive outlook and enthusiasm.

"Emily's already gone home for the day, but I'll ask her at the first opportunity tomorrow," I promised.

"We can go to the Christmas tree farm and ask." Juliet's eyes were bright.

"Let's not be too hasty. If you and I roll up to the farm, she'll think something's wrong. Give me one day to ask her."

She pressed her lips together as if she wasn't so keen on this idea. Then she sighed. "I suppose I can wait," she said. Her Carolina drawl was more pronounced when she was disappointed. "You need to ask her quickly, though, because Margot has already reserved the square for the shower this Saturday. We thought two in the afternoon would be the perfect time."

Ah, so that was the crux of it, but just to be clear, I asked, "Margot already reserved the square?"

"She had to. You know how busy the square can be

this time of year." She clapped her hands. "Jethro, it's time to go."

The pig lifted his head but didn't move from the spot where he was cuddled up with the cat and rabbit. They made an odd trio. My best friend, Cass Calbera, who was the head chocolatier at JP Chocolates in New York, insisted the three animals needed their own social media platform. I hoped that she never mentioned the idea to Juliet because she'd be all over that. Juliet already thought Jethro was a star. He'd appeared on several episodes of *Bailey's Amish Sweets*, and ever since his cameos, Juliet thought he needed his own talent agent. If you asked Juliet, he was right up there with Babe and Porky Pig when it came to notable swine.

Juliet marched over to the pig and scooped him up. At the door, she paused. "Don't delay on asking Emily, Bailey King. She needs a shower. The poor girl has been through so much. She deserves all the happiness we can give her."

She would have no argument from me on that point.

After Juliet and Jethro went through the front door, I closed and locked it behind them. I looked down at the cat and rabbit still snuggled together in the corner of the room. "Dollars to donuts we're hosting another party."

Nutmeg meowed as if to say, "You sure are!"

CHAPTER TWO

The next morning, the shop was busy. The more the popularity of *Bailey's Amish Sweets* grew, the busier our shop and the village of Harvest became. We were now on the routes of the major tour buses that drove through Holmes County. Before the show, Harvest had been largely ignored by the big tour companies driving through the county. The buses passed by Harvest for the better-known towns of Sugarcreek and Berlin. My television show changed all that. Now Harvest was on the map, and there was no going back. However, not everyone was happy with the increased tourist traffic.

May was just the beginning of the tourist season in Holmes County, and there were already signs of short tempers and aggravation at the changes. Of course, the shopkeepers loved the extra business. All the local businesses were doing better than they had a year ago. Swissmen Sweets' sales had doubled. Our biggest challenge was keeping up with the public's demand for more, more, more. More chocolates, more milk chocolate and white chocolate pig-shaped Jethro bars, more fudge. Community planner Margot Rawlings loved the crowds my show brought to Harvest.

On the flip side, the village council was receiving increasing complaints about traffic and congestion around the square, especially on Saturday afternoons. Ruth Yoder, wife of the bishop of the largest Amish district in the area and the district my grandmother belonged to, made a point of complaining about the changes to anyone who would listen. She was also quick to place the blame squarely on my shoulders, claiming Harvest had been a much sleepier, quieter Amish village before I arrived. She wasn't wrong.

I understood her concern. As great as the foot traffic was for the businesses downtown, I knew Harvest's sleepy, quiet reputation stood at risk. Some members of the community were loath to lose it.

When I finally saw a lull in customers at mid-morning, I told my grandmother I was headed into the kitchen to check in with Charlotte and Emily. As of yet, I hadn't told Emily about Juliet's idea of a baby shower.

If I didn't tell her soon, Juliet or Margot would move ahead. Emily needed to be warned, because this baby shower would happen with her blessing or not. I was sure of that.

"*Gut*," *Maami* said. "Make sure that Emily is not working too hard." She shook the spatula she was holding at me. "But don't tell her I said that. She is very sensitive right now about receiving special treatment."

I nodded. Emily's aversion to special treatment didn't bode well for her reaction to the baby shower.

Inside the kitchen, I found Emily and Charlotte sitting on stools next to the giant stainless steel island in the middle of the room. One by one, they moved chocolate-dipped cherries from the wax paper, where the cherries were left to dry, to candy trays for display inside the front glass counter.

Emily worked one-handed. Her other hand was pressed into her back.

I winced. "Emily, are you in pain? Maybe we should get you a chair to support your back."

She placed another cherry on the tray. "Don't you start, too, Bailey King! It's bad enough my husband is treating me like a fragile flower. I won't take the same at work." She blew a honey-blond lock of hair that had come loose from the tight bun on the nape of her neck out of her blue eyes. "It is so aggravating. Last evening, Daniel followed me around the house with a pillow and blanket as if I was a child who would fall to the floor at a moment's notice. I finally had to ask Grandma Leah to intervene."

I chuckled. Grandma Leah was Daniel's ninety-something great-grandmother. She was a spunky, no-nonsense Amish woman who still did a few chores around the Christmas tree farm. She also gave out advice like Amish kettle corn to anyone who would listen and some to those who wouldn't listen, too. I suspected she had choice words to say to Daniel about how he was treating his wife. Grandma Leah didn't abide coddling.

"I've told her to take it easy, too, Bailey," Charlotte said. "And she gave me the same warning."

I winked at my red-headed cousin.

"I'm much stronger than everyone thinks," Emily said with an uncharacteristic edge to her voice.

"Charlotte, can you give us a minute?" I asked. "There was just a big bus tour in the shop, and I'm sure *Maami* could use your help restocking the display counter. Those cherries would look great out front. Can you take the tray in to her?"

Charlotte gave me a curious look, and I knew she wanted to ask me what was going on. Typically, I didn't have anything to say to my shop assistants that they both weren't allowed to hear. Despite her expression, Charlotte didn't question me but took the tray through the swinging door that separated the kitchen from the rest of the shop.

I perched on the stool Charlotte had vacated and let out a sigh of relief. After such a busy morning, it was nice to be off my feet.

Emily continued her task of moving the chocolate-covered cherries to the tray. "Bailey, is everything all right?"

"Everything is great." I got up and washed my hands in the stainless steel sink at the back of the kitchen, then pulled on a pair of gloves. I sat back down on the stool and started filling another tray with the cherries. The urge to pop one into my mouth was great. They looked delicious. You'd think with all the time I spent around chocolate and sugar, I would have lost my taste for it. But I never have. My love of sweets was as strong as ever.

She eyed me. "Then why did you ask Charlotte to leave the kitchen?"

"Because I wanted to ask you a question in private." I smiled. "And I didn't want Charlotte's natural enthusiasm to influence you either way. It's your decision."

Her eyes went wide. I had always thought Emily could be a stand-in for a Disney princess with her big beautiful eyes. Her eyes became even larger when she was surprised or concerned.

"It's nothing bad," I said quickly. "I promise. It's actually something really fun. Or, at least I hope you'll think so."

"Bailey, you're making me nervous."

I set two more cherries on the tray and wiped my hand on a paper towel. "Okay, I'll just spit it out. Juliet and Margot had the idea of throwing you a baby shower this Saturday on the square. They wanted it to be a surprise, but I told them I'd have to ask you first. Everyone at Swissmen Sweets would help, and I'm sure the ladies of the district would also want to be involved."

She blinked back tears. "You all want to throw a party for *me*?"

I smiled. "We do. I know it's last minute, but we can pull it together. We've planned much bigger events with a lot less time."

"I—I don't know if I deserve a party."

My mouth fell open. "Why would you say that?"

She placed a hand on her stomach for a brief second as if she felt a kick. "Don't *Englischers* usually throw these sorts of parties for the first babies only?"

"Some do," I admitted. "But there are no hard-and-fast rules. There are no rules at all."

"But this isn't my first child." She whispered this so quietly I almost didn't hear her.

"I know . . ." I trailed off. When Emily was younger, she'd fallen in love and had a child out of wedlock. In secret, she put her first child up for adoption. I knew her story because it had been tied to a murder I'd solved not long after I came to Amish Country. But I'd never told another soul what I knew about my young friend.

"So it's not right to have a shower for me. I would not feel right about it."

I thought for a moment. I wanted to tread lightly on this subject. In many ways, Emily still hadn't forgiven herself. The fact that her sister, Esther, and her brother, Abel, were still angry at her about it made it worse. They refused to forgive her for what she had done, because it threatened their reputation in the Amish community. Emily knew how her brother and sister felt, and she had never completely forgiven herself either, even after moving away from her cruel siblings. Even after marrying a kind and gentle Amish man who loved her dearly. Even after all this time.

After a moment, I added, "Everyone in the village loves you and Daniel. They want to celebrate with you."

"I—I don't know. What would the church elders and the bishop think?" She licked her lips. "I've worked so hard to earn back my good standing with the district. I don't want people to think I am . . ." She trailed off as if she couldn't find the right word.

"Think you're what?"

"That I'm ignoring my mistake. That I forgot what I did." Tears in her eyes, she lowered her voice. "That I forgot my daughter."

"Oh, Emily," I said. "No one would think that. I didn't even know that anyone in the district knew about the baby."

"Not many do, but my sister knows, and she will think the idea of a party is wrong."

What I wanted to say was that Esther Esh thought the idea of *any* party at *any* time was wrong. I'd never met such a severe Amish woman. As far as she was concerned, there was no joy in life, just work. It was a hard way to live for her and the people around her.

"Emily, I know you care about your sister's opinion, but you have to remember that she hasn't been kind to you. You need to take her reaction with a grain of salt."

She moved more cherries and didn't say anything.

"How old would your daughter be today?"

"Six." Emily didn't meet my gaze. "I think about her all the time, but since I've been expecting this new child, I have thought about her more and more." She placed a hand on her stomach again. "I'm so happy about this child. I truly am. And Daniel is blissfully happy about being a father." She smiled. "He's terrified by the idea, too." Her face fell again. "But it makes me think about everything that I gave up."

"The choices you made in the past should not be your prison. You did what you felt was right for your daughter."

She didn't say anything to this.

"If you want, I could ask *Maami* to speak to the bishop for you about the shower. Or Grandma Leah could. She has no trouble talking to anyone, not even the bishop."

She looked at me with tears in her eyes. "No matter what they say, I don't deserve this kindness."

"Emily, I'm sure this pregnancy brings back painful memories, but you must learn to forgive yourself. You chose the best option you had at the time." I held a cherry by its stem, and it twirled back and forth in the air. "I think every choice is like that, especially life-changing ones. When you have to choose, you make the best decision you can with the information you have at the time. Then you move forward." I set the cherry next to the others on the tray.

She glanced at the closed door separating the kitchen from the front of the shop. "I've been dreaming about her. I woke up crying the other night, and Daniel asked me what was wrong."

"What did you tell him?"

"That I'd had a bad dream and to go back to sleep."

"He knows about your daughter, doesn't he?"

She nodded. "I knew it was important to tell him before we married. I told him when we were courting, and we've never spoken of it again."

I wasn't sure not talking about her first child was the best idea, but the Amish weren't ones to speak of difficult things. Not even with the people closest to them.

"If it's bothering you so much—" I paused, unsure if I should mention the idea that had come to mind. I took a deep breath. "Have you ever thought of looking for her?"

She stared at me. "How could I? I don't know where she is."

"But do you know the family that adopted her? Could you find out through the adoption agency?"

"It wouldn't be possible." She shook her head. "There was no adoption agency. I don't know where she went or how to find her."

"You didn't sign anything when the baby was born?" I asked.

"Sign anything? I don't know what you mean. The baby was just gone. My sister told me she went to a *gut* Amish family who wanted a child and lived far away. That's all I know."

I chewed on my lower lip. In the *Englisch* world, such an adoption would be illegal. But in the Amish world, Emily's baby would have been born without a birth certificate. A child could be taken without any legal record of her existence or her birth mother. It made me ill to think of it. All the red tape required by a legal adoption was to ensure the child was going to a safe place. Without it, children could be put in horrible situations.

"Would Esther know who adopted the baby?" I asked.

She looked me in the eye. "If she does, we both know she'd never tell me."

My shoulders drooped because I knew that was true.

"I'm not wishing to find the child. My sister promised me she went to a loving home. I have to believe her. I just don't want to do anything that would make it seem my first child doesn't matter." Tears came to her eyes. "Because she does. I pray for her every day."

"Anyone who knows you would never think that." I reached across the island and squeezed her arm.

"I don't think the baby shower is a *gut* idea."

I grimaced. "I can see why you would think that way, and you have made a very good point. Unfortunately, Margot has already reserved the square for Saturday. I'm afraid that the baby shower will go on whether you want it to or not. Trying to stop Margot and Juliet from organizing a party is like trying to stop a moving train."

She sighed. "And do you want to have this baby shower?"

I nodded. "I do, and so do a whole host of other people in the village because we all love you, Emily."

She chewed on her lip. "All right. I'll do it for you." She smiled. "And because Margot won't give me another option. The shower sounds very nice. I don't think I've ever had a party just for me before. I feel spoiled that you want to do this, and honored and surprised that Juliet and Margot came up with the idea."

"You deserve to be spoiled. Everyone does now and again. Does Saturday on the square work for you? I sure hope so, because that's when it's happening."

She nodded. "But that's not much time to organize a party."

I waved away her concern. "Let Juliet, Margot, and me worry about that."

"*Danki*, Bailey. You've done so much for me over the last several years. I could never repay you."

I smiled. "Then it's a good thing repayment is never required between friends."

"We are having a shower!" The kitchen door swung in, and Charlotte bounced into the room holding an empty candy tray.

CHAPTER THREE

Charlotte set the tray on the island. "I've always wanted to plan a party like this. Oh, please let me do it!" She clapped her hands together.

Emily's face turned pale. I knew what she was thinking. She wondered how long Charlotte had been listening to our conversation. I wondered the same. Daniel, I, and a few other people knew about Emily's first child, but Charlotte was not one of those select few.

"Charlotte, were you listening at the door?" I asked.

Charlotte's face turned the same shade as her bright red hair. "*Nee*! I would never do such a thing. Juliet just stopped by and told Cousin Clara and me about the baby shower for Emily this Saturday. I can't believe you didn't tell me, Bailey! You know how much I've wanted to plan more parties. I told Juliet that I wanted to help out. She said I was welcome to take the lead with the party theme. I'm so excited!"

I sighed. I knew I should have told Emily about the shower sooner. Not that I'd had much opportunity to discuss it with her outside of work. The shed phone at her farm was reserved for emergencies, and the Amish frowned upon unexpected social visits. But as far as Juliet was concerned, the shower would happen no matter what Emily said or wanted.

"I would never eavesdrop on you." Charlotte's face became pinched.

"I'm sorry, Charlotte," I said. "I just told Emily about the shower, so it was an odd coincidence that you should come in right after I brought it up." I sighed. "I asked Juliet to wait until I had a chance to speak to Emily first before going forward with the shower preparations."

"I don't think she did that." Charlotte chewed on her lip. "From what she said, she's already told the bishop and his wife and Margot Rawlings."

Emily shook her head. "I'm sure Daniel knows by now, too."

"And everyone else in the district. You know when Juliet becomes excited about something, it's all she talks about," Charlotte said.

I knew that all too well.

"So can I plan it?" Charlotte asked with hopeful eyes. "I have the perfect theme idea."

Emily and I waited.

"Lemons!" she cried triumphantly. "It's Emily's favorite flavor. We can make lemonade, lemon cake, lemon drops, lemon meltaways, and—" She took a breath.

I jumped in before should could name every possible lemon dessert. "We get the idea."

"I do love lemon," Emily said.

"Then it's settled." Charlotte clapped her hands. "It'll be so much fun! I've never been to a baby shower before. Let alone planned one."

"Are you sure you want to take this on?" I asked. "It's a lot of work with short notice."

"I do," Charlotte said.

I looked at Emily.

She smiled. "*Ya*, you can plan the party, Charlotte."

Charlotte jumped up and down. "I'm going to tell Cousin Clara right now." She ran out of the kitchen. "We can have games at the shower, too!"

Emily watched the door as it swung back and forth.

I frowned. She still didn't look certain about the baby shower idea. "Emily, I know both Charlotte and I are excited about this party, but more than anything, we want to celebrate you and your baby. If you really don't want a shower, we can skip it."

"*Nee*, we can have the shower. It's more than just about me." She paused. "But I have a condition."

I raised my brow. Emily certainly wasn't one to make conditions normally. "What's that?"

"I want you to invite Esther."

She must have seen the look on my face because she said, "I know you don't like the idea because you are my friend and protective of me. But no matter what, she will be my child's *aenti*. I want her to be there. I'm hopeful we'll be able to make amends. I want her to be able to tell my child his or her aunt was there for this special day."

I bit the inside of my lip. Emily's speech proved she was a better person than I was. If I were in charge, I wouldn't invite Esther. She had a sharp tongue, and there was a high probability she would say something to intentionally hurt Emily on the day of the shower.

"I'll invite her," I said.

"*Danki*, Bailey. You are a *gut* friend."

I hoped that proved to be true.

I was a firm believer in doing the thing you least wanted to do first. It might just be part of my makeup. I prefer to rip off the Band-Aid rather than prolong the process and be delicate about it. As a chocolatier in New York City, this was a part of my personality that I had to learn to tame. To make the delectable and gorgeous treats we sold at JP Chocolates, a candy maker had to take care and have finesse. My first year working for Jean Pierre, I broke three chocolate molds because I was too impatient when removing the hardened chocolate from the forms. Jean Pierre could have and maybe should have dismissed me after the third broken mold. Instead, my mentor took me under his wing and instructed me to take a breath and calm down. That was when he shared his mantra of listing all the different kinds of chocolate. It helped quite a bit. What helped more was when the chocolate shop upgraded its forms from plastic to silicone. The silicone didn't break.

I recited the list now as I walked over to Esh Family Pretzels to invite Esther in person to her younger sister's baby shower. Dark chocolate, white chocolate, milk chocolate, and . . .

It wasn't that I was afraid of Esther. She was a petite Amish woman who might have a sour disposition, but I knew she couldn't do anything to me. Not really. I dreaded the visit because I knew how the outcome could impact Emily. Emily was in a fragile state at the moment, and I'd be darned if I was going to let Esther make her feel any worse about herself.

When I walked into the Esh shop, I was relieved to find Esther alone. She stood at the counter writing on a piece of paper. She looked up from her task. Her forced friendly smile, which I knew was there only for paying customers, dissolved into a scowl.

There was no one I knew who could scowl as fiercely as Esther Esh. If it had not been for the sour expression on her face, she would have been a very pretty woman. Perhaps she wasn't as beautiful as Emily, who had gorgeous, honey-blond hair, glowing skin, and Disney-princess eyes, but few people were. I had no doubt that if Emily had been born English, she would have been scouted by a modeling agency by now. She was *that* beautiful.

Esther had the same color hair, but her skin had a more sallow undertone, with the result that her skin and hair were too close in hue to be pleasing to the eye.

"What do you want?" she asked as she folded the piece of paper she'd been writing on and tucked it into her apron pocket.

I sighed. I had not spoken to Esther in a few weeks. Anytime I saw her outside of the pretzel shop and tried to strike up a conversation, she'd either walk away or duck back inside to avoid me. I wasn't surprised that she wasn't happy to see me in her store.

Esther had disliked me since I'd first arrived in Holmes County. She was very traditionally Amish and believed that there should be a clear separation between English and Amish societies. Decades ago, this was much

LEMON DROP DEAD   25

easier, but the world had become smaller for everyone. That included the Amish. As Juliet had pointed out to me the day before, now many Amish had to use cell phones and other technologies. Even if it was for business, Esther hated the changes. Hers was one of the few shops on Main Street that didn't have a telephone. That wasn't because her bishop didn't allow such a convenience to run her business. There was a phone in Swissmen Sweets, and *Maami* and Esther had the same bishop. It was Esther's choice. She believed having a phone at the ready blurred the lines between the English and Amish worlds. That was something she could not abide.

Since I'd first moved to Harvest, she'd taken a particular dislike to me because she didn't like the idea that I, an English woman, should run an Amish business. It didn't make any difference to her that *Maami* was Amish. Or that my *mammi* and *daadi* had started the business and ran it themselves for decades. I'd only returned to Harvest to assist them when my *daadi* grew ill. I was very grateful to have had that time with him before he passed away. I'd stayed on to help my *maami*, and to claim my heritage. But as far as Esther was concerned, the only English people inside an Amish business should be paying customers.

To the right of where Esther stood, by the old-fashioned cash register, was a marble countertop dusted with flour. A dozen uncooked pretzels sat under plastic wrap waiting to rise. The finished pretzels were displayed in a warmer that faced the front of the shop. I examined the display case, and my stomach rumbled. I was especially drawn to the savory pretzels. There were rosemary, pumpernickel, cracked pepper, and cheddar garlic, to name a few. I wanted one of each. There were also sweet flavors like blueberry, cinnamon, and honey. I wouldn't turn one of those down either.

"What are you doing here?" Esther wanted to know. "Don't tell me you came over for a pretzel. You haven't bought a pretzel from this shop since Emily left."

Nice to know that she was keeping score.

"I would like to buy one of your cheddar pretzels," I said. "But you're right. That's not the only reason I'm here. I wanted to give you an invitation to Emily's baby shower." I held out the invitation to her.

She made no move to take the small yellow envelope from my hand. Charlotte—bless her—had already purchased "lemony" stationery from the shop down the street. She was taking her role in this party planning very seriously.

Esther frowned. "You did not have to bring me the invitation yourself. You could have put it in the mail or through the mail slot in the shop door. There's no reason for you to come here in person."

"Well, maybe not, but I do want that pretzel," I said, still holding the envelope in my hand as if I was serving a court summons.

"I'm not selling you one of my pretzels."

Well, that was disappointing. I'd really had my teeth set for one, as my *grossdaadi* would have said.

"That's your choice." I held the envelope up a little higher. "But will you take the invitation? My arm is becoming tired."

"I think it's time for you to leave. I have no patience for such foolishness. A baby shower for Emily? Who heard of a more ridiculous affair?"

I wanted nothing more than to walk out of the shop

and never come back, especially because I had been denied my pretzel of choice. Reminding myself that this wasn't about me—it was about Emily—I forged ahead. "In case you don't read it, the shower will be this Saturday at two in the afternoon at the gazebo across the street. You won't be able to miss it. We expect most of the women from your district to be there. You might have already heard about it from a friend."

She wouldn't take the envelope, so I set it on the counter. She didn't move to touch it, but she didn't throw it in my face either. I took that to be a good sign.

Her lip curled. "I see that your influence on Emily has grown even more in the last few months. I should have known that it would. It seems everything that you touch you change. The few of us in this county who don't fall for your charms should be considered lucky."

"I'm sorry you feel that way," I said, truly meaning it. All I had wanted since Emily got married was for her to make peace with her brother and sister. I wanted that because I knew it was what Emily wanted most, but it seemed to me a reconciliation would never happen if Esther continued to be so stubborn.

"The whole idea is disgraceful." She moved down the counter and removed the waiting pretzels from the plastic. She set them onto a tray and into the convection oven behind her to bake. Then she began cutting the remaining dough into balls that were each about the size of a nectarine.

I narrowed my eyes. "What do you mean?"

She didn't look up from her work. "A baby shower? That is an *Englisch* celebration. It's not something that the Amish in our district do."

"I know it's not something that has happened in the district before, but the bishop knows about the party, and he sees no problem with it."

"He would!" She began rolling one of the balls into a long rod of dough. "But what does his wife say? I'm sure she has another opinion on the matter."

"I don't know Ruth Yoder's opinion, but I heard she was planning to come to the shower." I didn't add that I thought Ruth was coming mostly to make sure that the celebration wasn't too English. Whatever "too English" might be.

"I am saddened to hear that." With a lightning-fast flick of her wrist, she twisted the dough into a pretzel. Her hands moved so quickly, my eyes were unable to follow the movement to see how she did it. "I would have thought that the bishop's wife would be against any celebration due to my sister's history."

I frowned. I knew what she was getting at, but I refused to take the bait.

"Emily would really like for you to be there. She asked me to invite you. Maybe it's not my place to say this, but this could be the chance for your splintered family to come back together."

"You're right; it's not your place to say it." She twisted another pretzel, and I had the sneaking suspicion that she was thinking about my neck.

I started to wonder why I was staying there any longer. I had kept my promise to Emily. I had invited her sister to the baby shower. It was clear that I wasn't going to get that cheddar pretzel. I took a step back toward the door.

Esther didn't say anything. She just made two more pretzels, slapping the dough on the marble with such ferocity, I was surprised it didn't bounce back and smack her in the face. "I'm saddened by the fact that so many people in the district are blind to what you are doing."

Against my better judgment, I stopped inching toward the door. "What *I'm* doing? I'm not doing anything other than throwing a party for my dear friend to celebrate her baby. I can't imagine that anyone would see my actions as anything more than that."

Her eyes narrowed. "You are leading the young and naïve away from the faith, so that they will become *Englisch* like you. It starts with small ideas like this, a baby shower. And then it moves on to cell phones and cars. Before you know it, the Amish society that has existed for hundreds of years is in shambles." She paused. "All because well-meaning *Englischers* like you think they are being nice."

I stared at her. "I think you're giving me way more credit than I'm due."

"That's how it starts," she said.

I frowned. I didn't even know why I was bothering to argue with her. Esther and I would never see eye to eye on this matter, just as we had never seen eye to eye on anything.

"Emily is your sister, and she specifically asked me to invite you. I've done my duty. Now it's up to you whether or not you decide to come. The ball is in your court."

She glared at me, and I turned to go. I'd almost reached the door when it opened and a tall man with reddish-blond hair filled the frame. He ducked his head slightly to step into the shop.

Despite myself, my stomach tightened. I was trapped inside Esh Family Pretzels between grumpy Esther and her even grumpier brother, Abel. I should have just tucked the invitation through the mail slot as Esther had said.

Abel would have been as handsome as Emily was beautiful if it were not for his nasty disposition. In all the time I'd been living in Harvest, I had never once seen him smile. Grin and sneer, sure. Smile, nope.

Abel had a particular dislike for me, going all the way back to childhood. Growing up, I spent my summers in Amish Country visiting my grandparents. When I'd been a tween, Abel had had a crush on me, and I rebuffed his advances. I'd told him that I liked a boy at my school back in Connecticut. I would have thought a grudge like that would be quickly forgotten. Not in this case. It seemed that Abel had a long memory and had held onto those hurt feelings for nearly twenty years. In different circumstances, I would've found that kind of determination admirable.

No one knew what Abel did for work. It was well-known in the village that Esther ran the pretzel shop by herself. Which was why she was still bitter about Emily leaving the family business to work for me. That betrayal was made even worse when Emily married Daniel Keim. With Emily's wedding, Esther really thought that she'd lost her younger sister. She might've been able to convince Emily to leave the candy shop, but there was no hope of getting her to leave her husband. As for her brother, Abel, there were whispers in the village that he was involved in some underhanded dealings. However, no one could prove anything other than that he occasionally partook of illegal moonshine.

"Hello, Bailey," Abel said. "It's a great surprise to find you in our shop. What are you doing here? Do you have another murder to solve? How very odd that Aiden Brody needs a candy maker to help him with his cases. That does not speak well of the Sheriff's Department."

I scowled. "I was just chatting with Esther, but I'm on my way out." There was no point getting into a conversation with Abel unless it was absolutely necessary. Thank goodness I didn't have to invite him to the shower.

He made no attempt to move.

"Can you step aside please?" I asked.

He took one step to the right, but it wasn't far enough away that I could avoid brushing against him when I tried to leave. The urge to push him out of the way was almost overwhelming.

I slipped past him and walked the few yards to Swiss-men Sweets, instinctively brushing off the arm of my coat. Against my better judgment, I looked over my shoulder at the pretzel shop and saw Abel watching me from the doorway with a smirk on his face. Abel Esh gave me the creeps. There were no two ways about it.

CHAPTER FOUR

What I had come to learn since moving to Ohio was that fine spring days were fleeting. The Midwest seemed to go from the dark days of winter to the humid days of summer in the blink of an eye. There were only a handful of lovely spring days when you could wear just about anything out in the sun and be comfortable.

The day of Emily's baby shower was one of those perfect spring days. Because Charlotte had begged to take over the planning, I had let her run with it. Whenever I asked her if she needed help or wondered what she had planned for the party, she waved me away and assured me that she and Juliet had it well in hand. The control freak in me had to let it go. Not easy, but I did my best.

I'd even convinced myself that I wasn't worried about the shower at all until that afternoon, when I arrived on the square just thirty minutes before it was set to begin.

Charlotte had insisted that I wasn't to come a moment sooner than that. I think she was afraid I might take over. I had a reputation for taking charge of things. As I walked across Main Street from Swissmen Sweets to the other side of the village square, I was more than a little nervous to see how Charlotte and Juliet had pulled it all off.

I reminded myself that Emily and the Amish women attending the party had never been to a baby shower before and therefore wouldn't know if anything was amiss.

When I came around the side of the gazebo, I realized that I didn't have any reason to worry. Everything was done. Folding tables and chairs had been set out for the guests. Every table was covered with a linen tablecloth, and glass bowls of lemons and white daisies served as centerpieces. The chairs had been covered with yellow seat covers. There was another table with a yellow linen tablecloth lined with sweets from the candy shop, small sandwiches, veggies and dip, tiny tarts, and every lemon-flavored treat that I could imagine. It even had the lemon drops that Charlotte promised.

Charlotte came up to me. A strand of her red hair fell out of the Amish bun at the nape of her neck. She held her hands in front of her, nervously waiting for my verdict. "What do you think?"

"Charlotte, this is amazing," I said. "I don't know what to say, other than great job."

She smiled and smoothed the skirt of her lavender dress. "Oh, I'm so pleased that you like it. I want to make Emily happy, of course, but I really wanted to show you what I can do."

I wrinkled my brow. "Do you think that I don't give you enough to do? I mean in the way of creative work?"

"I'm not sure that you would give me any work at all if

you didn't have your television show in New York, but I have been working at the shop for a long while now. I'm in my second year. I want more responsibility." She looked around the party with a smile. "I can do things like this."

"I—I didn't know that was something you wanted, but I'd be happy to talk to you about it. When Emily is on maternity leave, I'll need a lot more help. I was thinking of hiring more staff."

"Before you do that, let's see what I can do to help," she said. "I have some new ideas about the shop. I think there are many ways that we could shift things around to free up more time for you and your other projects."

I blinked. "Okay. I'm happy to hear them."

She nodded, grabbed the stray lock of hair, and with a twist secured it in the knot.

I smiled. "Charlotte, you are becoming quite a business-woman."

She didn't smile. "I've just been thinking a lot the last several months about what I want my life to look like. I'm not sure about most things, but I know I love working at the candy shop and want to keep doing that as long as you and Cousin Clara will have me." She looked around. "Are you sure you like it?"

Some of the confidence she'd showed when she'd given her speech about wanting to do more in the business faded away.

"I do like it. It's exactly how I would do it. Emily will be so pleased. I can't believe you did all this."

"Not all by myself. Margot, Juliet, and some of the other ladies from the district helped, and Deputy Little helped me put up the tables." She blushed.

"Deputy Little did?" I raised my brow.

She nodded. "He had the day off and volunteered. I thought it was very kind of him. He doesn't have much free time."

I nodded. Deputy Little worked with Aiden. I knew well the long hours the sheriff's deputies had to put in.

I didn't mention it, but it was very telling that Deputy Little would spend his rare day off helping my young cousin set up for a baby shower. I had suspected for months that the two were sweet on each other, as my grandmother would say. Their affection had become more obvious since Christmas. However, Charlotte was Amish, and Deputy Little was not. In order for them to be together, one of them would have to make a dramatic life change. As of yet, neither had made a move to leave their culture.

"I will definitely thank everyone who helped," I said, believing it was best to glaze over Deputy Little's involvement. "It really looks amazing. I've been thinking about expanding the business into planning more events. You might be just the person to take over that branch of Swissmen Sweets. We can talk about it more next week."

Charlotte beamed at me. "I enjoyed the research. I went to the library and got a bunch of books about *Englisch* baby showers. Do you know that the *Englisch* actually publish books on that topic—and more than one! It proves to me that the *Englisch* will read just about anything."

I didn't argue with her there.

"Wait until you see the games," Charlotte said. "I got the most wonderful ideas from the books!"

I looked around at the sea of lemon yellow before me. "I can see that. You really did a fantastic job. You should be proud."

She smoothed her apron. "I know it's not very Amish,

but I have to admit that I am proud. I can't wait for Emily to see it."

"She's going to love it," I said, not doubting that for a minute.

She blushed again. "I'm just glad that you're giving me the chance. When I first started working at Swissmen Sweets, you watched everything I did. Now I can take on a project and you trust me to get it done."

"Ugh, I'm sorry if I was that overbearing."

"*Nee, nee,*" she said. "It was what I needed while I was learning."

"Well, I like to think that I backed off as you've learned more, but I think it might have had more to do with the fact the shop is so busy now, I have to delegate to survive."

"Whatever it is, I appreciate it," she said cheerily.

I wished I had Charlotte's cheerful attitude sometimes. She had the ability to see the good in everything. When her parents and home district had turned their backs on her, she'd had every reason to be upset, but even in the face of their disapproval of her reluctance to be baptized into the faith, she remained positive. I could learn a lot from her.

I was about to tell her all this when Emily and Grandma Leah came up to us. Emily walked slowly to keep in step with Daniel's great-grandmother over the uneven grass. As Emily reached us, her eyes were wide.

"Look at all this!" Grandma Leah said. "It's like a lemon garden."

Charlotte beamed at her praise.

Emily smiled. "This is so lovely. These are the perfect decorations for someone who loves lemons as much as I do."

"It was Charlotte, Juliet, and Margot who put this all together. I take no credit," I said.

Tears filled Emily's eyes. "*Danki*, Charlotte. It is so kind of you to do this for me."

I had thought that Charlotte's smile couldn't get any bigger, but I was wrong. She positively glowed.

"This could be great fun," Grandma Leah said. "I have never been to a baby shower before. I don't know what to expect."

"Don't worry," Charlotte said. "I have it all planned. I checked out books from the library."

Grandma Leah laughed. "Then you must be prepared."

"We wanted today to be all about you, Emily. This is your day," Charlotte said.

Emily scrunched up her nose as if she wasn't comfortable with that idea. I remembered our conversation in Swissmen Sweets' kitchen at the beginning of the week and was certain she was not.

"Finally!" Margot shouted from the other side of the square.

As a group, we looked in her direction. I think we were all wondering what Margot could possibly be worked up about. As she hurried across the square, the short curls on the top of her head bounced up and down. Juliet followed in a lemon-colored, polka-dotted tea dress, holding Jethro under her arm.

Amish women had already begun to arrive for the shower, even though it didn't begin for another twenty minutes. The Amish were almost always early.

When they reached us, Margot wasn't out of breath. I suspected the petite woman spent most of her day running from place to place, making sure that everything in Harvest was in perfect order for the tourists, meaning that she was in excellent shape. If I were in her shoes, all the running and rushing would have me doubled over.

As was her habit, Margot patted her graying curls when she came to a stop, as if to make sure they were secure. "How lovely! The guest of honor is here. Emily, I speak for the entire village of Harvest when I say that we are just tickled over this new addition to the community."

Juliet hoisted Jethro up higher in her arms. "We are tickled pink over your coming bundle of joy. Aren't we, Jethro?"

Emily blushed. "It's so very kind of you both to say that. Jethro, too. I have to admit, I am quite overwhelmed by the attention. I feel very spoiled by all of this. Bailey tells me it was your idea, Juliet."

Juliet beamed. "Margot and I came up with it together. We can't have a new baby join our Harvest family and not celebrate the child and expectant mother!"

Margot shook her finger at Emily. "You deserve this. Ask anyone in the village, and they will agree with me."

Emily made a face, and I knew we were thinking the same thing. Emily's brother and sister wouldn't agree that their younger sister deserved such a celebration. I glanced around and saw no sign of Esther. I hadn't expected her to come, but still, a part of me—a very, very tiny part—had hoped that she would, just for Emily.

"I'm going to check on the food table one more time. Charlotte did an excellent job of putting it all together, but I want it to be perfect," Juliet said and hurried over to the food table.

Margot tapped me on the shoulder. "Bailey, I've been meaning to speak to you about an idea that I had."

A knot instantly formed in my stomach, as it always did when Margot said she had an idea. It wasn't that I didn't like Margot. I admired her a lot. She was a woman who took charge and got things done. But most of the times she'd said she had an idea for me, it had amounted to a lot of extra work. "Margot, whatever it is, I don't think Emily's baby shower is the right time to talk about a new project."

"Very true," she said with a shake of her curls. "But I like to prime the pump, as it were, so that you know something is brewing."

That didn't sound ominous or anything.

"I'll stop by the candy shop tomorrow so we can chat about it," she said.

"Tomorrow is Sunday. The candy shop is closed."

"I'll send you a detailed e-mail about it tonight. Be sure to read it." She glanced around the square. "Oh, there's one of the church deacons. I have a bone to pick with him." She scurried away.

I felt bad for the deacon.

"She scares me," Charlotte whispered.

"She scares me a little, too," I admitted.

As more guests began to arrive at the shower, both Amish and English ladies raved over Charlotte's decorations. Emily was shocked at the number of presents that were beginning to pile up on the gift table. "I can't believe this. It's just too generous," she murmured over and over again. "I won't ever be able to use all these things."

"You just might," I said. "I'm no baby expert, but I know from friends who've had babies, infants require a lot of stuff. Even Amish infants." I smiled at her. "Everyone is happy for you. Accept the gifts with a smile and thanks. Your friends are just showing how much they care about you and your baby."

She nodded, but I could tell from the expression on her

face that she remained overwhelmed by the outpouring of love.

Charlotte walked to the top step of the gazebo to address the guests. No one was looking at her. The women chattered and ate the food. They were all having such a wonderful time.

"Hello," Charlotte called.

I made a move to wave my arms to grab the group's attention, but Millie Fisher, a sixty-something Amish widow, put her fingers in her mouth and whistled the highest and shrillest whistle I had ever heard. The green went silent.

Millie shrugged. "If it works on the goats, I thought it might work on a crowd, too." She gave me a lopsided grin. "I'm glad to see that I was proven right."

"Thank you, Millie." Charlotte cleared her throat. "Hello, everyone! We are so grateful that so many ladies from the community are here to celebrate with Emily. I want to give very special thanks to Juliet and Margot, who made this day possible. I know I speak for everyone at Swissmen Sweets when I say that we love Emily like she was our sister."

I watched Emily as Charlotte spoke, and Emily blushed.

"We have a lovely afternoon planned. Please enjoy the food, and after we eat, there will be a number of fun games to play." She skipped down from the gazebo steps. I marveled at how much Charlotte had grown up over the last year. Across the square, I spotted Deputy Little wandering around. He was a short, compact man who was twenty-six, just a few years older than Charlotte. He always parted his hair precisely down the side, and even when he wasn't in uniform, like today, his clothes were neat and pressed.

He seemed to have one eye on Charlotte at all times.

Emily walked over to me. "*Danki* for doing this, Bailey. It was so kind of you."

"It wasn't me, Emily. Juliet, Margot, and so many other ladies were involved. They all care about you."

"I will thank them again, too." She bit her lip.

"Is something wrong?" My brow wrinkled.

"Esther isn't here," she whispered.

"I invited her."

"I know you did. I thought—maybe it was silly—but I thought that she would come. All the other women from the district are here. I think it makes it more painful to me that she's the only one who didn't come. It's a very pointed snub."

I couldn't argue with her on that. Maybe I was more cynical than Emily—in fact, I knew that I was—but I'd never thought for a moment that Esther would come to the shower. If she was asked about her absence by another woman in the district, I knew she would make up an excuse about needing to be at Esh Family Pretzels on a busy Saturday. That was true. She was the only person who worked in her shop, but that didn't mean she couldn't slap a BE RIGHT BACK sign on the door, run across the street, and make a short appearance at her only sister's baby shower.

"It's no matter," she said in a heavy voice that told me it mattered quite a lot.

I wanted to tell her not to worry about Esther. It would only lead to frustration, but then an Amish woman who I guessed was in her early fifties came up to Emily. She wore a navy blue dress and a white prayer cap. A pair of reading glasses hung from a beaded chain at her neck. "Congratulations on the baby. This is a lovely party."

Emily's brow wrinkled. "*Danki*. Have we met before?"

The woman smiled. "I'm not from your district, so I won't be staying long. I just wanted to tell you that I am so very happy for you. Your second child will be so well loved. It's clear that everyone in this village is ready to celebrate the birth."

The breath went out of Emily's chest in a whoosh. There were just a handful of people in the world who knew this was Emily's second baby.

"What did you say?" Emily asked.

"This *second* baby will be well-loved," the woman said, putting the emphasis on second.

"Who are you?" I stepped forward.

The woman looked at me. She had the darkest green eyes I had ever seen. They reminded me of the evergreens on the Keims' Christmas tree farm.

"I'm looking forward to your child meeting her sibling," she said. "The children should be together. It is right."

Emily gasped.

"It's time for the gifts!" Charlotte called to us. "Emily, we need you."

Emily was stricken, and I steadied her.

"Emily!" Charlotte called again.

"I have to go," Emily gasped and stumbled toward the folding chair that Charlotte had set up for her near the gifts.

I turned to speak to the woman, but when I did, she was gone. I looked around. Who was she, and how did she know anything about Emily's past? I had a sinking feeling in my stomach that this wasn't over. In my experience, things of this nature did not just disappear.

CHAPTER FIVE

For the rest of the party, I tried to tell myself the interruption was nothing to worry about. Perhaps the woman was someone from another district who wanted to make trouble. That wasn't typical behavior for an Amish woman, but I was grasping at anything to make sense of her visit and, more importantly, what she'd said.

As was to be expected, Emily was on edge during the remainder of the shower. She looked around frequently and seemed to be searching all of the faces for the woman. That, or she was looking for Esther, who never showed at all. If it would have done any good, I'd have gone to Esh Family Pretzels and dragged Esther across the street to raise Emily's spirits. However, that would only make matters worse between them.

Despite these setbacks, the baby shower was a success. Charlotte had done an amazing job. I thought a lot about how I could give her more responsibility in our business. I added that assessment to my list of things to do at the candy shop that night. I had planned to work late after the party, making supply orders and updating our online store. When I was a chocolatier in New York, I would typically do work like that on Sundays, but my grandmother was adamant that there should be no work on Sundays. On some Sundays, I was able to work at home, where I would not offend her, but because I needed to order supplies, it would be much easier to handle the ordering after hours at Swissmen Sweets, where I could see exactly what I needed.

Aiden was on the night shift again that Saturday for the Sheriff's Department, and working seemed the best way to pass the time.

After everything from the shower was cleaned up and put away, Emily went home with Grandma Leah. I didn't have a chance to speak to her in private about the mystery woman, and I was afraid it would have to wait until Monday. In the Amish world, Sunday was a day for church and family. It wasn't often that *Englischers* were welcome in Amish homes on those days.

Charlotte, *Maami*, and I went back to Swissmen Sweets. Charlotte took the leftover food containers into the kitchen, but I stopped my grandmother before she could follow her into the kitchen. "*Maami*, did you see a woman speak to Emily and me just before Charlotte asked Emily to open the gifts?"

She set the box of napkins and paper plates she was carrying on the counter. "*Ya*, now that you mention it, I do remember seeing a woman with you."

"Do you know who she was?"

The strange woman wasn't from the local district, and

I hadn't recognized her, but there was still a chance my grandmother would know her.

"*Nee*, I don't know who she was. I had never seen her before."

I wrinkled my brow.

"What is it, *kind*?" she asked.

I shook my head. I couldn't tell my grandmother. She didn't know Emily's secret. "She just said something odd to Emily, and I wanted to know who she was."

"What did she say?" my grandmother asked.

The kitchen door swung open, and Charlotte came through with a great sigh. "I'm so grateful that the shower went well, but part of me is even more grateful that it's over."

And I was grateful that Charlotte had interrupted us, saving me from answering my grandmother's question.

Customers started coming into the shop, as we'd re-opened for the last hour of the day. There was no time for my grandmother to ask me any more questions. For which I was also grateful.

Later that night, I sat at one of the café tables in front of the shop and worked on the online store. Puff and Nutmeg slept together on a pillow in the corner of the room. My back began to ache, and I soon lost track of how long I'd been sitting there. My grandmother and Charlotte had gone up to bed in the apartment above the shop hours ago. I was starting to think I should put off the rest of my tasks until tomorrow, when I could do them from the comfort of my bed. Then someone knocked on the front door of the shop. No, that wasn't accurate. The person didn't knock; they banged and shook the door. The noise was so startling, I fell out of my chair.

The wooden paddle-back chair crashed to the floor beside me, terrifying the sleeping animals. Nutmeg and Puff dove under the blond wooden candy shelves. Well, Nutmeg did. Puff couldn't quite get her back end to fit under it. Her rump and hind legs stuck out from beneath the shelf. Her puff of a tail trembled.

I scrambled to my feet and picked up the chair. Before I could reach the door, a knock came again. It wasn't as loud but was just as persistent. I peered through the front window to see if I could determine who was there. From the porch light, I saw the silhouette of a small person, but it was too difficult to distinguish the individual's identity.

I glanced back to the cowardly cat and rabbit. "You guys are my backup if this goes south."

Nutmeg mewed from his hiding place, and Puff's tail shook. I didn't think they would be much help if it was a masked man on the other side of the door. One thing I knew, it wasn't Aiden. He would have texted first to warn me.

I opened the door to find a blond Amish woman standing outside. It took me a moment to realize who it was. "Esther, what are you doing here?"

Under the glow of the porch light, her face looked yellowed and drawn. She whispered something I couldn't hear.

I leaned closer. "What did you say?"

She grabbed my hand and pulled me out the door. I stumbled onto the sidewalk.

"Esther, what's going on?" I cried as I righted myself.

"I need your help." She held my hand so tightly, I thought she might break my bones.

"Help with what?" I tried to pull my hand away, but she held it fast.

"Please. In the pretzel shop. I don't know what to do. You have to come now." Her eyes darted in all directions.

"Are you hurt?" Finally, I yanked my hand away from her grasp.

"Please. Aren't you listening to me? She's in the pretzel shop!"

I shook out my hand. "Who? Who is in the pretzel shop?"

She wouldn't answer me but just ran back toward her shop. I thought she would go in the front door, but instead she ducked down the alley between Swissmen Sweets and Esh Family Pretzels.

After just a moment of hesitation, I followed her. There were no lights in the back alley between the two businesses. I had been meaning to have a light installed on our building, but hadn't gotten around to it yet because I knew the Esh family wouldn't be pleased.

The back door to the pretzel shop stood wide open, and dim electric light came from inside. Having electricity in her shop was the only compromise Esther made to the *Englisch* world. She had to have it in order to acquire a license to sell fresh food. I stepped into the kitchen, which was a third the size of the Swissmen Sweets kitchen. The Esh family exclusively made pretzels and didn't need as much workspace as we did. At Swissmen Sweets, we needed a large kitchen because of the vast variety of candies we made.

The small kitchen felt even smaller when I saw an Amish woman slumped on the floor just by the open oven door; she was crumpled in front of the oven as if she had been a house of cards that had folded into itself.

"Is she alive?" I crouched on the floor next to the woman. I grabbed her wrist, and when I didn't find a pulse, I moved my hand to her neck. Her skin was clammy and cold to the touch. There was a red mark around her throat that was beginning to change to purple and blue. I was close enough to see her face and her blank dark green eyes. I gasped. It was the mystery woman from the baby shower. The one who knew about Emily's first baby.

When I was on the floor, the smell hit me. Like rotten eggs. I glanced at the open oven and jumped to my feet.

"Can you see her? You need more light? Can you help her?"

Behind me, I heard a clatter. I turned to see Esther holding a long lighter toward the lantern on the counter. "I need to see her better."

"No!" I knocked the lighter out of her hand and hit the lantern in the process. I caught the lantern before it could fall to the floor and shatter.

Esther stared at me.

"Gas," I said. "Can't you smell the gas? If you light anything, this whole place might go up."

She blinked a few times, and then realization dawned on her face. "I didn't notice it before. I was so shocked by what I found, I didn't notice anything else."

I pulled her by the arm to the open door. "We have to get out of here."

She didn't move. "What about her?"

"Esther, she's gone."

I dragged Esther out the door into the dark alley. But even in the open air, I was too afraid of the gas to light a match. Thankfully, there was a full moon that provided some light.

Esther wrung her hands. "What am I going to do? What am I going to do?"

As much as I wanted to comfort her, I had to call the police. The gas line to the shop needed to be turned off. If there was a spark, it could set off an explosion that would damage an entire block of Harvest's charming down-town, including Swissmen Sweets.

The dispatcher picked up on the first ring.

"There's a gas leak at Esh Family Pretzels." I swal-lowed. "And there's a dead body in the building."

"Did you say that there's a body in there?" the dis-patcher asked.

"Yes," I squeaked.

"Bailey King, is that you?" the dispatcher asked.

"Yes," I said with a sigh.

"Oh, my word." She clicked her tongue. "When Dep-uty Brody hears that you've found another dead body, he is going to flip his lid."

I didn't doubt it for a moment.

She then turned no-nonsense. "I have the gas com-pany, EMTs, and officers on the way. You know the drill. Don't touch anything."

Unfortunately, I did know the drill. All too well. That was Aiden's main complaint.

I ended the call and turned to Esther, who was folded at the waist, standing next to the dumpster. "Esther, are you all right?"

"Are you sure she's dead?" Esther whispered.

I nodded. "She's gone. Who was she?"

"I just found her. I walked in the back door, and she was like that."

"On the floor?" I noted she hadn't answered my ques-tion about the woman's identity.

"*Nee*, her head was in the oven. I pulled her out, but I wasn't strong enough to pull her from the shop. That's why I came to find help." She closed her eyes. "But I was too late. She must have already been dead. This is all my fault."

I touched her arm. "Esther, why is it your fault? Who is that woman?"

Once again, she ignored my questions, including the one about the woman's identity.

"I know that she was at the baby shower. She spoke to Emily. I was there when she did."

"She should not have spoken to Emily without me." Esther knocked my hand away. It made me feel better to see some of Esther's spunk back. A crying, insecure Esther was much more unnerving than an angry one.

Whether she admitted it or not, I was positive that Esther knew who the woman was. But if Esther and Abel weren't in the building, how had the woman gotten inside, and more importantly, why was she lying dead on the floor?

"What was she doing here?" I wrapped my arms around my shoulders. Even though it was May, it was chilly so late at night.

She still didn't answer my question.

"Esther, you're in a lot of trouble. The police are on their way. They're going to ask you all the questions that I'm asking you. You need to be prepared."

Her eyes met mine. "You mean that I need to have my story straight."

"I'm not telling you to make up a story, but you need to be prepared to answer questions."

She scowled at me and clamped her mouth shut. I wasn't going to get anything out of her. I wished Aiden the very best of luck. Even under duress, Esther was harder than day-old caramel.

CHAPTER SIX

"**B**ailey!" Aiden called from the alley.

"Behind the pretzel shop!" I shouted.

Aiden and Deputy Little appeared around the side of the building. Both of them were in their Sheriff's Department uniforms. After having the day off, Deputy Little had gone back on for the night shift.

"What's going on?" Aiden asked. He looked to me for answers. I wasn't surprised. Unfortunately, I'd learned to be concise when summarizing a crime.

"There's a dead Amish woman in the pretzel shop kitchen," I said.

"Little," Aiden said, "go to all the houses on this block and ask the residents to step out of their homes. Inform them there's a gas leak."

"Yes, sir." He looked at his phone. "The gas company

just arrived on the scene. I'll go out and meet them, and then knock on the doors."

Aiden nodded, and Deputy Little jogged back down the dark alleyway to meet with the gas company.

"*Maami* and Charlotte are sleeping in Swissmen Sweets," I said with anxiety in my voice.

"Little will get them out. The two of you need to move away from the building, too. Go across the street to the square. That's where we'll send everyone."

"I can't leave my shop," Esther said, speaking up for the first time.

Aiden looked at her. "I'm sorry, but you'll have to. This is a dangerous scene." He removed a compact flashlight from his belt. Although the flashlight was small, it had a strong beam that illuminated every pebble and stray leaf in the alley. "You can't stay here. I'm going to check inside the building."

"Are you sure you should go in there?" I asked. "The gas—"

He looked at me, meeting my gaze. "Bailey, I'll be fine. Take Esther to the square."

I nodded and pulled Esther along toward the street. As we emerged from the alley, I saw *Maami* and Charlotte stumble out of Swissmen Sweets onto the sidewalk in their nightclothes and coats. Charlotte carried Puff, and my grandmother had Nutmeg in her arms. I was relieved to see that they'd remembered the animals.

Deputy Little walked with them, murmuring to Charlotte as they went. She nodded at something he said. They crossed the street and stood by the gazebo until Esther and I joined them. Deputy Little ran to his squad car and came out with two blankets. He wrapped one around my grandmother's shoulders and the other around Charlotte's.

She gazed up at him with so much adoration in her face, I had to look away.

"Bailey, are you all right?" *Maami* asked as she tucked the blanket more closely around herself and Nutmeg. "When the deputy knocked on the door, I was so shaken I forgot to ask where you were. Had you already gone home? Did Aiden call you and tell you to come back?"

"I was still down in the shop, and it was a good thing I was when Esther came running for help."

"I need to get back to Deputy Brody," Deputy Little said somewhat reluctantly to Charlotte.

"Go," she said. "You have work to do. We'll be fine here."

He nodded and darted back across the street.

At the same time, Esther walked away from us back to the sidewalk. She stopped there and stared at her business as if keeping a vigil of some sort. I'd deal with her after I knew my family was okay.

Charlotte adjusted the rabbit in her arms. "She is an armful. You would think an animal that just ate vegetables wouldn't be this heavy."

"Keep hold of Nutmeg, *Maami*. He's been known to run away, but you can set Puff down," I said to Charlotte. "She never wants to go anywhere."

"Oh, thank goodness." She bent and set the bunny on the plush lawn.

Puff hopped one foot away and started eating the grass. My pet rabbit was very much an emotional eater. I suspected that she might have gotten that from me.

"Where is everyone else? Aiden told Deputy Little to go door to door and make sure that no one was in any of the other buildings. But you two are the only ones here."

"He did that," Charlotte said, coming to the defense of the young deputy.

"We are the only family who still lives over their shop," *Maami* said. "That's a *gut* thing, because no one is here at this time of night, especially when tomorrow is Sunday. Everyone is resting before church."

That was a relief. I shivered to think what would have happened if Esther had lit the lantern or if I hadn't been there to stop her.

Esther stood about ten feet away from us on the curb at the edge of the square. She continued to stare at the pretzel shop. There was a light on inside the shop now. Aiden and the police had put up some kind of lighting so they could examine the scene. I wished I was in there right now. Not because I wanted to be anywhere near the dead woman, but because I wanted to know what was going on. The woman who'd died was the same one who'd come to Emily's baby shower and knew about her first baby. Who was she? I had a feeling that Esther had the answer to that question, but good luck to me or anyone else who tried to get it out of her.

I don't know how long we had been standing by the gazebo when Aiden strode across the street. In the glow of the high moon and the streetlamps, the lines on his handsome face appeared more pronounced.

He was tired, and I knew the weight of another murder pulled him down. All he wanted was a peaceful, calm county. With death after death targeting Harvest, he was far from that dream. I worried about how this would impact him. It was becoming more apparent that the sheriff—who rarely left the department to assist with any investigation—was beginning to blame the uptick in crime in the county on Aiden. Of course none of this was

Aiden's fault, but Sheriff Marshall was a man who liked to point fingers, and his favorite person to blame was always Aiden. He resented Aiden for being so popular with the public.

Last year, the sheriff had been up for reelection, and no one, including Aiden, had the nerve to run against him. Aiden said he couldn't run because it would show disloyalty, which was a big no-no in law enforcement, but I wished he had. I knew he could have won, and then he wouldn't have had to deal with the disgruntled sheriff any longer. Aiden managed the department pretty much on his own already.

Aiden ran a hand through his hair and down his face. "The good news is that there is no gas leak. Someone just turned on the oven and opened the door."

"But there was no heat coming from the oven. Was the pilot light out?"

He nodded. "My guess is whoever turned on the oven blew it out. The rep from the gas company checked and double-checked for any other source of gas but found none. The fumes should be gone in a couple hours. There's no real danger, but I'd feel a lot better if you all didn't sleep in the candy shop tonight. Maybe I'm being overly protective, but I'm fine with that."

"I'd feel better if you didn't, too," I added to my grandmother and cousin. "You can spend the night at my house. I'm sure Puff would love to show Nutmeg around."

Maami nodded. "All right. Charlotte and I will drive over in my buggy so we'll have it handy to go to church tomorrow."

Charlotte glanced at Esther, who continued to stare at her pretzel shop. Esther's arms were wrapped around her body so tightly, her fingers almost touched at her back.

"What about Esther?" Charlotte asked. "Where is she going to go? I doubt that Abel will come and take her home at this time of night."

I thought the same. Perhaps it was one of those nights when Esther worked late and slept on the cot in Esh Family Pretzels in order to finish all her work. That was often what Emily had done until she finally had had enough and left.

"She can stay at my house, too," I said. "If you don't mind sleeping on the floor, Charlotte." I wasn't going to ask my grandmother to sleep on the floor.

"That would be okay, but I can also grab the cot from the candy shop. It's the one I used to sleep on until you moved into your house. It's quite comfortable." She smiled. "I sort of miss sleeping on it. The bed is just so big."

Leave it to Charlotte to find a silver lining.

"I'll go tell her," Charlotte said and walked off in Esther's direction.

Maami, Aiden, and I watched as Charlotte hurried over to Esther. Esther shook her head. But Charlotte didn't take no for an answer. She grabbed Esther's arm and pulled her toward us.

"Are you all right, *kind*?" *Maami* asked Esther. "That must have been a terrible discovery."

Esther looked as if she might cry. Or it could have just been a trick of the light. I'd never seen her cry before, but she had found a dead body tonight. That would shake even the most stoic soul.

"I will be fine. Charlotte has told me that I have to leave." Esther shuffled her feet. "I can't leave. It's my job to make sure that everything is put away and ready for Monday morning."

"I'm sorry, Esther, but you can't go back into the pretzel shop tonight," Aiden said. "Honestly, I don't know if you'll be able to enter the building on Monday. It's a complicated scene."

"Is it because of the gas? Maybe we can put fans in there to blow it out. It can't last that long. I can wait." Esther grabbed the edge of her apron and twisted it in her hands.

"It's not just the gas that's a factor," Aiden said. "The kitchen is a crime scene. You can't go back in there tonight or tomorrow."

"You can't close my kitchen," Esther said. "This is my business and my family's livelihood. How do I know my shop will be safe with so many *Englischers* going in and out of it without me knowing?"

Aiden frowned. "The people working the scene are all professionals. You have nothing to worry about. However, I'll station a deputy outside of the building to be safe. You have my word that nothing will happen to the shop while we are investigating this crime."

Esther looked as if she wanted to argue some more.

My grandmother touched her arm. "Come, dear. Charlotte and I are going to go to Bailey's house for the night. You're welcome to stay with us."

She jerked her arm away. "I'm not spending the night in an *Englischer*'s house. I want to go home. I will walk if I must."

I sighed. I should have expected a reaction like this from Esther. "You're not walking to your farm in the middle of the night," I said. "I'll drive you."

"Fine," she said without so much as a thank-you.

Aiden glanced over his shoulder as the coroner's car arrived on the scene. When he turned back, Aiden's wry, almost-smile was just for me. He knew that Esther was no fan of mine. "That actually works better, Bailey. I have to check in with the coroner. Clara and Charlotte, you're free to go. Esther and Bailey, can you hang around for a bit longer?"

I nodded, knowing that Aiden needed to get our official statements while the events were still fresh in our heads. I imagined that Esther would not be happy with any of those questions.

Aiden's face softened as he looked at me, and my stomach did a little flip. I knew there was more he wanted to say to me, but he wasn't going to do that in front of Esther.

"Can we grab a few things from inside?" *Maami* asked.

He nodded. "That would be all right. I'll send over Deputy Little to help you carry what you might need to your buggy."

"*Danki*, Aiden," *Maami* said.

Charlotte scooped up Puff from the grass, and then *Maami* and Charlotte, carrying the rabbit and the cat, respectively, went back to the candy shop. Deputy Little waited by the door.

Aiden watched them go and then turned to me. "Can you stay here with Esther? I won't be long."

I nodded and then bit my lip. There were so many questions that I wanted to ask him. How long had the woman been dead? What was the murder weapon? Esther denied letting her into the pretzel shop, so how did she get inside?

He kissed me on the cheek before jogging back across Main Street and down the alley.

Esther scowled at me. "I don't know why we can't leave now. I have nothing to say to the police."

"If you have nothing to say to the police, why don't you just tell me what happened?" I knew it was a long shot that I could convince Esther to talk to me, but I was willing to try. Perhaps she would be more forthcoming with me than she would be with Aiden.

She folded her arms. "There's nothing to tell. I already told you everything I know."

I also folded my arms and took the same stance she did. "I don't believe you. The dead woman in your shop is the same woman that came to the shower and spoke to Emily."

"That doesn't mean I know the woman."

"She knew about Emily's first child."

My statement hung in the air, and a slew of emotions crossed Esther's face in the light of the streetlamp.

Her back went rigid. "All sins are found out in the end."

CHAPTER SEVEN

Esther stomped away from me and went back to her post, staring at Esh Family Pretzels. Thankfully, Aiden came back a few minutes later, as promised. He said something to Esther, but she turned her back to him. Aiden shook his head and walked over to me.

"Esther's not making this any easier," Aiden said when he reached me.

"I'd be surprised if she did. Esther isn't known for making anything easy for anyone. Not even herself."

"That may be so, but I still have to talk to her about this. Before I do, I'll take your statement. Maybe something you say will help me get through to her how important this is."

I had my doubts, but agreed to answer his questions in any case.

"What did you see when you went into the shop?"

I described the scene to Aiden. The woman on the floor in a heap, the open oven door, the smell of gas, and the marks on the woman's neck. "The gas was a cover-up, wasn't it? This wasn't a Sylvia Plath–style death. The woman was dead before whoever did it even turned on the stove . . ."

Aiden rocked back on his heels. "You know I can't share details of an active murder investigation—no matter how astute your observations might be."

Ha! It was as I suspected. Although one detail struck me in a way that made my stomach tighten. "Did you find her reading glasses?"

"Reading glasses?" Aiden asked. "Do you know who the dead woman is?"

I shook my head and bit my lip.

Aiden studied me. "Bailey, if you know something that might lead to what happened to this woman, you have to tell me."

I frowned. "I don't know anything for certain, but I think Esther knows who she is, even though she won't admit it to me. I saw the woman this afternoon at Emily's baby shower. That's how I know about the reading glasses. They hung from a beaded chain around her neck at the shower. I don't remember seeing them when I was inside the pretzel shop, not even when I took her pulse." I paused. "I wonder if that chain might have been used to kill her."

Aiden rubbed his chin. "It's possible. The ligature marks are peculiar. I've never seen anything like them before. We didn't find any glasses, but I will tell the coroner this detail. It might help us narrow down what was used to strangle her.

"Was she a woman from Emily's Amish district? Was that why she was at the shower?"

I shook my head. "She wasn't."

"Then what makes you think Esther would know her?"

"Umm," I stalled. I didn't want to bring Emily and her first child into this conversation if I could avoid it. At least, I didn't want to mention either of them before I had a chance to speak to Emily in person. "The woman is dead in Esther's shop. It'd be very strange for someone to be there at night if Esther doesn't know the person, wouldn't it? Maybe I'm making assumptions, but a middle-aged Amish woman wouldn't be my first guess as to someone who'd break and enter."

"Mine either," he said. "She doesn't have any ID on her, although that's not unusual for an Amish person. She might not be from this district, but someone must know who she is. The Amish world isn't that big. And I have something else that might help."

"What's that?"

He paused. "I shouldn't be telling you this."

"Probably not—but, Aiden, I can help. Haven't I been able to help you before?"

He sighed. It wasn't a point he could argue, because I had helped him on numerous occasions with his homicide cases involving the Amish community. "Does the name Rosemary Weiss mean anything to you?"

I shook my head.

"The coroner found a letter in her pocket addressed to Rosemary Weiss in Wooster. As of right now, I'm under the assumption that's our victim." He reached into the inner pocket of his jacket and brought out a plastic bag. There was a letter inside. He showed me, but made no move to let me hold it. "Does anything about it jump out at you?"

I stared. "The return address is Esh Family Pretzels."

He put the letter back into the pocket of his coat. "Exactly. Esther wrote and mailed this letter."

"Have you read the letter?" I studied his face.

He blew out a breath. "I have."

"Is it from Esther?"

"Yes." He pressed his lips together. "And the letter is, in a word . . . harsh."

"What did it say?" I was breathless.

He sighed and tucked the letter away back inside his pocket.

"Aiden, I can help. I have a much better chance of getting Esther to tell me what she knows than you do."

"That's true, but your chances remain slim. Esther has never been a fan of yours."

I couldn't argue with him on that, so I didn't bother to try.

"The letter said that Rosemary should honor their agreement and not come to Harvest. If Rosemary did visit Harvest, Esther claimed there would be repercussions."

"Repercussions?"

"That was her exact word," he said with a nod.

"That sounds like a threat."

"It is a threat, and not a veiled one either." He patted the pocket where he had placed the letter as if to reassure himself that it was still there.

"What kind of agreement?"

He shrugged. "It doesn't say. Apparently, Rosemary would have known when she read the letter."

"What else did the letter say?"

He shook his head.

I let out a breath. I wanted to know more, but realized that was all Aiden was going to share with me about the letter. Perhaps he hadn't even meant to say that much.

Even so, I asked another question. "Can you at least tell me Esther's wording of the threat?"

Aiden looked at me with those chocolate-brown eyes of his. I couldn't read his emotion.

"Aiden, I'm asking to help. I can help. How many times have I been able to assist on a case for you because of my closeness to the Amish community? They trust me because they love and trust my grandmother. I can ask questions and go places you can't."

He seemed to be weighing everything in his mind. "Stay away, or you will be sorry," he said finally.

"I know that Esther can be prickly, but it's hard for me to imagine that she'd actually threaten anyone."

"She's threatened you before."

I frowned. He had a point, but that felt different. Maybe because I knew that Esther didn't have any power over me, her words never felt like a threat.

I almost said that she was Amish and wouldn't kill anyone, but stopped myself. Both Aiden and I knew that Amish people—including women—could do terrible things. "Another murder in Harvest," I said.

"Yes," Aiden said.

"It just doesn't seem likely there would be so many in such a small town."

"Never bet on something like that. Life isn't like the lottery."

"Maybe I should play the lotto," I said.

"Maybe. But your odds of winning wouldn't be as good as those of finding another dead body. You have a knack for that." Warmth came back into his dark eyes.

"It's a knack I could live without, but I'll do anything to help you."

He chuckled. "Oh, I know, you will be meddling all the way."

"Meddling, helping. It's two sides of the same coin."

He rolled his eyes. "In any case, the sheriff will want this buttoned up quickly. Another murder is bad for his image."

"But he was just reelected a year and half ago. I thought the term was for four years. Why would he be worried now?"

"It is, but just like any politician, he's always thinking about reelection. There are no term limits for sheriff. He could be in office until he decides to retire."

"When would that be?" I raised my brow.

"I can't see him ever walking away from the job." Aiden wouldn't look at me. "It might be time for me to consider my options."

"Options?" I asked. "What are you talking about?"

He shook his head. "We can talk about it later. Right now, I have to solve this case and do it fast."

Great. He'd given me something else to worry about. Wasn't murder enough?

Both Aiden and I tried to speak to Esther again to find out what she knew about the victim, whose name was most likely Rosemary, but she refused to answer any questions. Even when Aiden threatened to take her to the county jail, she refused to talk.

Aiden let out a breath. "Esther, I don't think you understand the gravity of the situation."

"I understand it just fine," she snapped. "I would like to go home now."

Aiden's face fell, and he glanced at his departmental SUV, which was parked on the street. I knew what he was thinking. He had more than enough evidence to take Esther to the station for questioning, maybe even enough evidence to arrest her. But I knew Aiden when he was torn about making a decision; he always erred on the side of compassion.

"Very well," he said, proving my assumption right. "You can go home, but I will talk to you again tomorrow."

"Tomorrow is Sunday."

"And this is a murder investigation. It does not matter what day of the week it is."

She scowled at him and marched away. I walked to the corner of the square.

"You could have taken her in," I said.

He stared down at me. He looked so tired. I wanted to reach up and wipe the exhaustion from his face. I touched his cheek. Out of the corner of my eye, I saw Esther, in silhouette, tapping her foot. "I'd better go."

Aiden held my hand against his cheek for a moment more. "Please be careful. I can't live without you, and I couldn't live with myself if something happened to you because you were helping me with my job."

"Don't worry about me, Aiden Brody," I said with a smile and dropped my hand. "This isn't my first rodeo."

He groaned.

After I said good night to Aiden, I walked to my car, which was parked around the corner on Apple Street.

Like Emily, Esther looked petite standing under the gas streetlamp. With her cloak hood up over her head, she appeared more like a child dressed up for Halloween than a thirty-year-old Amish woman and successful business owner.

"Esther?" I asked as I approached.

She turned around, and the moonlight caught her pale face. She seemed even younger than Emily in that moment. Esther was frightened, which frightened me because I didn't know how this would all impact Emily's life. I'd be kidding myself if I said I didn't think the murder had something to do with the birth of Emily's first child.

"Are you ready to go?"

She nodded but made no comment.

Esther's silence was more disconcerting than finding Rosemary's body in the pretzel shop—and that was saying something. Because I'd never forget the expression on Rosemary's face, or the stillness in her unusual, dark green eyes. The details of her murder were ingrained in me now and would stay with me forever. It saddened me. And on the heels of that thought, I was saddened further thinking about Aiden. How many horrific images did he carry with him? Not necessarily murders, but there were other crimes, the faces of other victims, I was sure. It was almost one in the morning now. Esther must be exhausted. I knew I was.

I unlocked the car, and we both climbed in. "You live on Barrington Road." I knew this because I'd taken Emily home a handful of times before she'd gotten married.

Esther nodded and turned to look out the passenger-side window.

I put the car into gear and pulled away from the curb. It wasn't a long drive to Barrington—just under ten minutes—so that didn't give me much time to grill Esther for information. However, I had to try. I'd told Aiden that I would do my best. Though she might not like it, she'd likely rather talk to me about Rosemary and the letter the police found on the body than to Aiden or one of his deputies.

"Inside the pretzel shop, you said you didn't know who the dead woman was. Except the police found a letter addressed to Rosemary Weiss in the woman's apron pocket. They'll have to verify it, but the police are assuming that the woman is Rosemary. Even more interesting, the letter came from you."

She didn't respond.

I glanced at her across the car's dark interior. With no streetlights in this part of Harvest, I couldn't see her face.

"I don't know a lot about police work," Esther said. "But I'm certain Aiden Brody was not supposed to tell you that sort of information. You're not a deputy."

I didn't argue with her because she was right.

"Can you tell me who Rosemary is?" I asked.

"I don't have to tell you. You're not the police."

"You're right. But Aiden will ask you again. He might have let you go home tonight because he's a compassionate man and it's so late, but he will ask you again. When he does, he'll expect an answer. He'll keep asking until you give him one. You could even go to jail if you refuse to cooperate."

She turned to me. "Why would I go to jail? I've done nothing wrong."

"If you hinder the investigation, you could. That can definitely get you sent to jail. I bet Aiden already told you that, too."

She didn't answer, which told me I was right.

She turned back to the window and said, "The woman's name is Rosemary Weiss."

I let out a breath in surprise. I'd hoped that Esther

would tell me, but I'd also expected her to put up more of a fight. "Why didn't you tell me as soon as you saw her body?"

"I didn't say who she was when you came into the shop because I was shocked and scared. I didn't know what would happen."

I bit my tongue to keep from saying that lying was frowned upon in the Amish community, especially when it came to women who were praised for their honest virtue.

"How did you know her?"

She pressed her lips together.

"Esther?" I asked.

"Why does it matter?" she snapped.

"It matters because the sheriff's deputies found a very damning letter from you on Rosemary's person. The letter sounded threatening."

"A threat? I would never threaten anyone. And how do you know what the letter says? Did you see it?"

"I didn't."

"But Deputy Brody told you, didn't he? If I were *Englisch*, I would file a complaint about his behavior."

"He told me because he assumed that you would be more comfortable talking to me about Rosemary than talking to him."

"He was wrong," she said.

We turned onto Barrington Street. The Esh farm was at the end of the road. I didn't have much time. I slowed down the car just a tad, hoping she wouldn't notice.

"Tonight wasn't the first time that I saw Rosemary," I said.

She didn't say anything.

The Esh farm came into view. "I told you earlier that she was at the baby shower and said something to Emily about her daughter."

Esther stiffened.

"We both know that she wasn't talking about Emily and Daniel's unborn child because the Amish don't find out the gender of their children."

Esther smacked her hand on the dashboard, causing me to jump. The car swerved slightly, but I quickly regained control.

"She had no right to go up and speak to Emily like that," she said as she had before. "I told her not to do it!"

I took a breath, trying to calm myself after being startled so badly. "Why not?"

"Turn here." Her voice was clipped. "This is my driveway."

My heart sank. I was so close to finding out the truth, and I'd run out of time. "Would Emily know who that woman was?"

"*Nee*, don't involve my sister in this. She has nothing to do with it. She does not work for our family any longer."

"Esther, Rosemary spoke to Emily just a few hours before she died. It doesn't matter if you don't want Emily to be involved or not; she is. The police are going to want to know about that conversation."

"Emily does not know who the woman is," she snapped.

"Then how does Rosemary know her?" I asked as the car came to a stop.

She opened the car door. "I have said enough."

"Esther, I can help you if you'll let me." I heard the pleading in my voice.

"I don't need any help from an *Englischer*." With that,

she got out of my car and stomped toward the small ranch home.

The lights were on inside. There was no electric porch lamp to light her way to the door, but she was sure-footed. She must have made that walk in the dark a thousand times before. I idled in the driveway until she went inside. A light shone out from the front room.

In the window, a curtain moved, and a large shadow crossed through the light. I knew that it had to be Abel. I hoped he would be kind to her after what she'd discovered.

I sighed as I turned onto the street. Esther might think she didn't need my help, but this wasn't the first time I'd been a witness in a murder investigation. I knew the rules, and she did not. She needed my help, all right, and she needed it badly.

CHAPTER EIGHT

When I woke up the next day, I couldn't remember what time I'd gotten home the night before. I'd walked into the house and fallen onto the couch in my living room. I was only awake long enough to acknowledge that Charlotte was curled up on the cot on the other side of the room.

Bright sunlight flooded through the windows on either side of my door. I'd been meaning to buy thicker curtains for the windows to keep my nosy next-door neighbor, Penny, from peeking in, as she was prone to do. However, like so many things, I hadn't gotten around to it. It seemed that every day I wrote my to-do list with the very best intentions, and every day those intentions were derailed by other events . . . like murder.

I groaned and dropped my hand to the floor. Puff was there. Her soft fur was comforting.

"What time is it?" I asked the rabbit.

As usual, she didn't have an answer for me. Sometimes I wished Puff was like my smartphone and could answer simple questions about time, weather, and what was next on my calendar.

I vaguely remembered dropping my phone on the floor next to the couch before falling asleep. Through squinty eyes, I looked down. There was no sign of the phone. I was willing to bet Swissmen Sweets that it was under the giant white rabbit. For whatever reason, Puff loved to lie on electronics. It could be a phone, a remote, or even a computer. She wanted to lie on them all. Whenever my cell phone was within her reach, she turned up her nose at the cushy pet bed I'd bought her and placed under the window.

"Puff." I tapped her side. "Get off."

The rabbit didn't move an inch. I had to hang over the side of the couch and shove my hand under her to fish out the phone. My other arm was behind me, holding onto the back of the couch so I wouldn't fall.

I grabbed the phone and hoisted myself back on the sofa. Now that the phone was gone, Puff hopped away. She sat a few feet from me and narrowed her blue bunny eyes. If one day she went Bunnicula on me, I wouldn't be the least bit surprised if it was over my cell phone.

I checked the time. It was nine in the morning. I shot up. Nine wasn't late for some people to wake, but I was a candy maker who'd been trained to believe that sleeping any time after six was a crime.

I was late to the candy shop. Way late. Just as I had this thought, another one hit me. It was Sunday. The shop was closed. After that realization, the night before came into my mind, like a movie streamed across the front of my brain. Esther, the body in the pretzel shop, the smell of gas, Charlotte and *Maami* standing on the village green in their nightgowns, coats, and prayer caps. It was all too hard to believe. I was certain Aiden's head was reeling as well. Maybe he'd even wanted to arrest Esther last night, but as always, his compassion had won out. To drag her to the station in the middle of the night after such a gruesome discovery seemed cruel.

Despite Aiden's kindness, Esther wasn't doing herself any favors by not telling him how she knew Rosemary.

I padded into the kitchen and found a note from my grandmother.

Charlotte and I have church today. We took the buggy. After the night you had, we didn't want to wake you before we left. Maami

I let the note fall back onto the kitchen counter. One way that the Amish differed from other church groups was they didn't have church every week. Services were held at one of the church members' homes every other week. To their way of thinking, Sunday was for church, but it was also for family. On the off-church Sundays, the district members were expected to hold devotions in their own homes and educate their children about their faith.

As I stood there, it dawned on me that Emily would be going to church, too. That was terrible news. Not that she was going, but what she would be hit with when she went. The entire district would be talking about the events of the night before at the pretzel shop. Even though the only Amish there had been Esther, *Maami*, and Charlotte, I knew how the Holmes County gossip mill functioned. Everyone in the district would know about the murder before the end of the first hymn.

I had to warn Emily, but I also had to tell Aiden what

I'd learned from Esther. I didn't want to call him because he would ask what I planned to do that day and wouldn't like the answer. Instead, I shot him a text saying that Esther had confirmed that the victim was Rosemary but had given me nothing else.

I ran upstairs. I had to get to Emily. I had to comfort her. I also had to find out what she knew about the dead woman, because if Esther knew her, there was a good chance Emily did, too.

Penny waited for me by my garage. Penny Lehman was a conservative Mennonite, which meant she dressed like the Amish but drove a car. That stated the two cultures' differences in the simplest of terms, which I realized was not fair to either religion. Conservative Mennonites dressed in a plain style but were allowed to use all the technology they wished for home and business. The Amish were not.

"Oh, Bailey," my next-door neighbor said. "You're getting quite a late start this Sunday. You're usually out the door before the sun comes up."

I tried not to be irritated that she noticed my comings and goings. When I was in a hurry, it was much more difficult. I typed the code into the garage-door opener attached to the side of the one-car building.

Penny didn't take the hint. "I must say, I was very surprised to see your grandmother's horse and buggy parked on the street this morning. Both she and Charlotte stayed the night? Did you all have a girls' night in?"

"They just needed a place to sleep," I said. "For one night."

"I suppose that's because of the murder!" She paused. "You found the body, of course. A very unlucky talent you have for finding dead bodies."

I sighed when she finally got to the heart of the conversation. She wanted details about the murder.

"Umm, Penny, I'm surprised to see you at home at this time on a Sunday. Don't you have church today?" I asked pointedly. It was only fair to let her know that I kept tabs on her, too. Not very close tabs, though. Who had the time to be as nosy as Penny?

She rubbed her hip. "I couldn't go to services today. My arthritis is acting up again. It's difficult for me to sit in one place for long. It's much easier to stand and walk about. Our pastor doesn't like when I do that in the services. He claims it distracts him from his message. He invited me to stay home on the Sundays when my leg is bothering me."

I bet.

"What happened last night?" she asked. "I can't believe that another person has been murdered in our little village. It makes you want to hide in your home all day and all night."

"I can't really say. The Sheriff's Department would be upset with me if I said too much."

"Of course, you need to be careful because you don't want to jeopardize your engagement to Aiden Brody. Everyone is looking forward to the wedding. Have you set a date yet?" Her face was eager.

"Aiden and I are not engaged." I did my best to appear neutral and not show the irritation I actually felt at her question.

"That's not what his mother says." Penny stepped behind my car.

Oh, I know.

"I'm sorry, Penny, but I do really have to run. As you mentioned, I got a late start. Lots to do!"

She didn't move.

I sighed. I couldn't back up the car as long as she stood in the middle of the driveway. "Penny, can I ask you to step to the side so . . ."

"Oh, of course." Again, she didn't move. "You know, there are rumors flying through the village that Esther Esh killed that woman. It's hard for me to believe. Esther is as sour as they come, but murder? I never would have guessed that."

"Some probably made that assumption because it was Esther's shop."

"Yes and no. You're right, that's part of it, but Esther and the dead woman were seen on Apple Street having a terrible argument during Emily Keim's baby shower. One friend said that she saw Esther yelling and pointing at the woman." She brushed nonexistent lint from her skirt. "It's also hard for me to picture Esther yelling."

Apple Street ran perpendicular to Main Street, where Swissmen Sweets and Esh Family Pretzels were located. The fight must have happened just a few hundred yards from the party, but because it was around the corner, I hadn't seen it.

"Who saw the fight?" I asked.

"I—I don't know exactly who. I heard about it from my cousin, who heard it from an Amish friend."

"Which Amish friend?"

She shrugged. "She didn't say, but my cousin wouldn't tell tales that weren't true. She is an upstanding Mennon-ite woman, just as I am."

I chewed on my lip. Esther *would* be considered a sus-pect because of the location of the murder and the threat-ening note, but this evidence would make her appear even guiltier. I had a feeling that if she didn't speak to

Aiden or cooperate, she'd be spending the night in jail. Aiden's compassion would only go as far as his position as an officer of the law allowed.

"I'm sure Aiden will find out what really happened."

She finally stepped off the driveway and into the grass. "I'm sure *you'll* find out what really happened. If we're honest, you're the one who usually does."

CHAPTER NINE

As I drove to the Keim Christmas tree farm, I tried to call ahead on my cell phone. The answering machine picked up. I wasn't surprised. It was a church Sunday. I couldn't be certain that anyone in the family was at home, and if they were, the likelihood that they would be near the farm's shed phone when I called was slim. Not for the first time, I wished my Amish friends had cell phones.

I understood their reasons for not having phones. It was a way to keep friends and neighbors together. Instead of a quick phone call to tell someone something, they were encouraged to have conversations face-to-face. The in-person meetings allowed the Amish to settle disputes more quickly and to better understand intentions on both sides, whereas words could be misconstrued on a call or via text. However, when I needed to warn a friend about something bad, it was super frustrating and inconvenient.

As I drew closer to the home, I could see the little *daadihaus* that Grandma Leah lived in. It was like a miniature version of the large wood-framed home. A few chickens pecked at the ground outside the barn, but they were the only movement I saw. The farm was quiet, just as I had expected. The entire family, including Emily, Daniel, Daniel's father Thad, and Grandma Leah, must have gone to church. That could only mean that Emily already knew about the night's events.

I wondered if I should have told her the night before. I shook my head as I turned the car into the driveway. It would only have scared her and most likely the entire Keim family if I'd shown up at their farm after midnight.

I put the car in park and debated going up to the door to knock. I'd come this far; I might as well confirm my suspicions. I got out of the car, and the chickens—all five of them—came running to peck at my feet.

I hopped from foot to foot. "Hey, stop that. I didn't do anything to you!"

The largest chicken was all black with red wings. She flapped those wings and took off a couple feet from the ground.

"Ahh!" I cried and made a dash for the Keim front porch.

The chickens followed in hot pursuit.

Just as I made it up onto the porch, the front door opened.

"What on earth is going on out here?" Grandma Leah shouted from behind the closed screen door of the *daadihaus*.

"The chickens!" It was all I could get out before she

pushed open the screen door and came out waving her cane.

"Shoo, back to the henhouse with the lot of you," Grandma Leah cried.

The chickens clucked and cackled but flew or ran down the steps, back toward the barn.

I put a hand to my chest, feeling out of breath. "I didn't know chickens could fly."

She eyed me. "Of course, chickens can fly. They're birds, aren't they?"

"Penguins can't fly."

"Do they look like penguins to you?"

There was a black-and-white chicken that could double as a penguin, but I didn't say that.

"Now why are you here tormenting my chickens on a Sunday, Bailey King?" Grandma Leah demanded. Grandma Leah had snow-white hair pinned neatly back in an Amish bun at the nape of her neck. She wore a gray Amish dress and prayer cap, but no apron. Circular glasses perched at the end of her nose, and her trusty cane was always at her side. She might be over ninety, but she could easily pass for someone twenty years younger.

"Your chickens were tormenting *me*," I said.

The chickens had drawn together in a huddle, and I couldn't help but think they were regrouping for the next strike.

"I can't believe that you've lived in Holmes County for this long and are afraid of chickens." She set her cane down on the wooden boards at her feet.

"I'm not afraid of chickens, but when an animal that I don't know starts chasing me for no reason, it's a little unnerving."

"I'm sure the chickens had their reasons," she said.

I did not find the statement comforting. "I didn't know you had chickens anyway."

"New additions," she said with a smile. "I'm far too old to be much help with the tree farming, but there's no reason I can't take care of a few chickens and collect their eggs. I have to do something to keep myself busy. *Gott* wants us to work for his kingdom as much as we can while we're here on earth. I'm not dead yet. I have to do my part."

I was always a proponent of hard work; I just preferred it if chicken rearing wasn't part of it.

"Now, what are you doing here, *kind*?"

"I wanted to speak with Emily. I know that she's probably not home because church is today, but I have a very important matter to discuss with her."

Grandma Leah nodded. "It's about the dead woman at the pretzel shop, isn't it?"

I sighed, even though I wasn't surprised that she already knew. "Who told you?"

"Deputy Aiden Brody was here bright and early this morning and told us the news. He also had a number of questions for Emily. Daniel wasn't so keen on letting him speak to his wife, but I told him to let the deputy get on with it. After Deputy Brody left, it was difficult to convince Daniel and Thad to go to church without us. They can be so overprotective. Men!"

"Did you stay home from church because of what Aiden told you?"

"*Nee*, Emily and I were already planning to stay home. She was feeling poorly last night after the baby shower, so Daniel ran and fetched the midwife. The midwife said that Emily was overtired. I volunteered to stay home with her."

I bit my lip. "Do you think, if I talk to Emily, it will tire her more?"

"*Nee*, she's been up and doing a little knitting for the baby. I think she just needed a quiet day. It's not easy for a shy soul like Emily to be the center of attention the way she was at the party. Not all of us like that many people focused on just us. I personally haven't ever had that problem, but different personalities make the world go 'round."

Wasn't that the truth?

"Come on in." She shuffled to the big house, opened the screen door, and stepped inside.

I followed her.

"Emily, you have a visitor," Grandma Leah said as Emily walked into the living room from the kitchen.

"A visitor? It's not the police again, is it?" She placed a protective hand on her stomach. "Oh, Bailey. As soon as Aiden left, I expected you."

"Are you okay, Emily? Grandma Leah said the midwife was here."

She waved away my concern. "I'm fine. I'm much better than that poor woman who died in my family's pretzel shop." Tears pooled in her eyes. "I suppose you want to talk to me about her, just as Aiden did."

I gave her a sad smile. "I do."

"I'll get the Sunday roast on and let the two of you talk." Grandma Leah's cane made a rhythmic thump-thump on the wide plank floor until she disappeared into the kitchen.

"Have a seat, Bailey." Emily pointed at the sofa under the window, while she sat in a padded rocking chair by the potbellied stove. She ran her hands along the arms of the chair. "I love this chair. Daniel made it for me so that I could rock our baby to sleep at night. It should be in the nursery, but I asked him to put it here by the stove. I think the baby will like the warmth while being rocked."

"I'm sure you're right." I sat on the sofa.

She stilled her hands on the arms of the chair. "I hope I am. Being a mother is terrifying to me, Bailey. What if I'm not up to the task? What if I can't raise this child the way that he or she needs to be raised? What if I have to give this child up like I did the first one because I fail?"

I hinged forward in my seat. "Emily, I know that won't happen. You are one of the kindest and sweetest women—Amish or English—I've ever met. You'll be a wonderful mother."

"I failed before." She said this barely above a whisper.

"You made the choice that you felt you had to make at the time. You didn't have the support system you have now. Daniel, Grandma Leah—none of us will let you fail. We'll be there when you need strength or support."

Tears ran down her beautiful face. "But I didn't make the choice before, Bailey. I wasn't given a choice. The baby was taken from me. I was told what was best. I was too frightened and ashamed of what I had done to argue."

My hands curved into fists on my thighs as I heard that, but I couldn't let Emily see how much that revelation angered me. What a great injustice to lose her child that way. But what was done was done.

Still, a small part of me wondered if it could be undone.

CHAPTER TEN

"Can you tell me what happened with your first child?" I asked.

She looked down at her hands. They were bone-white from the pressure of holding them in place so tightly.

"I know it's difficult to speak about, but I really think your baby's adoption has something to do with Rosemary's murder." I shifted forward on the sofa, which was so big it threatened to swallow me.

She chewed on her lower lip. "I was young, and I thought that I was in love. The man—boy, really—who I loved was a few years older than me. I didn't understand . . . how children come into the world. It isn't something that the Amish talk about. Maybe I would have known better if my mother had lived. She might have told me, but no one else did. When I found out that I was pregnant, I was terrified. But the most terrifying thing was telling my sister and brother. I knew they'd be ashamed of me, and I was right."

"Who was the baby's father?" I asked.

"I can't tell you that. He's not Amish any longer, so it doesn't matter." She clenched her jaw closed.

I wasn't so sure about that, but I decided to drop that line of questioning for the moment.

"Whose idea was it to give the child up for adoption?"

"Esther's. I agreed because I didn't know what else to do. I was so frightened. By that time, the boy I loved had left the Amish faith, and I knew that I would never see him again. Esther had an *Englisch* friend in Indiana, so she decided to send me there. The friend lived near an Amish community, so I could go to a birthing center to have the child. Esther and Abel swore me to secrecy."

And I knew it was a secret they were determined to keep. When I'd first moved to Harvest, a developer was blackmailing the Esh family with Emily's secret. His goal was to convince them to sell the pretzel shop to him. When that developer turned up dead, the Eshes became suspects. It was the first case I'd helped Aiden with, and during that investigation, I had learned about Emily's first child.

"When you were in Indiana, did you see any other Amish?" I asked.

She clasped and unclasped her hands. "Not really. We were close to an Amish community, but I lived with an *Englisch* family for the last four months of my pregnancy, when I could no longer hide it. The family kept me out of sight. After the child was born and I was feeling better, I came home and went back to work at the pretzel shop."

"And you never knew who took the baby?" It was hard

for me to believe that she wouldn't have asked. I was certain I would have.

"I was told that my daughter was sent to a childless Amish family and the family was overjoyed. That's all I know." She let out a sigh as if she had been holding her breath. "I know that look on your face. I know that I should have asked more questions. I just did what I was told. I was so ashamed over what I'd done, I felt I didn't deserve a say in what happened to me any longer."

I bit my tongue to stop myself from correcting her. I knew Amish culture had its own way of dealing with children born out of wedlock and members whom the community believed had made poor choices. However, I didn't believe that anyone should be denied a say in the course of their own life.

She looked out the window. "She'd be six years old now. I wonder about her every day. I don't regret Esther's decision. I wouldn't have been a *gut* parent to her so young. If I'd kept my baby, my siblings would have turned me out of the house in order to save themselves from shame. Then where would we have gone? This way, she is growing up with a mother, father, and maybe aunts, uncles, and cousins. It's more than I ever had, and all that I would want for her."

"Did you talk to your bishop or a church elder about any of this at the time?"

She stared at me as if the suggestion was completely ridiculous. "*Nee*, no one in the church could know I was pregnant. Esther and Abel were very clear on that. We had to keep it a secret in the family."

I thought back to when I'd first come to Harvest and learned of Emily's secret. The blackmailer had died before he could act out his plan to acquire the shop, but

Emily's secret had come to light as a result of his death. How had the developer learned about it? Someone else must know. Could it have been the child's father who had told the blackmailer?

"I know it's difficult, but it might be helpful to know the name of the baby's father."

She wouldn't look me in the eye. "I can't tell you that."

"I'm afraid you might have to tell me or the police. Presumably, if he's still around, he'd be a suspect in the murder. Rosemary's death appears to be tied to the baby you gave up for adoption."

"He didn't know about the child. My brother and sister told me not to tell him."

I could hear the old hurt in her voice, and I balled my fists at my sides, close to my legs so that Emily couldn't see how upset I was over the way she had been treated. She had been coerced from the beginning to the end of her first pregnancy. I blew out a breath, hoping I'd be able to speak without revealing my emotions. "What about his family? They must still be here."

She nodded. "They're in Holmes County, but they are in a different Amish district. It's a blessing that I don't have to see them at church. I think that would have been very hard after I returned to Harvest."

"Have you seen the baby's father since you gave birth?"

She glanced at me. "Once. Just once. It was right before Daniel and I married. It was winter, and Margot had organized a hot chocolate sale on the square. I was there working for the sweet shop."

I wrinkled my brow. "I don't remember this."

"You were in New York at the time, filming your show. You and Charlotte were both gone. It was just Clara and I there to mind the shop, so I volunteered to work in the hot chocolate stand. I didn't want Clara to have to sit out in the cold. That's when I saw him."

I leaned forward. "Did he see you?"

"I don't think so. As soon as I spotted him, I put on my bonnet to hide my face and kept my head down. The only people who saw my face that day were the people who bought hot chocolate."

"What was he doing here?"

"I suppose he was visiting his family. He was in *Englisch* clothes and walked with an *Englisch* woman. They were holding hands. Even though I was about to be married, I felt like I'd been punched in the stomach. I'm happily married now to a *gut* man. He knows all I've done and still loves me. That is rare. I could never have hoped for such a husband as Daniel. He cares for me so well. But seeing the first man I loved with someone else, it was difficult. I wouldn't say it was because I wanted him to love me instead, but it felt odd. For a moment, I had this flash in my mind that what I was seeing could have been my life. I could have been the woman in the *Englisch* clothes walking beside him and holding the hand of a little girl."

"You thought of being *Englisch*?" This surprised me.

"*Nee*, but I know that's what he wanted. I was weak and young. It's clear that I was, or I would not have become pregnant in the first place. However, I didn't want to leave the Amish way, while he was very certain that he did."

I knew it wasn't my place to judge this young man

whom I didn't know, but I didn't approve of how he'd treated Emily. Emily might have not been aware of the ramifications of sex, but I bet the young man knew full well.

"That day I saw him, I remember feeling surprised that he would come back to Harvest. He knew my pretzel shop was across the street, even if I didn't work there any longer, though he couldn't have known I'd left."

I wasn't so sure about that. The Amish gossip mill was strong. If one Amish person wanted to find out what was happening in another Amish person's life, it wouldn't take a lot of work to get an idea.

"When I was in Indiana, my sister forwarded me a letter from him saying that he was leaving the Amish way for *gut*." She took a breath. "I was crushed." She dropped her head. "My sister had been right to tell me to give up the baby. The child would have no father. That is not the Amish way to raise children."

I bit my lip to keep myself from saying what I really thought. Emily had been naïve. I wanted to give Esther the benefit of the doubt and believe that she'd tried to do the right thing for her sister. But I couldn't help feeling she'd made her choices based on what was best for herself and the Esh family's reputation.

"What's his name, Emily? You have to tell me. Aiden will want to know."

"I can't tell you that," she whispered.

"You have to, and if you don't, I'll find it out another way. Even if people didn't know of the baby, I'm certain there will be someone in the district who will remember the young man courting you. Probably a lot of someones, based on how rumors fly around the district."

She took a breath. "Gideon Glick."

I felt as if a huge weight had been lifted when she said

that. Now, finally, I was getting somewhere in the case. "Thank you for telling me. I know this conversation must be hard, must remind you of old hurts."

She put a hand on her stomach. "This whole pregnancy has been difficult for me. It's been even more difficult than the first one because it brings back so many memories. So many regrets. I should have stood up for myself back then. But I was so young and scared, and Esther and Abel were so strong. I didn't have many choices, or at least it felt like I didn't have many choices. Maybe if I'd gone to the district bishop and the elders to confess, things would have turned out differently. Not only for my daughter and me, but for Rosemary, too." She looked at me with those wide eyes. "Do you think she was killed over the mistake I made all those years ago? How did she know about the baby?"

"It's hard to believe that would be the reason," I hedged, knowing it wasn't the definitive yes or no she'd been searching for. I wished I could give her more, but I didn't want to lie. Emily had been lied to too many times before.

"Is there anything I can do for you?" I wanted to get to my car, so I could call Aiden and tell him what I'd learned. I also wanted to ask him to tread lightly with Emily.

She looked up at me with tears in her eyes. "I'm worried about Esther. Is she in much trouble?"

I suppressed a wince. Esther was in a whole heap of trouble, but I couldn't tell Emily that without upsetting her more. "She is a suspect."

She gripped her hands a little more tightly in her lap. "I thought so. In that case, I do have a request. Can you find out who killed Rosemary Weiss to clear my sister's name?"

I didn't say anything.

"Please, Bailey. If this is tied to the child that I had years ago, I can't allow my sister to be punished for my mistake."

What if I discover that Esther did kill the woman? I wanted to ask, but I stopped myself. "I'll do my best."

"*Danki,*" she whispered and began to softly cry for Esther, her children, herself. I didn't know, and I didn't have the chance to ask because the front door opened and Daniel came running into the house.

He hurried over to Emily and knelt in front of her. "Are you sick?"

She shook her head. "I need to talk to you."

Daniel looked from me to Emily and back again. "What is it?"

I stood up. "Emily, I'll see you later. Why don't you take tomorrow off from the candy shop and rest? It's a Monday. Things will be slow."

She didn't respond, so I opened the door to go out.

"Where are you going?" Daniel asked me.

"You need to talk to Emily alone."

My heart hurt for her. It would be difficult for her to tell him what she had to say, and it would be hard for him to hear again the story of her first child. I prayed that Daniel would be understanding and not punish Emily any more than she had already punished herself for what had happened in the past.

I let myself out of the house. This was one time when eavesdropping wasn't the least bit tempting. I didn't need to hear the outcome of this conversation.

CHAPTER ELEVEN

Here's the thing about social media that most people don't think about: it makes it super easy to track a person down. As long as a person has a profile on the Internet and you have a few clues as to the people they might know and where they live, you can probably find them. Also, a startling number of folks don't take advantage of the privacy settings on their accounts. They might think that the picture of their dog is just going to their friends, but it's actually out there for all the world to see.

I knew this from my own experience at JP Chocolates. When I worked there as Jean Pierre's second in command, I was in charge of hiring sous chefs for the shop. The first thing I would do when reviewing applicants was to look them up on the Internet. There were many times I didn't even interview a candidate because their online persona appeared problematic. I'd also not dated someone for the same reasons. A boss or girl can never be too careful.

Aiden had told me many times that he'd used social media to track down criminals, and it's standard police procedure now. Of course, it doesn't work with the Amish criminals. But Gideon Glick was English now.

While driving away from the Christmas tree farm, I called Aiden to tell him what I had learned, but he didn't pick up. I pulled over to the side of the road and texted the highlights to him. While the car was stopped, I decided to take a peek on the Internet for one Gideon Glick. I found him with very little effort. According to his profile on a business networking site, he worked at an accounting office in Millersburg.

It was Sunday. The office would be closed, but I was out and about already, and I thought it wouldn't hurt to have a look at the place.

Millersburg was the county seat of Holmes County and a short drive from Harvest down a county road lined with Amish farms and stores. However, as I drove through the busiest part of the county, including the Amish town of Berlin, more of the businesses started to look English. It turned out that Millersburg was an English town in an Amish county.

The best indication of its Englishness was the impressive county courthouse. It rose hundreds of feet in the air. In the cupola, there was a clock, and a statue of the blind Lady Justice stood on a ledge near the top of the giant structure holding her scales.

Even though Millersburg was an English town in an Amish county, not many of its storefronts were open on a Sunday morning. Some would open at noon for the after-church crowds, but an accounting office probably wouldn't fall into that number.

There was ample street parking, so I pulled in next to the courthouse and decided to walk to the accounting firm. It was in one of the two-story brick buildings that lined the street across from the courthouse.

I walked over and studied the plaque screwed on the brick wall. The third listing down was Glick and Marin Accounting. I tried the door. No surprise that it was locked. I frowned at the door, and to my shock, it swung open. I jumped back just in time to avoid the door hitting me in the nose.

"Oh my God! Are you all right?" asked a thin woman in a bright blue wrap dress. She wasn't Amish, of course. She wore makeup, jewelry, a form-fitting dress, and super high heels. The Amish would never wear an outfit that was so impractical.

Before I could answer, she added, "You shouldn't be standing outside the door like that if you don't want to get hit."

I raised my brow. "I thought the place was closed. I was just locating the offices of Glick and Marin."

"Oh!" Her demeanor changed again, giving me mental whiplash. She was all smiles. "I'm Leslie Marin. Can I help you?"

"I was looking for an accountant." That was technically true. "Gideon Glick was recommended to me."

"What kind of accounting do you need?"

"Well, I'm a small business owner."

Her eyes sparkled. "We love small businesses. Would you like to come in for a moment and talk things over?"

"I—I didn't expect anyone to be here today."

"It's May—we're still in cleanup mode after tax season. It's easier to get catch-up work done when the rest of the county is sleeping or at church." She sighed. "Taxes are such a gauntlet every year. I told Gideon that we have to think about hiring some more help to get through the first four months of the year."

"Gideon is your business partner?"

"Yes, and he's my husband, too. I'd tell anyone to think twice before going into business with their spouse. I can't say that we're always on the same page." She laughed at her own joke.

"Oh." I didn't know why it surprised me that they were married. I supposed it was her name. A woman keeping her maiden name wasn't common practice in Holmes County. "Maybe he's that way because he was Amish."

Her eyes narrowed. I affected my most innocent expression. "His name is Glick, isn't it?"

"Oh, right," she said, slightly appeased. "I guess anyone who has lived in Amish Country for any amount of time knows Amish names. I'm not from here. I grew up in Cleveland."

"What brought you to Holmes County?"

"My husband. He wanted to be closer to his family, which surprised me. When I first met him, he didn't have many favorable stories about his life growing up Amish. I suppose age mellows a person out to old hurts."

Age? Leslie was twenty-four if she was a day. I guessed that Gideon was the same age. It was impressive that they'd been able to open their own office at such a young age.

"Would you like to come up and talk about how we could help grow your business? What kind of business are you in again?"

"I have a shop in Harvest." I waited to see what her re-action would be.

"Harvest?" She looked me up and down. "I thought all the businesses there were Amish. You would think with Gideon's Amish connection that we'd have luck drumming up business in that community, but they're another breed. They seem to think they can manage their own money. Maybe they can. But can they make it grow?"

I bit my lip to keep from saying that the Amish wanted to be comfortable, but they certainly weren't a culture concerned with accumulating wealth. They wanted to make money to help their families and the members of their district in case of illness or disaster. Having more than that would be a very foreign and *Englisch* concept to them.

Her phone rang. "Oh, I have to take this call."

She reached into her purse and came up with a busi-ness card. Judging by how quickly she was able to come up with the card, I guessed it was constantly at the ready. "Here's my card. Drop by sometime later this week. Both Gideon and I would love to speak to you about what we can do for you and your business." She smiled brightly. "What was your name again?"

I had never said. "Bailey."

"Well, Bailey, I think you would be pleased with the full-service accounting services we offer. You know, some-one your age should begin thinking about retirement. We can help you with that, too, and your employees." She waved the card in my face.

I arched my brow, not amused by her hard-sell tactics. However, I accepted the card. It couldn't hurt to have a suspect's phone number. I wondered if Rosemary had in-terrupted this high-strung woman's plan for her life, especially if Rosemary knew about the child that Gideon had had with Emily. Did Leslie even know that Gideon had a child out in the world somewhere?

Her phone rang again. "I have to jet. Talk soon." She waved to me, put her phone to her ear, and hurried down the street. From where I stood, I could hear her yelling into the phone.

I looked down at the business card. It seemed that my visit to Millersburg had been worth it. I had a new suspect to add to my growing list. I sighed, knowing what Aiden would say about my having a suspect list in the first place. I'd made Emily a promise that I would clear Esther's name, but I still had to entertain the possibility that Esther actually was the killer. Rosemary was a few inches taller than Esther, but there wasn't a huge difference. If Esther had caught Rosemary by surprise from behind . . .

I closed my eyes, trying to remove the image from my head, but it was too late. I had already allowed it into my mind.

As I walked back to the car, my phone rang. I looked down at the screen and saw the smiling face of Cass Calbera, my best friend and the head chocolatier at JP Chocolates in New York.

I answered the call.

Without preamble, she asked, "Find any dead bodies lately?"

"Ummm."

"OMG, Bai, are you serious?"

"I didn't find it first."

"Like that makes it okay."

"Why on earth would you ask that question anyway?"

"Well, it's been about a year since you found your last one—I figured you were due."

"Cass . . ."

"Hey, if I can't make jokes about your weird gift for finding dead people, what can I do? I mean, seriously, Bailey, it's kind of ridiculous."

I couldn't argue with her about that. I did seem to have a knack for finding dead bodies. It wasn't a skill I was proud of.

"Okay, give me the lowdown." I walked back to my car, giving Cass the highlights, but I left out any news about Emily and her past. I wasn't going to betray my friend.

"Are you okay?" Cass asked, sounding concerned. "I mean, Esther has been nothing but horrible to you. Why would you want to help her?"

"She's Emily sister," I said. "And maybe a small part of me hopes that if I prove she's innocent, she'll make amends with her sister. I know their bad relationship weighs heavily on Emily, and I've seen firsthand how Esther and Abel treat her."

"Bai, you continue to prove that you are a much better person than I am."

"Cass, under that tough exterior, you have a big heart," I argued.

"Maybe, but nobody has as big a heart as you do, Bai. Nobody."

CHAPTER TWELVE

I drove back toward Harvest and had just gotten through Berlin when an SUV from the Sheriff's Department pulled in behind me. It sounded its siren and lights. I smiled. I supposed that wasn't the normal reaction when one was pulled over by the Sheriff's Department, but I knew that car. I turned into a warehouse parking lot. Aiden followed me.

I got out of my car and leaned against it, folding my arms, "Are you allowed to pull over citizens when they're obeying all the traffic laws?"

He laughed. "I can always think of a reason to pull someone over. That's what safety checks are for."

I wrinkled my brow. "Is that what this is? A safety check?"

He came and stood next to me, leaning on my car. We stood hip to hip. "Sure. We can call it that, and the term works because you sometimes seem to find your way into a whole mess of trouble. If anyone under my jurisdiction needs a safety check, it's you, Bailey King."

I sighed. "I suppose you're right."

"So, it seems to me that you're coming from Millersburg. You wouldn't happen to be coming from Gideon Glick's accounting office, would you?"

"Who, me?"

He shook his head. "I do appreciate your speaking to Emily. When I talked to her, she didn't tell me the name of her first baby's father. He lives in the county, so he is a suspect."

"I thought as much, which is why I went to the office." I reached into my jeans pocket and came up with Leslie Marin's business card. I held it out to him. "While I was there, I ran into Gideon's wife."

He took the card. "Wife?"

"Yep." I went on to tell him about my brief conversation with Leslie. "She really wants to be my accountant."

"I bet she'd want that even more if she knew you have a show on Gourmet Television."

"Hmm . . ."

"Bailey, I'm not saying that to encourage you to interview her again." Aiden fell quiet.

I shifted my position to face him. "What's up, Aiden? You're not telling me to back off the investigation. You're not telling me what you plan to do next. It's not like you to be so quiet about this sort of thing."

He pressed his lips together.

"Aiden?" I asked, growing worried.

"An opportunity has come up."

I wrinkled my brow. "What kind of opportunity?"

He turned to look at me. "A job opportunity. I've been recruited by BCI."

"BCI?" I repeated dumbly, feeling like a parrot. All I knew about BCI was that it was the FBI on the Ohio state level, Ohio's Bureau of Criminal Investigation. I'd met one of the agents last year when there was a murder case that dealt with an illegal still. The illegal still had brought BCI in on the case.

"Do you remember Agent Robbie Bent?" he asked, mentioning the name of the agent I had met. "She's the one who put in a good word for me with the agency."

"Did you ask her to?"

"No." He shook his head. "I wasn't looking for other work, but she was impressed by how I handled the case and my efforts to bridge the culture gap between the Sheriff's Department and the Amish community. She thought those skills would translate well to BCI as the Amish population in Ohio continues to grow. It's important that there's cooperation between law enforcement and the Amish."

"She was here in Holmes County last summer because of the illegal still in Harvest. Have you seen her since?"

"On other cases in the county," he said. "Nothing as big as the murder last summer."

"What does the offer entail?"

"It's a sizable bump in pay, for one thing, and I would be in charge of my own unit, focusing on crimes in Amish communities across the state."

"It sounds like a great fit." Even as I said this, I felt apprehension grow, and my right arm tingled as if it were about to go numb. "What did you tell her?"

"Nothing yet, but I have a week to make a decision before they open a statewide search and give it to someone else."

"Just a week? That's not a lot of time to make this kind of choice."

"Actually, they gave me two months. I'm just down to the wire now."

I bristled. "You had two months to make this decision, and you're just telling me now?" I couldn't keep the accusation from my voice.

"Don't be like that, Bailey. I had to know how I felt about the new job before I came to you with it."

"You didn't want my opinion." I winced.

He looked at me. "Did you consider my opinion when you agreed to take on the television show?"

"I—I—" He had a point, but to me that was different. At that time, we hadn't been together long. We hadn't been seriously talking about getting engaged like we had recently. What would this mean for us? Where would he live? How would this impact our life together?

I told myself to settle. "What have you decided?"

"You don't sound enthusiastic about this opportunity."

"You've had a while to sit with it," I said. "It's just hitting me now. I'm trying to process this and what it means."

"What do you mean, what it means?" He frowned. "It means that I might have a promotion."

I bit back a sharp retort because the truth was I *hadn't* consulted Aiden when I'd made my decision about working for Gourmet Television. It hadn't even entered my mind to ask him. At the time, I hadn't been used to consulting someone else when making choices about my life. I'd been on my own since I was eighteen. "Can you tell me what you think about the opportunity?"

"The money would be helpful if . . ." He trailed off.

"If what?"

"If we get married." He studied my face. "Don't you want the fairy tale, Bailey? The house, the white picket fence, the dog, the children?"

I forced a laugh. "I don't know where the dog would fit in with Puff and Nutmeg," I joked. "And Jethro is with me half the time, too."

His face fell. "Every time we speak about marriage, you make light of it. I don't think it's a laughing matter."

I grabbed his hand. "I'm sorry, Aiden. I don't think it's a laughing matter either. I do want to marry you, but when you talk about the Norman Rockwell version of married life, I don't know. I never saw myself in that place. It doesn't change the fact that I love you and want to marry you."

He studied my face. "I love and want to marry you, too, but this job, well, it could put those plans on hold. We haven't been talking about a specific timeline, but I would be lying if I didn't admit that I had one in mind." He held my hand tightly. "I want to begin my life with you, but I don't want to start it and then leave for this job."

My stomach twisted in a knot. I didn't want Aiden to go, but I would not say that. It would not be fair to him to say that.

He rubbed the back of his head. "I can't deny this is a great opportunity. It's becoming increasingly difficult to be an effective officer of the law in this county with the sheriff undercutting me at every turn." He licked his lips. "At BCI, I'd have my own unit. Sure, there'd be more levels of bureaucracy, but I'd be calling my own shots within the unit, and Agent Bent would be my supervisor.

We have a good working relationship. She trusts me. She trusts me more that the sheriff ever has."

"The sheriff shouldn't even be in office anymore. If someone . . ." It was my turn to trail off.

He sighed. "I know that you think I should have run against him at the last election, and maybe you're right. But things just don't work that way in law enforcement. Respect for those in authority is a very real thing."

I stared at him. "Are you going to take the new job?"

He swallowed. "I don't know. The main BCI office is in London, Ohio. After training, I could be sent anywhere in the state. Commuting to the office is something to consider. The main office is about two hours away, and the closest field office is an hour away. My lease is up on my apartment. Perhaps it would make sense to get a place closer to where I worked."

My stomach tightened more as he said this. "It would be a long commute."

He nodded.

I couldn't tell Aiden not to take the job just because I'd miss seeing him at Swissmen Sweets every day or that I hated the idea that it would push the timeline of our getting engaged and married into the distant future. He'd never tried to talk me out of my candy shop show, which had me traveling back and forth to New York for days at a time. "How long is the training?"

"Six months, and it's pretty intense. We aren't allowed to leave the training center even on weekends for the first few weeks."

"You'll be gone for six months." I said this barely above a whisper.

He studied my face. "If I decide to take the job, yes."

I bit the inside of my lip.

He leaned back on the car and faced forward. "I just always thought that I'd be sheriff of Holmes County someday."

"Aiden, you're young. You have a long and great career in front of you. Even if you take this job at BCI, that doesn't mean you can't be sheriff someday. Perhaps it will give you the distance and experience that you need to be an even better sheriff."

"Does that mean you want me to do it?"

I sighed. "Do I like the idea of your being gone for six months? No. Not even a little bit. Do I like the idea that we might not get engaged for a while? No. I understand it, though. But it's not my place to tell you what to do when I'm gone for weeks at a time filming my show. Perhaps being a BCI agent, you'll be taken more seriously as a candidate for sheriff. Sometimes a person has to break away from the place he was raised and then come back to be taken seriously."

"You think I'm not taken seriously?"

"You are by the public, but I know you aren't by the sheriff. Aiden, you haven't been happy in your job for months. I've seen it."

He nodded.

I took his hand again. "Whatever you decide, I support you. I just want you to be happy." I looked deep into his chocolate-brown eyes. They reminded me of milk chocolate, which as a chocolatier, I had always found dependable in my work. Aiden was dependable in my life. "It's your choice. Your choice alone. I love you and if you have to go, I'll wait. I'm not going to disappear."

He kissed me. "I love you, too, and talking to you makes me feel better. I should have told you sooner, but I was a chicken." He sighed. "I have other concerns, too. I worry about the department after I leave and what will happen to the Amish if I'm not here to protect them from the sheriff."

"I can understand that, but Deputy Little will still be here. You've been training him for years. Perhaps it's time he stepped into the limelight." I couldn't believe I was trying to talk Aiden into this, but everything I said was true.

Aiden nodded and straightened. "I should go. I have to get back to the office."

"It's Sunday."

He smiled. "And there's a murderer on the loose. I can't rest until this person is caught and everyone in Harvest feels safe again, including you. So please, please be careful." He looked deep into my eyes. "I don't know what I would do if something happened to you."

"Can I ask you the same thing?"

"Sure." His lip curved up in a smile.

I hugged him and buried my face in his chest so he wouldn't see my worry. Worry for him every day on the job. Worry for what would happen to us if he left for so long.

CHAPTER THIRTEEN

The next morning, when Margot Rawlings and Ruth Yoder walked into my candy shop together, I knew I was in trouble. The two of them were always at odds with each other. Margot wanted to move the village into the twenty-first century and beyond, while Ruth wanted to keep it firmly in the Amish tradition, so circa 1800.

Charlotte stared at them from her spot behind the candy counter. "Are you two here . . . together?"

It was a fair question and one that I had been wondering about, too.

Margot and Ruth were about the same age, somewhere in their sixties. Ruth, the bishop's wife, wore a pressed plain dress, black apron, and perfectly positioned prayer cap on her gray hair. In contrast, Margot's graying brown curls sort of bounced on the top of her head, and she wore a flowered blouse and denim capris. However, Margot's casual attire didn't fool me into thinking that she wasn't dropping by Swissmen Sweets on business.

Ruth glanced at Margot with a pinched look on her face. "Margot and I have spoken, and we are very concerned about the reputation of Harvest."

I tried not to make a face, because this wasn't my problem—well, not completely—but I had a feeling that both Margot and Ruth were about to make it my problem.

"There have been so many murders in the village, it's making us look bad in the eyes of the rest of the county," Margot said.

"But there are more tourists than ever in Harvest because of Bailey's show. It doesn't seem to me that anyone is staying away because of the murders." Charlotte wrinkled her nose.

"They aren't staying away yet," Margot said. "But it's just a matter of time before they do. Who wants to go to an Amish town where the Amish are killing each other all the time?"

Ruth glared at her. "The Amish aren't killing each other. The upswing in crime, is, of course, because of the increased *Englisch* influences in the village."

Margot put a hand on her hip and stared at Ruth. "You have it in your head that the Amish can do no wrong. There are law-breaking Amish just as there are law-breaking English. The sooner you realize that, the better."

"Perhaps there have been some unfortunate events when an Amish person was pushed too far by an *Englischer.*"

Margot threw up her hands.

"What does this have to do with me?" I interjected before the two of them could come to blows.

"Deputy Aiden Brody needs to clear up this murder

case as soon as possible, but we know that he can't do without your help." Margot folded her arms.

I was relieved that there weren't any tourists in the shop at the moment to overhear our conversation. I didn't think talking about murder was conducive to selling candy. "What am I supposed to do about it?"

"We need you to help Aiden solve this case," Margot insisted.

I made a face. I wasn't about to tell them that I was already planning to do that. To be honest, with my history of solving several murders in Holmes County over the last few years, I didn't think I had to.

"It doesn't look good for the village when a shop-keeper is suspected of murder." Margot shook her head.

"You mean Esther Esh," I said.

"Yes, of course, I mean Esther," Margot replied curtly.

"And it doesn't look *gut* for our district," Ruth said, "when a member of the church is suspected of murder." She narrowed her eyes at Margot. "The church is more important than the town."

"No, it is not!" Margot cried. "This is the place where you live. How can you even say that?"

They looked as if they were about to come to blows again. It seemed to me that Margot and Ruth's teaming up to talk to me about this matter had been a very bad idea. One or the other should have come to deliver the message. However, knowing them, they wouldn't have liked that either because the one not delivering the message would be certain that the presentation was skewed, which it would be.

I held up my hands. "What information can you share that would help me solve this murder? You were both at the baby shower; did you see Rosemary there? Do you know her?"

Margot looked at Ruth and waited. Charlotte and I turned our attention to the bishop's wife and waited, too.

"I do not know Rosemary from Holmes County, but yes, I knew who she was and where she was from."

I stopped myself from throwing up my hands again. I wished she had just said that at the beginning. "And?"

"There's no reason to get all riled up over it, Bailey," Ruth snapped.

I closed my eyes and quickly recited the different types of chocolate, as Jean Pierre at JP Chocolates had taught me to do when I was upset. It always had a way of calming me. I opened my eyes. "How do you know Rosemary?"

Ruth pressed her lips together, and I worried she wouldn't answer my question. Finally, after what I could only believe was an intentional beat, she said, "As you know, my husband is the bishop of the largest Amish district here in Harvest."

Next to Ruth, Margot rolled her eyes. I had to avert my own.

"As bishop of such an important district, he interacts with bishops and Amish communities all over the area. He is the particular friend of a bishop in Wayne County. Rosemary attends services in that district."

"Attends," I said, noting the word. "Attends is a lot different than belongs to."

"She has attended at the district of my husband's friend for many years, but she is a member of a district in Indiana."

Indiana. That's where Emily gave up her baby for adoption. It could not be a coincidence that Rosemary was from that state, could it?

"How do you know about her?" I asked. "I'm sure there are many people in that district that you don't know by name."

"This is true. However, Rosemary was in a women's group from that district, and we raised money together to build a school that had burned down in Wayne County. No one was hurt in the fire," she added quickly. "Our district became involved because a young member of our church was the teacher at the school." She took a breath. "As you know, whenever our ladies help with a project, I want to know how everything is going to come together."

I knew this well. "Delegate" was not a word in Ruth's vocabulary. "Micromanage" was, though.

"So," Ruth went on, "I insisted on meeting with all the women involved. Rosemary was in charge of collecting the donations from the Wayne County district that were to be auctioned off. She was keeping them in her family bakery. I went there to make sure everything was organized and ready. I was surprised to see that she had it all well in hand." She sniffed.

Beside me, I heard Charlotte stifle a chuckle. I thought we were both thinking that Ruth had likely been disappointed that Rosemary did such a good job.

"When I was there, I met her cousin, who owned the bakery, and Rosemary's young daughter."

My chest constricted. "Daughter? How old was she?"

Ruth thought about this for a moment. "She couldn't have been more than five or six. She was a lovely girl. Quiet and pretty. The way all girls should be."

Next to Ruth, Margot grunted. I was on Margot's side on this one.

An idea tickled in the back of my mind, but I pushed it away. I couldn't be right. "What was her cousin's name?"

"Dinah Stoltzfus," Ruth said.

Another suspect.

"Did you tell Aiden any of this?" I asked.

Ruth folded her arms. "I did not. The deputy has not come to talk to me about the murder. I suppose you can be trusted to relay this information."

"I can," I said, but even as I spoke, I realized that Aiden might already know. He did have the letter that Esther had sent Rosemary. It had a Wooster address on it. Was it the address of the bakery?

"What's the name of the bakery?" I asked.

"The Dutch Muffin. It's within walking distance of the College of Wooster." She wrinkled her nose at this.

I wasn't the least bit surprised that Ruth viewed higher education with disdain.

"What do you plan to do about all of this, Bailey?" It was Margot who asked the question.

"Do about the murder?"

"Yes, about the murder. These deaths seem to be occurring again and again, and we just can't have it," Margot said with click of her tongue. "How are we supposed to attract more tourists to the village if people keep being murdered here? It's so bad for tourism."

Ruth gave her a look. "We aren't concerned about the impact on tourists. We're worried about the people who live here in the village. We're worried about the impact on the Amish in particular. We are a quiet and kind people. We don't want the *Englisch* to think otherwise."

Margot shook her head. "The point is that we both want the same thing. We want you to fix this. You have to solve this murder and do something to keep any more from happening," Margot said. "We have complete faith in you."

After Ruth and Margot left the shop, Charlotte and I shared a look.

"You're going to the Dutch Muffin, aren't you?"

My mouth curved into a smile. "How did you know?"

"Let me go with you."

"Charlotte . . ." I began.

"I can help! I really can. You won't be going into an Amish business in Holmes County. The Amish there won't know you. They won't trust you. It would help to have an Amish person with you to show you are okay." She pointed at herself. "Me!"

I wrinkled my brow, but I had to admit, she had a point. I did have a reputation in Holmes County for poking my nose in Amish business. But Charlotte was right; it might not have reached Amish districts outside of the county. "I need to go now if I want to get there before the bakery closes. If you come too, that will leave *Maami* alone in the candy shop for the rest of the afternoon because Emily isn't here today. We'll have to ask *Maami*."

"Ask me what?" *Maami* queried as she came into the front of the shop from the kitchen.

Charlotte beamed at her. "Whether I can leave with Bailey to interview a murder suspect."

I sighed.

"Bailey, are you pulling Charlotte into your detective work, too?" *Maami*'s eyes were wide.

I held up my hands in surrender. "It's not my fault. It was her idea."

CHAPTER FOURTEEN

Charlotte and I were walking to my car, which I'd left on Apple Street, when someone shouted my name. "Bailey! Bailey!"

Even if I hadn't recognized Juliet's voice, the Carolina accent would have been a dead giveaway. Usually, Juliet's accent was more pronounced when she was stressed, excited, or upset. It was rare that Juliet was running at me when she wasn't experiencing one of those three emotions. I turned to see Juliet rushing to me as quickly as she could while balancing on polka-dotted heels, with Jethro cradled in her arms like a baby. "Bailey!"

Charlotte and I stopped in the middle of the sidewalk.

"She's going to ask you to pig sit," Charlotte said.

I gave her a look, but I knew she was right.

"Bailey!" Juliet skidded to a stop in front of us.

I put out my hand to steady her. "Juliet, please be careful. Those shoes were not made for sprinting."

She laughed. "Oh, you sound just like Aiden. It's no wonder the two of you make such a perfect pair." She smiled at Charlotte. "I don't have much time."

She held Jethro out to me.

I didn't move.

"Can you take Jethro for me? I was just at Swissmen Sweets to ask you if you would watch him. Clara told me that you and Charlotte were leaving on an errand, so I hurried to catch you." She let out a breath and pushed Jethro toward me.

I accepted the pig. I don't even know why I bothered to hesitate. It wasn't as if it was ever in question whether I would pig sit or not. "What are you about to do that Jethro can't stay with you?"

She clasped her hands together. "Oh, Bailey, you have no idea what a responsibility being a pastor's wife is. I have so many activities with the women's league of the church. I lead the meetings now, you know, and I just can't keep an eye on Jethro during those get-togethers." She shook her head. "You know how curious he can be. The last time we had a gathering, he broke into the church kitchen and ate an entire bin of potatoes. I can't have that, Bailey. I have to keep up my reputation and the reputation of Reverend Brook as well."

I bristled. There was that word again. Reputation. It seemed to be following me everywhere today.

"Please take him. It's only for a few hours. Bring him back to the church after. Say, around six? That way he can have dinner at home with Reverend Brook and me."

I looked down at the pig. Of course I would have to get the little bacon bundle home in time for his dinner.

"Okay," I said with a sigh.

"You're the best daughter-in-law a woman could have!" She kissed Jethro on the snout. "Now, you be good for Bailey. No potato stealing!" She scratched him between the ears and then finger-waved at Charlotte and me before hurrying back to the corner of Main and Apple Streets on the way to the church.

Charlotte started to chuckle.

"Don't say anything about the pig," I muttered.

"I wasn't going to," she said. And then she laughed out loud.

The drive to Wooster from Harvest took close to forty minutes in late-afternoon traffic. Or what rural Ohio considered late-afternoon traffic. I couldn't imagine what it would have been like to travel between the two towns by buggy. It would really feel like a world away.

Charlotte stared out the window as we drove. "It's nice to get out of Holmes County, isn't it? Even if we are just one county over, it's nice to see something new."

I glanced at her. "It is."

"Ever since our trip to New York, when you took me to the filming of your show, I keep thinking that I'm missing out on a lot. There's so much more out there to see. And they aren't things I have access to as an Amish woman."

I made a noncommittal sound. As long as I had known her, Charlotte had been struggling with the idea of being baptized into the Amish church.

"There are so many things I want to do. I loved planning Emily's shower, and I still love playing the organ at the *Englisch* church. You inspire me, Bailey. Nothing and no one holds you back. I want to be like that, but I'm not sure I can and be a *gut* Amish woman at the same time.

There are places I want to see and plans I want to make with . . ."

I turned my head for a second and looked at her. "With whom?"

She shook her head. "I just have to make a choice, Bailey, and soon. It's eating away at me."

"You will," I reassured her.

"I want to make the right decision for me, and not worry about anyone else."

I couldn't help better wonder who else she could possibly consider.

Wooster was adorable, but very much a college town, too. There were a few bars, bookstores, coffee shops, and even a few boutiques that catered to college students. It definitely had a different vibe from Harvest. In the middle of the main street was the Dutch Muffin.

I parallel-parked on the street, and Charlotte looked out at the bakery.

"It's so cute," she cried. "It's like a cottage out of a fairy tale that I read in a book from the library."

I glanced at her. "I didn't know Amish children were allowed to read fairy tales."

"I'm not saying my parents knew I read them."

I smiled and glanced into the back seat at Jethro. "We had better leave him in the car. It's not hot today. He'll be fine with the windows rolled down a bit."

Jethro grunted as if he understood everything I'd just said. If you asked Juliet, he had.

"It seems as if Juliet asks you to take care of Jethro more and more lately."

I made a face. "I guess she didn't realize how much responsibility being a pastor's wife would be. I know she was involved in Reverend Brook's church before they got married, but now she's there all the time."

"Can't she take Jethro with her? I never knew Reverend Brook to say the pig wasn't allowed in the church. He was in their wedding, for goodness' sake."

"I think Juliet is beginning to realize that she can't run programs at the church and watch the pig at the same time. There have been more than a few mishaps."

"Like the potatoes?" Charlotte asked.

"Yes, but before that, he knocked over the baptismal font."

"He's basically like a human toddler." Charlotte chuckled.

I laughed. I'd never heard of a better description of the pig before. I got out of the car, making sure the windows were rolled down a little ways. Jethro placed a hoof up against the back glass and stuck his snout through the crack in the window.

"Making me feel guilty won't help. We'll only be gone for a few minutes."

He fell back onto the seat with a soft squeal.

"He's one dramatic pig," Charlotte said.

That was the understatement of the millennium.

Charlotte had been right; the bakery was like a cottage in a fairy tale. There was a small garden by the front door filled with spring flowers. A stone plaque had a Bible verse on it. A cheerful pink and white wooden WELCOME sign was on the front door. It was all so charming and so not Amish. There were too many frills. Too many embellishments. I couldn't help but wonder what the rules of plainness were for this district of Amish. When we stepped inside, a bell chimed.

A round Amish woman with pink cheeks stood behind

the counter, beaming at us. On the tiled counter, there were five different platters covered in glass domes that held the most delectable treats I had ever seen.

My stomach growled. I swore the blueberry muffins were twice the size of my fists.

Charlotte bumped me with her elbow. "Cousin Clara warned you not to skip breakfast."

I shot her a look. I had skipped breakfast and lunch, too, if I didn't count the piece of fudge I'd eaten back at the candy shop.

"*Gude mariya, wilkumm* to the Dutch Muffin. Can I help you?" the Amish woman asked.

"Yes," I said. "Charlotte, why don't you pick out something to eat?"

In my experience, shopkeepers were much more likely to answer my questions if I bought something from them first.

"Oh, it's so hard to choose." She clasped her hands together. "I never met a baked good that I didn't like. What do you recommend?"

The woman chuckled. "I'm told often it's difficult to make a choice. I just pulled a lemon tart out of the oven. It's one of my favorites."

Charlotte wrinkled her nose. "Sounds lovely, but I just spent the last week up to my elbows in lemons. Do you have anything with chocolate?"

Charlotte really was a girl after my own heart.

"I have double chocolate muffins."

"Perfect! I'll take one of those. Anything that has double chocolate is sure to be a winner."

"I'll take one, too," I interjected. They just looked too good to pass up, and I was hungry.

The woman nodded and picked up two plastic containers from a stack. She placed the muffins into the containers and closed them. "That will be six dollars."

Charlotte accepted the containers, and I set a ten on the counter. "Keep the change."

The woman stared at the bill. "That's most generous. *Danki*!"

When Charlotte and I didn't move, she asked, "Is there something else I could help you with?"

"Are you Dinah Stoltzfus?"

She smiled uncertainly. "I am."

"This is the shop that Rosemary Weiss worked in?"

Tears gathered in her eyes, and she grabbed a dish towel from the counter. "I'm so sorry. It has been difficult."

I nodded. "I can understand that. We're from Harvest."

"Are you from the pretzel shop?" she gasped.

I shook my head. "Charlotte and I work at Swissmen Sweets next door. When the owner of the pretzel shop found Rosemary, she ran to our shop for help. We are friends with Ruth Yoder. She said that she knew Rosemary and told us about your shop."

Charlotte made a sound. Okay, maybe technically we weren't friends with Ruth, but we knew her pretty well. It was close enough in my book.

Dinah touched the cloth to the corner of her eye. "I—I don't understand. Why are you here?"

"We wanted to share condolences from our village."

Her face reddened. "*Danki*. That is very kind."

"And we are very good friends of Emily Keim," I added.

Her face went blank.

"You might know her better as Emily Esh."

A light dawned in her eyes, and she looked down for

just a moment before making eye contact with me again. Then she glanced at the floor again. "Is Emily with you?"

I shook my head and started to wonder what kept grabbing her attention at her feet. "Do you know why Rosemary was visiting the pretzel shop? Did it have something to do with Emily?"

She wrung the towel in her hands. "It was about Hannah. My cousin wanted Hannah to meet her mother. Rosemary is the only mother that Hannah has ever known, but Rosemary thought it was important that the child knew she had another mother, especially because . . ." She trailed off and looked at the floor again.

I peered over the counter to see what she was looking at. I gasped. There was a young girl on the floor, flipping through a picture book. Her honey-colored hair was twisted in a long braid that hung over her shoulder.

"Oh hello," I said to the girl, but she didn't look up.

"She can't hear you," Dinah said. "She can't hear anything."

"She's deaf?" Charlotte asked, looking over the counter, too.

Dinah nodded. "She's been that way since birth. She's never even heard Rosemary's voice and never will." She stepped toward the child and touched her shoulder.

Hannah looked up in surprise. Dinah pointed at us, and the child closed her book and scrambled to her feet. When she made eye contact, I gasped. It was like looking into a younger version of Emily's face. I could see Emily everywhere, from the large, blue Disney-princess eyes to the pert nose and the honey-colored hair that I knew would sparkle in the sunshine, just like Emily's.

CHAPTER FIFTEEN

I guessed that Charlotte also saw the resemblance to Emily in Hannah's face because she gasped. I'd guessed that Rosemary had adopted Emily's daughter—that had been my suspicion from the start, but I had not expected to come face-to-face with the child so soon.

Dinah shook her head. "You can understand my distress. I don't know what to do with Hannah. She was Rosemary's daughter and now has no one in the world."

"Wait, didn't Rosemary have any other family? Was she married?" I asked.

Dinah's expression was pained. "She was technically still married when she died, but her husband, Isaac, will have no interest in an Amish child. He had no interest in anything Amish at all."

"But if they are married, isn't he Amish?" Charlotte

asked. "I've never heard of an Amish person marrying a non-Amish person and remaining Amish."

"They are separated and have been for many years." She glanced at Hannah again. "Perhaps you can help me."

"What do you mean?" I asked.

Dinah sighed. "Let's sit." She folded the dish towel and set it back on the counter. "If you are friends with the Esh family, perhaps you can help me with the problem of Hannah."

I glanced at the beautiful young girl. How could anyone think a child was a problem?

Dinah came around the counter, and Hannah followed her. Charlotte glanced at me and then touched the child's arm. Hannah looked up at her, and Charlotte reached into her pocket and pulled out a piece of lemon-colored ribbon. I recognized the yellow ribbon from Emily's baby shower. She handed it to the girl. Hannah's eyes lit up, and then Charlotte took her by the hand, walking her to a quiet corner of the bakery. Charlotte sat cross-legged on the floor, and Hannah sat with her. Charlotte began to tie a bow with the ribbon, slowly showing Hannah how to do it. Then she gave the ribbon back to the child.

I let out a breath, grateful for the compassion of my young cousin. I needed to speak to Dinah about Hannah, but I didn't want to talk about her mother's death in front of her. I knew she couldn't hear me, but it still felt wrong.

Dinah gestured for me to sit at one of the café tables in the front of the shop. The tables and chairs were so similar to the ones in Swissmen Sweets, I almost thought I was back in my shop. However, I knew I wasn't. I was surrounded by baked goods, not candy, on all sides.

Dinah didn't sit but went back to the counter. She lifted one of the domes off a plate of chocolate chip cookies. Each cookie was the size of my hand. She selected four cookies and divided them between the two plates. She handed one plate to Charlotte, and the other she set in the middle of the table where I sat, but I had lost my appetite.

Dinah sat across from me at the café table. "You will have to excuse me; if a customer comes in, I'll need to get up."

I nodded. "I understand. I have a shop of my own."

"That's right. I had already forgotten. Ever since I heard the news about my cousin, I haven't been thinking straight."

"Rosemary was your cousin?"

"Distant cousin. Our grandmothers were first cousins, but that still made us family. When she called and asked me for help, I had to try. That's what family does."

"I think you'll have to start at the beginning for me to understand," I said.

She picked up one of the cookies, took a big bite, and set the rest of it on a napkin in front of her. After she swallowed the bite, she said, "I always tend to eat more when I'm under stress. I'm sure you can tell this from my appearance, but I have been stressed most of my life. I can't say I've lived up to the Amish teaching of a peaceful spirit."

Perhaps Dinah was a little overweight, but it hurt me that she would talk about herself like this to a stranger. "I think everyone has to deal with stress and anxiety. If someone says they don't have any, they're lying. I eat the candy in my shop when I'm stressed," I admitted. "Chocolate is my weakness. I never tire of it."

She picked up the cookie and took another bite as if she was trying to gather her courage and the cookie was in some way helping. After she swallowed, she said, "Any time someone tells me that they don't like chocolate, I wonder if they have ever eaten a proper chocolate chip cookie. How could you not like a cookie? I can understand maybe not liking cake, but a cookie?" She shook her head as if this was beyond comprehension.

To be polite, I broke off a piece of my cookie and put it in my mouth. The cookie melted on my tongue. "Oh, wow, that cookie is amazing."

She smiled. "My chocolate chip cookies are the very best. I have customers that come here every day for one cookie and a cup of coffee, and students from the College of Wooster are frequent visitors, too."

"I can see why," I said and broke off another piece. "Now, tell me why Hannah is alone. You said that she has no family, but Rosemary's husband is alive. Wouldn't he be her adopted father then?"

She pushed her cookie around the plate with her finger. "I think I need to go further back in the story."

I nodded, unsure of what I was about to hear.

"Rosemary and Isaac married young. I believe my cousin was seventeen when they married. They were from the same community in Indiana. They had courted ever since they were old enough to do so. Everyone thought they were the perfect Amish couple. Attractive, hardworking, and active in the church. There was just one problem: they couldn't have children. For fifteen years, they tried to have a baby. Rosemary got pregnant so many times." Dinah's face fell. "Each time, she lost the child. She thought that was her punishment from *Gott*."

"Punishment for what?" I asked.

Dinah shook her head. "In that time, Isaac grew restless. He had always toyed with the idea of leaving the

Amish way but was baptized into the faith so that he and Rosemary could marry. As the years went on and Rosemary struggled with losing her babies, he became more discontent. He told Rosemary he wanted to leave. She believed the only way to convince him to stay was to have a child."

Then I remembered that Emily had been sent by her sister to live with an English family while she was pregnant. She had been sent outside the Amish community so that the pregnancy would remain secret. I realized now that I had never asked Emily who that English family was. Could they somehow be involved in the murder, too?

"Rosemary cleaned houses for wealthy *Englisch* families who lived near her home to make extra money. One of the families she cared for had a pregnant Amish teenager living with them."

"Emily," I said.

She nodded. "Emily."

"Do you know the English family's name?"

She shook head. "*Nee.* I never thought to ask. It was so long ago."

It might be long ago, but it could still be important. I couldn't go to Indiana to interview the family, but Aiden could send someone or call the police department in that area for support. Dinah might not know, but I was certain both Emily and Esther would.

"Rosemary thought if she and Isaac had a child, that would fix everything, so she spoke with the family about the Amish girl and what was to happen to the baby. They told her that she was going to give the child up for adoption. Rosemary said she wanted the child."

"What did Emily say?" I asked.

She shook her head. "I don't know that they asked her. From my understanding, she was told that the baby went to an Amish family, and that was the end of it."

That fit with what Emily had told me, so I assumed it was true; the two stories matched. I wanted to ask about the legality of the arrangement, the protocol, and the paperwork. When I lived in New York, one of the chocolatiers in the shop had adopted a child. The process had cost the couple sleepless nights, thousands of dollars, and endless paperwork. In the end, it had been worth all the stress and heartache, but getting a child without jumping through all those necessary hoops had never been an option.

I couldn't imagine that it was legal to hand over a baby, even an Amish baby, without some kind of paper trail. Perhaps the Amish involved could claim that they didn't know how the system worked, but the English family that had taken part in the secret adoption couldn't make the same claim. It was very possible that they could still be in a great deal of trouble if the police could prove they were involved in an illegal adoption. It could even be considered human trafficking.

A sour taste rose up in my throat. Emily was a victim. Her daughter was a victim. My heart ached at the thought of what had transpired, and when I glanced across the room at beautiful little Hannah, all I could think was, "Thank God, she has been loved. Thank God, she was safe."

I was breathless. "What happened after Rosemary took the baby?"

Dinah sighed. "It seemed at first that things would be better with Isaac. He had always wanted to be a father." She glanced at Hannah, who was quietly eating a cookie with Charlotte. "But when they learned of Hannah's limitations, he became restless. He finally left for *gut* when Hannah was three."

I could not imagine how hard that must have been for Rosemary. She'd adopted a child to save her marriage, and it had failed. I guessed that it was always bound to fail. Saving a marriage wasn't the best motivation to have children.

"So Rosemary was living in Indiana. How did she end up here?"

"She learned that Isaac had moved here to Wooster, where I was living. She thought if she could see Isaac again, she would be able to convince him to come back home and return to the Amish faith."

"He's no longer Amish?" I tried not to look at the cookie plate. Just the thought of food at the moment made me feel ill.

"He told Rosemary that *Gott* had turned his back on him, not letting him have a child, so he would turn his back on *Gott*."

Charlotte gasped behind us.

"When Rosemary found out that her husband was here in Wooster," Dinah said, "she wrote me a letter, asking if she and her daughter could come and work with me. At the time, I was in need of more help at the bakery, and I always like to work with family. I'm a widow, and my son had no interest in working here." She swallowed. "He has other ideas for his career. It seemed like a perfect solution."

"Did Rosemary ever speak to her husband after moving here?" I asked.

She eyed my cookie. "Several times over the last two years. He came here often, trying to talk to her as well."

I pushed the cookie plate closer to her. "Really?"

She broke off a piece of the second cookie. "He wanted a divorce so that he could remarry another woman, an *Englischer*. Rosemary refused to sign the papers to make their divorce official. I suppose he's free to marry now that she's dead."

I shivered. That was a motive for murder if I had ever heard one. "What did she say when he asked?"

"She always said *nee*. She loved him, blindly loved him. Have you ever cared for something for no logical reason? That was the way Rosemary was with Isaac." She shook her head over the sad, sad tale.

I bit my lip and couldn't think of anyone or anything that I had loved that much in my life. However, my tendency was to question, and trust was not something that came easily to me.

In any case, Isaac was a suspect, especially because Rosemary would not grant him a divorce and he was dating another woman. The other woman would not like the idea of the man she was dating being legally married to another woman. That made the girlfriend a suspect as well.

"Do you know the name of Isaac's girlfriend?"

Dinah shook her head. "I do not."

"Do you know where I can find him?"

She chewed her lip. "I don't think you want to. He's a very unhappy man. In my opinion, Rosemary was better off without him. But she couldn't shake the idea that as an Amish woman, it was her job to keep her marriage together no matter what. Even though she herself was not happy with Isaac, she made a commitment to stay married to him. That is our way."

"So that meant she would stay in a loveless marriage just because she agreed to it years ago?"

Dinah shrugged. "If that was their marriage, *ya*. Marriage is not always easy. Much of it is very hard." She said this as if she spoke from experience.

I frowned. I had never been married. The closest I had ever gotten was with Aiden, and we were just beginning to toy with the idea of becoming engaged. Even so, if I was miserable with the person I'd married, I couldn't imagine staying married. Especially if all attempts at reconciliation had been exhausted.

"Now maybe you can help me with Hannah." She leaned across the table.

"Help you with Hannah how?" I glanced over my shoulder at the young girl.

"I can't care for a child with her special needs," she said as if "special needs" was some sort of disease. "She should be with her family."

I frowned. "What are you proposing?"

"Take her with you and give her to Emily. She is the child's mother. She is the one Hannah should have been with since birth. I don't believe that a child should ever be removed from her mother. I did not like the idea of Rosemary adopting the child in the first place, but her bishop allowed it. It was not my place to question the word of a bishop."

I could not believe what she was suggesting. "I can't just take a child."

"You have to. The church elders don't know what to do with her. She is not from our district. If you don't take her, she will likely be given to another family in my district. It will be another family that is not hers. With her limitations, that will be challenging for both her and the family."

I pressed my lips together and stopped myself from saying that being deaf was not a limitation. There was no reason Hannah couldn't have a full and happy life. However, I knew that might not be the general Amish view. "I—I can't—"

I was starting to tell her a second time that I couldn't take Hannah when the front door smacked against the wall and a young Amish man stormed inside, his face a mask of anger.

CHAPTER SIXTEEN

"Mason, I have customers," Dinah said, and her face turned an even deeper shade of red.

He glanced at Charlotte and me and then he said something in Pennsylvania Dutch. While he spoke, I studied him. He had, dark curly hair and a wide mouth. He was a handsome young man, and I guessed he was in his early twenties. To my surprise, instead of the standard black tennis shoes or work boots that most Amish men wore, he wore cowboy boots. They were simple in design with no embellishment, but I couldn't think of any time that I had seen an Amish man in cowboy boots.

Charlotte gasped at whatever he said to Dinah. I didn't understand it, of course, but I could tell by the tone that it was not friendly.

Hannah's eyes went wide, and she scooted closer to

Charlotte and ducked her head. It was as if she thought that if she couldn't see Mason, he couldn't see her either.

"Mason, please," Dinah said in English. She glanced at me. "These are friends of Rosemary's. They are here to tell us how sorry they are for our loss."

That wasn't technically true, but I didn't bother to correct her. I stood, too.

The young man seemed to relax and said in English, "I'm sorry for my outburst. It has been a difficult time for all of us."

"Because of Rosemary?" Charlotte piped up.

I raised my eyebrows, thinking how far my young cousin had come in the last several years. Raised in a conservative Amish district, she'd been taught not to speak to a man, Amish or English, whom she didn't know without being spoken to first.

He glanced at her in surprise. "*Ya*, that is true, but it has been a difficult day at work."

"Where do you work?" I asked.

"I work at the racetrack. I train horses."

"My son is the best Amish horse racer in Wayne County," Dinah said with pride in her voice.

He frowned at his mother and shifted his stance. "I *was* the best horse racer in Wayne County. I'm not anymore."

It was then that I noticed he seemed to take extra care with his left side, and his left foot dragged on the floor just a little bit. The weakness didn't seem to hinder him too much, but it looked as if it must have been caused by a painful injury of some sort.

Dinah noticed me looking at his leg, even though I did my best not to stare. "Mason was in a racing accident eighteen months ago. It was terrible, but he's healing well.

At first, the doctors didn't think he'd walk again, but look at him now. He's doing so well." She smiled at her son.

"How did I heal well if I can't race anymore?" His voice was sharp again, and then he shook his head as if he remembered whom he was with. "I'm sorry. It was just a hard day at the track. People aren't doing what they need to race well. I see these young Amish men come to the track to try their hand at racing. They act like it's a joke. It's not a joke to me. It was my life. It was all I cared about."

"Mason," his mother said softly.

"I am sorry to hear about your injury . . ." I said.

"Everyone thinks I'm done when it comes to racing, but I will come back. I'm feeling stronger every day. I just have to keep working at it. Soon the stable will see that I'm better in my current state than all these young fools will ever be in their young and healthy bodies." He balled his hands into fists at his sides.

Mason sounded determined, but his foot dragging on the floor told me another story. I wondered if he would have surgery to fix his leg and how he would pay for it. Non-Amish think that the Amish are averse to doctors, but nothing could be further from the truth. The Amish do tend to rely on home remedies that include plants and herbs, but if they have a major illness or injury, like the one Mason had, they would gladly turn to an English doctor for help. They weren't doctors themselves because of their lack of education, which ended at eighth grade. I'd always thought it was ironic that the Amish stopped education so early yet depended on outsiders for such critical help.

"You are young, too, son," Dinah argued. "You're only twenty-one. You have your whole life ahead of you."

"I am older than my years because of what I have seen and what I have been through."

I tended to agree with him this on this point. I believed experience—good or bad—could age a person.

Charlotte handed the rest of her cookie to Hannah, who accepted it with a smile. She really was a lovely girl. I had no idea how Emily would react when she saw her daughter. Also, I didn't know how her husband would react. Emily said that Daniel knew about her past and had forgiven her for it, but coming face-to-face with Hannah would be another thing entirely.

Mason glanced at Hannah. "I thought the bishop was going to take her tonight. Please don't tell me you've decided to keep her. She's not our responsibility. We have enough concerns without a crippled child."

Charlotte gasped. I didn't react, but I did have an urge to punch him despite his injury.

Dinah winced. "Mason, the bishop said he would consider taking the child tonight. We don't know yet what is to happen."

"You are too busy to have a deaf girl here in your shop. What if she gets too close to the oven or a blade?" he asked. "You won't always be able to reach her in time, and shouting will be no help at all. You are too old to be a mother again. You should be thinking of slowing down, not the opposite."

I bristled. Again his words made it sound as if being deaf was some unsurmountable thing.

"Bailey and Charlotte might take her," Dinah said. "They know the child's first family. I was just telling them that it is important for the girl to be with her real family."

"*Ya*, take her," Mason said. "Our burden is too great already to have her here."

I wondered what he meant by that. What was his burden? His injury? Or was there something else under the surface? "I don't know that we can take her from your community without permission."

"Whose permission?" Dinah asked. "If you need it from me, you have it. Rosemary didn't have anyone else."

"What about her family in Indiana?" I asked. "They must have been informed of her death by now and will be worried about Hannah."

"They will not worry about Hannah. They didn't want Rosemary to take the girl in the first place. They all but turned their backs on her when she adopted Hannah. They will not want her."

I frowned and bit the inside of my cheek. Hannah was just a child, and she had nowhere to go, at least nowhere that she was wanted.

I walked over to the table where she had been sitting with Charlotte and touched her arm.

She looked up at me with wide eyes.

I touched my chest and fingerspelled my name, "Bailey."

She stared. When I was growing up in Connecticut, there was a girl in my class who was partially deaf. She was able to hear most things at school, thanks to her hearing aids, but our teacher still thought it was important that the children in our class learn some American Sign Language.

Her face lit up, and if possible, she was even lovelier. She touched her chest and spelled Hannah, and then she began to sign quickly. I shrugged my shoulders to tell her

I didn't understand all that she was saying, but then I
pointed to Charlotte and with clumsy fingers spelled her
name.

"You know sign language, Bailey?" Charlotte asked.

"Very little," I said. "Hello, yes, no, and how to finger-
spell. Oh, and I know the sign for 'cat.'" I made a motion
as though I was pulling a whisker away from my face,
which meant cat.

She made the sign for "cat," too, and we both smiled.

I signed, "I cat."

I hoped she would understand that I had a cat, not that
I was a cat.

She grinned, and I assumed that she understood my
point.

"Oh," Dinah said. "This is a gift from the *gut* Lord and
a sign that you are the one to take her. No one else can
communicate with her as you can."

Okay, that gave me pause—really, so many of the circumstances surrounding Hannah were raising alarms.
*How was it that no one had been able to communicate
with her?* The thought was deeply disturbing.

"I really don't know if I can take her with me." I
chewed on my lip. I wanted to help Hannah, but moving
a child to a new home when I had no real claim to her
could cause just the kind of trouble Aiden had warned me
against. There were strict laws in place—and rightfully
so—for the very purpose of protecting children.

"You need to take her," Dinah said. "You can help her
better than anyone else in our district. I have not seen
anyone else who can talk to her the way Rosemary
could." She shook her head. "I always meant to learn to
sign, but I never spent the time on it."

"Does she know about Rosemary's death?"

Dinah licked her lips. "*Nee*, I didn't know how to tell her, and she is too young to understand."

I frowned. "She's six years old. She will know that her mother is not here."

Dinah wrung her hands. "I don't know how to tell her. I can't communicate with her, not like Rosemary could. Not like you can."

"Have the police been here?"

"*Ya*, there were officers from Holmes County here. They were the ones who told me about Rosemary's death." She put a hand to her chest. "I could not believe it."

"Did the police try to speak to Hannah?"

"An officer did, but he didn't know she was deaf."

"You didn't tell them that she couldn't hear?" I asked.

"I—It's not something that we talk about in the Amish community. We don't share the failings of others outside of the community."

I balled my fists at my sides. Hannah's deafness wasn't a failing. It was just a fact. Neither good nor bad. I glanced over at Hannah, who was smiling at me. It was the first true smile I had seen on her face since Charlotte and I had stepped into the bakery. And it happened because I'd attempted to communicate with her using my awkward fingerspelling. "I'll take her."

"Bailey . . ." Charlotte began.

I glanced at Charlotte. "*Maami* can look after her at the shop until the proper authorities decide what we should do. Aiden will know what to do or at least who to ask."

Dinah let out a sigh of relief. "*Danki*, you don't know what a great weight this is off me. I know that Hannah will be much happier with you than she would be here. You said that you have a cat? She loves animals. I don't have any myself."

Well, that was a plus because if Hannah came with me, she certainly would be surrounded by animals. Puff, Nutmeg, and Jethro, just to name a few.

I wasn't sure that I was doing the right thing, but I had to move Hannah to a place where she would be cared for. Not to mention that Emily was her biological mother. I chewed on my lip. I would have to warn Emily before she saw the child. It would be a great shock if she came into the shop and ran into a miniature version of herself. Thankfully, Emily wasn't scheduled to work at the candy shop that day. I would have enough time to warn her and talk to Aiden. He would know if social services would need to be involved.

Hannah smiled at me, and my stomach twisted again. I prayed that I was doing the right thing.

I held out my hand to her. She took my hand in hers and stood. It seemed she was ready to go.

CHAPTER SEVENTEEN

It took some awkward fingerspelling and gesturing to explain to Hannah that she was leaving the bakery with Charlotte and me. She was a trusting child, and she came with us when she understood what we were saying. That made my stomach hurt a little. It was too easy to convince her to leave. I wished that she had a little more "stranger danger" ingrained into her.

When we got outside the bakery, Charlotte held Hannah's hand and stopped in the middle of the sidewalk.

"What's wrong?" I asked.

"We forgot about Jethro. What should we do about the pig?" Charlotte asked. "Should I sit in the back with him?"

I shook my head. "Hannah is too small to sit in the front seat. You can hold him in your lap in the front." I frowned. "I don't have a booster seat for her, but we'll buckle her in as well as we can."

"A booster seat?"

"It's to secure children in the back seat," I said. "It's required by law for children under a certain weight. I can tell just by looking at her she is under that weight."

"The Amish don't use booster seats," Charlotte said.

"Oh, I know," I said, thinking of the children I had seen riding on the outside of buggies on summer days.

"Okay, I guess I can hold the pig then." She sighed, looking down at her pale blue skirt. "I just made this dress."

I opened the back door of the car, and Jethro hopped out. He shook his head, and his collar jangled. Hannah's face lit up, and she squatted on the ground so she was eye to eye with the pig. Jethro bumped her cheek with his pink nose, and she put her arms around his neck, giving him a gentle hug.

I laughed. "Looks like he can sit in the back with Hannah."

Charlotte smiled. "Friends at first sight."

I nodded and gestured for Jethro and Hannah to climb into the car. I buckled her in, and she wrapped her small arm around the pig's shoulders. Instant best friends. I was never so grateful to have Jethro with me. For his part, the pig pressed his nose against the girl's cheek, and she giggled. I smiled. The little bacon bundle did have many redeeming qualities. I would never complain about pig sitting again. Okay, I would try to never complain about pig sitting again.

"Why don't you get in the car with them? I have to call Aiden. I can't take a child without letting the police know what happened." Truthfully, there was no way that I would consider leaving a child with people who so obviously did not want her. But I would do whatever I could by the book.

Charlotte walked around the car to hop inside. Through the opened windows, I heard the girls laughing as they played with the pig.

I tapped my phone screen, and for once, Aiden picked up on the first ring.

"Aiden?" I asked.

"What's wrong?" He must have known from my tone that something was off.

"Are you sitting down? This is a long story," I said.

"Oh-kay," he said in a measured voice. "I'm sitting."

As quickly as I could, I told him about the visit to the Dutch Muffin and how I ended up with Hannah.

"She's in my car with Charlotte." I paused. "And Jethro."

"Jethro?" There was resignation in his voice.

"Your mom had a meeting at the church and said Jethro needed a sitter so she could concentrate and not worry about him eating all of the church's potatoes."

Aiden sighed.

"It's actually a good thing. Hannah was taken with the pig right away. She seems to really have connected with Jethro."

Aiden sighed again. "I need to make some calls to see what we should do. Moving a child around without a legal guardian is a tricky business and could get you and the Sheriff's Department in a mess of trouble. I assume that the child doesn't have a birth certificate because she's Amish."

"I doubt it, and I don't think her adoption is on any official records either."

He was quiet for a long moment. "What does that mean?"

I told him what I knew about Hannah's adoption.

Aiden groaned.

"Aiden, one more thing."

"What else could there possibly be?"

"Hannah is deaf."

"Deaf?"

"Yes."

"But I saw her the day that I interviewed Dinah. I spoke to her."

"Did she speak back?" I asked.

"No, now that you mention it, but it's not unusual for Amish children to be quiet around English people, especially with police they don't know. She was so small, I didn't even know if she spoke English. I assumed all she knew was Pennsylvania Dutch."

"She's deaf," I reiterated. "That's really the reason I decided to take her. Dinah was reluctant to keep a deaf child. I know a handful of signs. I know the word for 'cat.'"

"She knows American Sign Language."

"Apparently Rosemary learned it and taught her."

"Why didn't Dinah tell me the child was deaf? That changes everything. We really have to take that into consideration when trying to find the right place for her. Dinah doesn't want her at the bakery? Why didn't she say that when Deputy Little and I were there yesterday? We could have gone through the proper channels to find care for the child."

"Dinah didn't want to tell you because it's not something that the Amish talk about with *Englischers*. And to answer your question, no, Dinah doesn't want her at the bakery. She practically pushed Hannah out the door with me."

He sighed. "This case is one of the most complicated I've ever had. The most important thing is to make sure that girl is safe and cared for. She is now the number one priority, even above finding the killer."

"Agreed."

"Let me make those calls," Aiden said. "I'll meet you at Swissmen Sweets."

He ended the call.

On the drive back to Harvest, I glanced in the rearview mirror. Hannah held Jethro's head close to her chest as she stared out the window and watched the countryside buzz by. Jethro had his eyes closed and snuggled close to her. Having the pig with us really was the best thing that could have happened.

I'd hoped that Aiden would be there when we arrived at Swissmen Sweets, but I didn't see his departmental SUV anywhere close to the square. I parked right outside of the candy shop in a spot that I usually left for customers. I wanted to get Hannah settled and comfortable as quickly as possible.

As we walked to the shop from the car, Hannah insisted on carrying Jethro. The little girl had her hands wrapped around his middle as if she were carrying a sack of potatoes. The comparison seemed fair to me, considering his potato caper at the church.

We walked into the shop, and I was grateful to see that there were no customers inside. *Maami* stood in front of the domed counter, cleaning the glass with a cloth. The sharp scent of vinegar cut through the smell of chocolate that typically permeated the air in Swissmen Sweets.

Maami looked up from her task. "How was your visit?" Her mouth fell open as Hannah came into the shop after Charlotte with Jethro in tow. "Oh my, who is this?"

"This is Rosemary's daughter," I said.

"Rosemary's?" she asked. "She looks just like . . ." She trailed off, but I knew she was going to say Emily. The more time I spent with Hannah, the more she looked like Emily to me.

Maami spoke to her in Pennsylvania Dutch, but the child just stared, holding onto Jethro until the little pig's eyes bugged out a bit. *Maami* looked to Charlotte and me for an explanation.

"She can't hear," Charlotte said. "Bailey knows some sign language."

"Not nearly enough. She doesn't know about Rosemary's death yet." I bit my lip.

My grandmother stepped forward and hugged the child. "You poor thing. We will care for you."

Even though Hannah couldn't hear her, she accepted the hug, at least until Jethro squealed and kicked as he was squashed between them.

"Has she eaten anything?" *Maami* asked.

"I don't know." I pulled up my phone and googled the sign for "eat." I made the sign, and Hannah nodded. "She's hungry."

"Well, we shouldn't give her candy if this is her first meal of the day. Let me run upstairs. We have some left-over chicken soup and homemade bread that Charlotte and I had for dinner last night."

"You stay with Hannah, Cousin Clara," Charlotte said. "I'll go get the soup ready."

Nutmeg came into the room, and Hannah's eyes lit up when she saw the small orange cat. Of all the animals that frequented the shop, including my rabbit, Puff—whom I'd left at home today—Nutmeg was the smallest. He was almost three years old but had always remained a small cat, so he'd never lost his cuteness. Hannah kissed Jethro on the nose, set him on the floor, and knelt in front of the cat.

Maami picked up the small cat and pointed to a chair. Hannah sat, and *Maami* set him on Hannah's lap. The cat circled twice, settled into her lap, and began to purr. Hannah beamed at me and made the sign for "cat." I did the sign right back.

Jethro seemed to frown, though, and bumped Hannah's leg with his snout.

"The pig is jealous," *Maami* said. "Have you ever seen such a thing? It's almost as if these creatures know what's going on."

I knew that they did.

I shook my finger at the pig. "Don't be jealous. She still loves you, too."

As if she understood his expression, too, she leaned down and gave Jethro a kiss on the top of his head. The pig smiled.

Just then, Charlotte came down the stairs from the apartment with the warm soup. It did smell heavenly. I was tempted to ask her if there was any more upstairs so I could make myself a bowl. But I refrained.

"I'll start cleaning up the kitchen for the end of the day," Charlotte said.

"Thank you, Charlotte," I said as she disappeared through the kitchen door.

Hannah took the piece of thick homemade bread from the tray and took a bite. She ate the bread quickly.

Maami frowned. "When was the last time the child ate?"

"She had a large cookie when we were at the Dutch Muffin," I said.

"I like sweets as much as the next person, but a child needs real food to grow."

The door to the shop opened then, and Aiden filled the frame, pausing as his eyes fell on Hannah. He stepped inside.

Aiden looked at me then, and his eyes were full of compassion for the child. "She doesn't know about Rosemary?"

I shook my head.

He nodded and pulled a chair out in front of the child. He began to sign. Hannah perked up and signed back. Their signing was so fast, the only thing I caught was that Aiden was telling her his name.

I stared at him. "You never told me that you could sign."

"Why would I? It's never come up," he said, looking at me. "I also speak Spanish. I felt it was my duty as an officer of the law to be able to communicate with those I'm helping. In the summer, there are many people from Mexico here working on the English farms to pick the berries and other crops. Someone in the department should know it."

I felt my heart swell. What was this incredible man with so much compassion and goodness in his heart doing with me? It was one of the many times I told myself that I didn't deserve him.

Aiden looked at me. "Someone needs to tell her about Rosemary, but I think I need to call children's services. I want to do this right, with the least amount of trauma to Hannah."

Aiden signed something to the little girl. She laughed, and then he stood up, removing his phone from its clip on his belt. "I'm just going to step outside for a minute to make the call."

I nodded. *Maami* sat next to Hannah and held her hand. The two of them took turns petting Nutmeg, who purred furiously with all the extra attention. Jethro bumped one and then the other with his snout to remind them not to forget that he was there, too.

I walked to the window and looked outside. I watched Aiden pace up and down the sidewalk as he spoke on the phone. Whatever he heard on the other end of the conversation, he wasn't happy about it.

Aiden ended the call, and I jumped away from the window before he saw that I'd been spying. However, if he knew me at all, he wouldn't be the least surprised that I had been.

Maami pointed at the bowl of soup, and Hannah seemed to get the hint that she should eat. She tucked into the soup eagerly. *Maami* held Nutmeg for her.

Aiden gestured for me to join him in the corner of the room. "I spoke with the county's children's services. It's the end of the day. They can't send a social worker until tomorrow to assess Hannah."

My eyes went wide. "What do we do until then?"

"Keep her here. Would it be okay if she spent the night with Clara?"

"I'm sure my grandmother wouldn't mind, and I think Hannah would be more comfortable in an Amish home instead of my little rental house. Maybe you can teach

Charlotte some signs before you leave, so that they can communicate." I glanced back at the little girl.

She laughed as Nutmeg made a motion with his paw to reach her soup. He likely smelled the chicken. The little orange cat was a chicken fiend.

Maami swatted away his paw, and Hannah giggled.

"I can show Charlotte some signs. Hannah's a bright girl. I hate to keep this secret from her, but because no one has a claim to her, social services has to make an assessment."

"Even though she's Amish."

He nodded. "Yes."

I stepped closer to him. "I think she's Emily's first child."

"I thought the same thing when I saw her." He ran his hand through his hair.

"Does that mean Emily has a claim to her?" I asked.

"I would think so, but would she want her? She gave the child up originally."

I pressed my lips together. "I don't know. From what I understand of the adoption, I'm certain that she wasn't given much other choice."

"That may be, but we can't make any assumptions about what Emily wants now. Someone did that to her before, and as you can see, it didn't end well for Hannah. Hannah must come first in all of this."

"Agreed." I paused. "I have to tell Emily that her daughter might be here."

Aiden shook his head. "Let's wait until Hannah meets the social worker."

I frowned.

"Bailey, please. We have to do this right in order to make sure Hannah goes to the best home for her."

"Okay," I whispered, but in my heart, I knew it was a mistake.

As promised, I took Jethro back to Juliet around six. Hannah was sad to say goodbye to the pig.

I searched the sign language gestures on my phone and fumbled through to tell her that she would see the pig again soon. Thankfully, at the church Juliet seemed to be preoccupied with her women's program and didn't ask me any prying questions about the murder or about why I wasn't engaged to her son yet. I handed over the pig and made a run for it.

That night, I stayed at Swissmen Sweets long after closing to spend time with Hannah. As the evening went on, she became more and more uncertain. She must have wondered when she was going back home to Wooster. Aiden had explained to her before he left that she would be spending the night at the candy shop, but she was still a small child. How could she really understand what he meant? The language barrier didn't help.

I stayed until *Maami* tucked Hannah into bed. I left my car parked on the street, deciding to walk home. I had a lot to think about. I'd become involved in this case as a favor to Emily, but now I had a much more important reason. A child had lost her mother. What if Hannah was the reason for the murder? If that was the case, then Hannah wouldn't be safe until the killer was brought to justice. I paused on Apple Street. I was halfway home to my little rental house. It was eight-thirty in the evening. The sun had just set over the village.

I had an unexplainable urge to return to the candy shop. I spun on my heel and began walking, and then my walk changed into a run. I came around the corner onto

Main Street just in time to see a large form standing outside of Swissmen Sweets.

I couldn't see the person's face, but it was a man in
Amish clothes, and he cupped his hands around his face,
staring into the window.

"Hey!" I cried and ran toward him.

Without looking at me, the man took off.

I ran as fast as I could, but he sprinted down the street,
outpacing me with his much longer legs, plus he had had
a head start. At the end of the block, I bent at the waist,
gasping for air. I hadn't run that fast since I was in high
school. Honestly, it was possible that I hadn't run that fast
in my entire life.

Footsteps approached me from behind. I spun around
with my fist up, ready to strike.

Deputy Little yelped. "Bailey, don't hit me."

"Little? What are you doing here?"

"Deputy Brody asked me to keep watch on Swissmen
Sweets because of the little girl who's staying there."

"Did you see a man running away from the shop?" I
asked. "He was looking in the window."

He grimaced. "No, I didn't. I went to my car to get a
book to read. I was going to sit at the gazebo and keep an
eye on the candy shop from there." His face turned red as
he said this.

I glanced at the gazebo and thought I saw a shadow
move.

"No, there is no one over there," he said a little too
quickly. "I was just there."

I frowned. "Well, I'm going to stay here for the night.
We can both keep watch on Hannah."

He nodded and glanced nervously at the square one
last time.

CHAPTER EIGHTEEN

The next morning, I had an ache in my back from sleeping on the floor in the front room of the candy shop. I hadn't gone upstairs to my grandmother's apartment after seeing Deputy Little on the sidewalk. I didn't want to scare my grandmother, Charlotte, or Hannah. Instead, I'd made a makeshift bed out of two of the ladder-back chairs in the front of the shop. It had been a fine idea until I fell off one of them in the middle of the night. I guessed that Deputy Little had been more comfortable sleeping in his car than I had been sleeping on the cold pine floor with just a threadbare blanket that I had found in the hall closet to keep me warm.

By three in the morning, I decided to get up and start working on the candies for the day. If I couldn't sleep, I might as well make candy.

"Bailey? What are you doing here so early?" my grandmother asked when she came into the kitchen at four-thirty.

I told her about the previous night's events.

A fierce expression crossed her usually gentle face. "We will protect the girl."

I smiled, and we worked in silence for over an hour until Charlotte and Hannah wandered into the kitchen rubbing their eyes. Hannah looked even smaller in the nightshirt that she must have borrowed from Charlotte to sleep in.

"You know what?" I said. "We should do something fun. Why don't we all go to the Sunbeam Café for breakfast? They open at seven. That will give us enough time to eat and come back to open the shop by ten. I've already done most of the prep work for the day."

"That's a great idea," Charlotte said with a yawn. "They make the best pancakes. I want a double stack!"

We were all in agreement. A double stack sounded just about right to me. After the night I'd had, I might make mine a triple.

The Sunbeam Café was on the other side of the playground in the village square, near Juliet's church. It had opened about a year ago and was owned by Darcy Woodin, a young English woman with the curliest blond hair I had ever seen. It was as if she styled her hair with a corkscrew, but it was completely natural. I knew because I'd asked her once.

Darcy was usually in the back cooking, while her grandmother, Lois Henry, ran the front of the café. I felt a kinship to the Sunbeam because it was a grandmother-granddaughter business, just like Swissmen Sweets. It was a nice place to go for lunch or dinner when I became tired of the heavy Amish food that was served in most restaurants in the area.

Also, Lois was a hoot, and I thought she would be just the one to distract Hannah from becoming homesick. That, or she'd scare her to death.

Lois and her granddaughter weren't Amish, but Lois was *really* not Amish. She was in her late sixties, styled her fiery, red-purple hair in spikes, and adored heavy makeup and costume jewelry. She also had a big personality. All the same, she'd grown up in Holmes County and knew the Amish way of life well. Somehow, despite her outlandish appearance and behavior, she had the ability to put people at ease and was accepted in the Amish community. I knew a lot of that had to do with her best friend, Millie Fisher, the Amish matchmaker in the village. The two women could not have been more different, yet they were a perfect fit, like yin and yang. Although that was a reference that Millie mostly likely had never heard.

I held open the café door, and Charlotte, *Maami*, and Hannah went in. I followed a few steps behind.

Charlotte hugged herself. "I'm starved. Bailey, when was the last time we ate?"

I shook my head. I couldn't remember. I'd been so wrapped up in helping Hannah that food didn't seem to matter in the least. I'd claimed to be too anxious to eat dinner the night before, but I might have snuck a couple of pieces of fudge while everyone else was sleeping.

The inviting scents coming from the café made my stomach rumble. I decided Charlotte was right. A double stack was definitely in order.

Lois looked up from the counter. "Well, what do we have here? The whole crew from Swissmen Sweets! This is quite a treat for us. Coming in for breakfast?"

"Yep," Charlotte said. "I already know that I want a double stack of Darcy's pancakes."

Lois shook her pen at her. "As if there is anything else worth eating to get your day going." She bent at the waist and peered down at Hannah. "And who is this adorable young lady with you?"

"This is Hannah. She's staying with my grandmother for a few days. She's from Wooster," I said, keeping my explanation simple.

Lois wasn't buying it. "Where is her family then?"

I made a face.

Lois folded her arm. "Spill, girl."

"She was Rosemary's daughter," I said.

"The woman who died at the pretzel shop?" she whispered. Lois didn't know that she could have shouted and Hannah still wouldn't have been able to hear her.

I nodded.

"Poor child." Her face fell. "Doesn't she have anyone else?"

"Aiden is going to find out where she should go. Until then she's staying at Swissmen Sweets with Charlotte and my grandmother."

"Of course she is," Lois said and then turned to Hannah. "And would you like pancakes, too?"

Hannah stared at her. She then grabbed *Maami*'s skirts and ducked behind her.

"I didn't mean to scare her." She patted her spiky, red-purple hair. "I know this look is not very Amish, but I mean well."

I smiled. "I know, Lois. Hannah just can't understand what you're saying."

She looked up. "Doesn't she speak English? Is she not in school yet?"

"It's not that." I lowered my voice. "She can't hear you. She's deaf. She knows sign language. Aiden knows it, too, which is a real blessing. I don't know what we would do if he didn't." I made a face. "Until Aiden returns, we have to do a lot of pantomiming." I glanced at Hannah. "She is such a sweet and trusting child. She just follows us wherever we take her."

Lois pressed her hands to her heart. "How sad. But if she knows American Sign Language, then that's all we need." She waved at Hannah. The young girl looked at her with those big blue eyes that were so much like Emily's.

Lois moved her hands rapidly. Hannah's eyes lit up, and she signed back.

I stared at Lois. "What did you ask her?"

"I introduced myself. Then I asked her what she wanted to eat." She grinned. "She wants pancakes and a piece of lemon pie. I think you should allow the pie in this case."

"She can have whatever she wants," I said as relief flooded me. It was such a blessing to have someone else close by who could communicate with Hannah. I knew Aiden wouldn't be available to translate for us every time we might need him. "Where did you learn to sign?"

She grinned. "My second husband had a deaf brother, so I took it upon myself to learn when we were married. The whole family could sign, and I felt I should be able to as well. The skill was the best thing that came out of the marriage. The rest of it was a total waste." She waved at Hannah again, and the young girl beamed at her. "You all take a seat, and I will come by and grab the rest of your order." She pointed at a table near the window.

After we were settled, Lois came back with a tray holding three mugs of coffee, four glasses of water, and a giant piece of lemon meringue pie. She set the piece of pie in front Hannah. Hannah beamed. We gave our orders, and Hannah dug into the pie.

Maami added cream to her coffee and passed it to Charlotte. Charlotte, knowing I had a terrible sweet tooth, slid the cream and sugar in my direction. Hannah hummed softly to herself while she ate the pie. She was happy, and she was unaware she was making a noise to express it. I wondered the last time I had been so happy that I hummed just because I could not hold in my joy. I swallowed hard as I doctored my coffee. For this brief moment, with three generations around this small table, all seemed to be right with the world. Sustained by coffee and lemon meringue pie, we could not be touched by the outside world. We could forget about such things as murder.

Charlotte cocked her head. "She really loves lemon. Doesn't that seem like a sour flavor for such a young girl to love? The only other person I know who enjoys lemon that much is Emily."

I nearly choked on my coffee.

Maami patted my back. "Bailey, are you quite all right?"

The strong coffee burned the back of my throat.

"I'm fine," I croaked like a frog.

In short order, Lois returned with our food. There was a stack of pancakes for Hannah, scrambled eggs and French toast for *Maami*, more pancakes for Charlotte, and a western omelet and toast for me. I'd decided I needed some protein for breakfast instead of pancakes. I was so hungry that I didn't doubt for a second that I could eat every last bite of every dish.

"That was fast," Charlotte said when Lois finished setting out the food.

Lois tucked her serving tray under her arm. "Well, I knew you and Hannah wanted pancakes, and Bailey and Clara always order the same thing for breakfast when they come here, so I had Darcy get a start on it. I figured that Bailey would be sleuthing to find the killer." She winked at me.

For a second time, the coffee burned the back of my throat. At least I didn't choke this time because I was ready for it.

Charlotte sighed as she took a bite of her pancakes. "I could eat pancakes for every meal."

It didn't sound like a bad idea to me.

My grandmother smiled at Charlotte. "Perhaps you say that now, but everyone tires of the same thing day in and day out. Change is *gut* for the soul, even difficult change."

I spread strawberry jam on my toast, and Aiden's new job opportunity came to the forefront of my mind. He had been working as a sheriff's deputy for so long. Maybe he needed this change.

The café door opened, and Millie Fisher walked in. "Oh my word, we have the whole group from Swissmen Sweets here this morning."

I smiled at her. Millie was a petite Amish woman Lois's age. She was also the village matchmaker and helped Amish couples find love. She had an innate talent for knowing when a couple would fail and when a couple was meant to be together. She had once told me that Aiden and I were meant to be. I took that encouragement to heart, no matter what Aiden might decide about his job opportunity with BCI.

Lois and Millie had grown up together, and despite their very different lifestyles, they were the best of friends. In a way, I kind of imagined they were what Cass and I would be like in forty years, minus the Amish part. I was definitely Millie to Cass's Lois.

"We came for the pancakes," Charlotte said.

"Very wise choice!" Millie said. "All is well, Charlotte." Charlotte blushed and nodded.

I wrinkled my brow. What was going on here?

"And who's this little girl?" Millie asked.

Maami told her in a hushed voice.

"Oh," Millie said. "The poor thing. It's a *gut* thing that Lois can sign with her."

Lois came back and warmed up our coffees. "Millie, there you are! You are late today."

"Goat problems," Millie said.

Lois nodded as if this made complete sense. Millie waved to us and went to sit in her normal spot by the counter.

"Lois," I said when she buzzed by again, "would it be possible for you to teach us some of the most useful signs so we can talk to Hannah?"

Lois's eyes lit up. "I would love to do that. I have to tell you, I am a bit rusty. I divorced my second husband over twenty-five years ago."

"Anything will help," I assured her. "The only signs I know are fingerspelling, yes, no, and cat." I made the sign for cat, and Hannah smiled as she continued to happily dig into her pie, ignoring the pancakes in front of her altogether. Charlotte was right; I had never seen someone who loved lemon so much. Other than Emily Keim.

"Right now we're in the middle of the breakfast rush, but if you come back after two this afternoon, I can give you a crash course. That's our slowest time—after lunch and before we gear up for dinner."

"Sounds perfect," I said. "Even if I can't come, you can teach Charlotte. I think Hannah will enjoy the lesson, too, watching us fumble as we try to learn."

"Why wouldn't you be able to come?" Charlotte asked.

"Don't you know? She needs to solve a murder." Lois gave me another wink.

I didn't correct her because it was true.

CHAPTER NINETEEN

W hen we got back to the candy shop, Hannah was in much brighter spirits. Lois had given us a stack of children's books, crayons, and coloring sheets to entertain her, saying, "We keep these in the café to entertain the kiddos that come in so their parents can have a quiet meal. I can't say that it always works, but it might help Hannah get through the day at Swissmen Sweets. If you need anything, or need me to come over and sign for you, just holler. I'll come as quick as I can."

I hugged her. "Thank you. You can't know how much this means to us. You are the best neighbor we could have at a time like this. You have a pretty big heart, too, Lois."

"Don't you let that get out." She winked at me.

Back at Swissmen Sweets, *Maami* got Hannah settled at one of the café tables at the front of the shop with a few of the books that Lois had given her.

Maami smiled at me. "I know better than to give her all the books and coloring books at once. Children are soon bored with activities that are no longer new to them. You certainly were that way when you were young." She tucked the rest of the books, coloring books, and crayons on a shelf under the cash register.

Then she filled a small white box with lemon drops and set them on the table next to Hannah. Hannah looked up from her book with glowing eyes. She popped one of the lemon drops in her mouth and went back to the book.

"*Maami*, she just had pie and pancakes with maple syrup at the Sunbeam Café. I doubt she needs any more sugar."

"I know we can't just feed the child sugar, but a few lemon drops never hurt anyone."

I smiled. "Okay, *Maami*." I glanced back at the table where Hannah sucked on lemon drops and flipped the book pages. She didn't know what had happened to the only mother she had ever known. It made me ache to think that I neither had the authority nor the ability to tell her.

I texted Aiden and asked about the social worker he had promised. I got a frowny face in response. SHE'LL BE THERE LATER THIS AFTERNOON. I THINK CLOSE TO THREE. SHE HAS A LOT OF CLIENTS.

I UNDERSTAND THAT, I texted back. BUT IT DOESN'T SEEM RIGHT TO KEEP HANNAH IN THE DARK ABOUT HER MOTHER'S DEATH. EVERYONE IN THE VILLAGE KNOWS. IF SHE COULD HEAR, SHE WOULD ALREADY KNOW BECAUSE PEOPLE ARE TALKING.

I AGREE, BUT THE SOCIAL WORKER SAID THAT SHE NEEDS TO ASSESS HANNAH AND BE THERE WHEN SHE IS TOLD

ABOUT ROSEMARY. I'M SORRY. MY HANDS ARE TIED. WITH NO LEGAL GUARDIAN ALIVE, SHE IS A WARD OF THE COUNTY.

BUT HER BIOLOGICAL MOTHER IS ALIVE.

EVEN IF I AGREE WITH YOU, THAT'S AN ASSUMPTION YOU ARE MAKING.

I stared at the screen. Dots flashed as Aiden was typing; then I read, WE DON'T EVEN KNOW IF EMILY WANTS HER. SHE'S NOT MARRIED TO HANNAH'S FATHER, AND SHE HAS ANOTHER BABY ON THE WAY. SHE MIGHT WANT TO KEEP HANNAH IN HER PAST.

EMILY WILL WANT HER, I texted back. I HAVE NO DOUBT IN MY MIND.

I waited for a response text, but there was none. I told myself that wasn't a reflection on how he saw Emily, but that he'd been called away. Countless times, our text or phone conversations ended abruptly because Aiden was called away by his job. However, he was always nearby. I knew I would see him if he had a moment to pop in and say hello at Swissmen Sweets or even at the end of the day for dinner. Would that still be the case if he took the job with BCI? His jurisdiction would be the entire state of Ohio. There'd be many nights that he might not come home to Harvest. Could I live with that?

I shook the dark thoughts from my head. What Aiden decided to do for his career wasn't as important at the moment as Hannah's well-being. An even darker thought hit me. Was Hannah safe? I felt she was safe at the candy shop, but I had seen that figure outside Swissmen Sweets the night before. Was it possible that the killer believed Hannah knew something about the murder? If that was true, I had a greater motive than ever to solve Rosemary Weiss's murder. I had to protect this young girl at all costs.

Hannah was happy, and we had everything ready to open the shop, so I turned to my grandmother. Before I could even speak, she said, "Go."

"Go?" I asked. "I didn't even say I was going some-where."

She shook her head. "You didn't have to. You have that look in your eye like you do when you feel you need to make a move. Charlotte and I will be fine here in the shop today. We will care for Hannah. I know you're wor-ried about her."

"I am," I admitted.

"We both know the way to keep her safe is to find out what happened to Rosemary. You are the best person to do that."

I raised my brow. "What about Aiden? He is a sheriff's deputy."

She smiled. "Aiden will do what he can, but you have a way of getting people to speak to you that I have rarely seen in another person, Bailey. Some might even say it's your divine gift."

"I have never thought of having a divine gift before."

She shrugged. "Just because you have not thought about it doesn't mean it's not there. *Gott* gives each and every one of us gifts. Each is different. Each is special. It is up to you what you do with them." She patted my cheek. "You, my granddaughter, are using them well. You make me very proud, and pride is not something I am eager to admit."

I held my grandmother's hand as she pressed it against my cheek because I knew how true that was. In the Amish world, pride of any kind was sin. Even knowing that, knowing her church would see it as a fault, I was joyful that she was proud of me. For her and my grandfather to be proud of me was all I'd ever wanted. I'd thought for a very long time that I had to earn that pride by becoming the top chocolatier in New York City. I had since learned my grandparents were prouder of me when I cared for others.

I said goodbye to Charlotte and waved goodbye to Hannah, who was halfway through her box of lemon drops already.

I was off to find the man Hannah had known as her father when she was very young: Rosemary's husband, Isaac Weiss. I hoped he wouldn't be hard to find. Dinah had said that he worked in a hardware store in Wooster. After a quick search, I found only one Amish hardware store in Wayne County, so I guessed that was my best bet. It was time to drive back to Wooster and see if that bet would pay off. For Hannah's sake, I prayed it would.

Forty minutes later, I sat in the giant parking lot outside of Mueller Hardware Store and stared. It wasn't a hardware store; it was a hardware palace. It was a giant warehouse that could rival any big-box home-improvement center in the state. Could such a giant enterprise really be Amish? If the line of Amish buggies and wagons hitched to the long posts behind me were any indication, it could. The numerous Amish here told me I was at the right place.

Shaking my head, I got out of the car. I walked to the front of the massive building and stepped through the automatic doors, which, to be honest, didn't seem very Amish either. My head was spinning. I found myself in a giant rotunda, which seemed better suited to a grand hotel than a place to buy a lawnmower.

An Amish man in a bright white shirt, jeans, and tan suspenders appeared to be speaking to a customer. He had a trim salt-and-pepper beard, and his belly hung out over the waistband of his jeans.

Even more shocking than the store's grand entrance or overall size was the person I saw speaking to the man in suspenders. It was Abel Esh. The two men laughed at something Abel said, and then Abel glanced over his shoulder. When he saw me standing there, he narrowed his eyes. He said something to the other man in Pennsylvania Dutch. They laughed again and split up.

"Are you lost, Bailey King?" Abel asked as he marched by.

"What are you doing here?" I asked.

"I'm shopping. I could ask you the same thing." Then he marched out of the store, but I noted he wasn't carrying any shopping bags with him.

"Welcome to Mueller Hardware. Can I help you find something?" asked the man who had been talking to Abel.

"Why was Abel Esh here?" I asked.

"Oh, you know Abel?"

I nodded.

He broke into a wide smile. "I was just giving him some advice on tractors. It is one of our specialties."

I frowned. Something about this felt off . . .

"Do you work here?"

He laughed as if that was the funniest question he'd ever heard. "If I didn't, why would I ask to help you?"

"Oh, then I think I might need your help. This place is so big. It's not really what I expected of an Amish hardware store." I marveled at the size of the place. I noticed that, outside the rotunda, there was a staircase that led to a second floor and an elevator. An elevator in an Amish business? Now I had seen everything.

He chuckled and looped his thumbs around his suspenders. "We get a lot of tourists coming in here and gawking at the entrance. It is something, isn't it? The owner wanted to make a statement and show off Amish craftsmanship at the same time. I guess it is more grandiose than what people expect in this part of the world."

I stared at the skylights that were twenty feet above my head. The bright blue sky was clearly visible through the crystal clear glass. All I could think was that it must be a historic pain to keep those skylights that clean.

"So what can we do for you? If you're just visiting, I can direct you to the Amish-made goods. Those are always crowd pleasers with people from out of town. Every *Englischer* wants something handmade by the Amish." He chuckled at that.

I didn't correct his assumption that I was a tourist. I was often mistaken for a tourist in Holmes County as well. By those who didn't recognize me from my cable show, at least. As he was an Amish man, I thought it was a safe bet that he had never seen *Bailey's Amish Sweets* on Gourmet Television.

"I would love to see those Amish-made gifts. I have a friend who lives in New York City, and she cannot get enough of anything made by the Amish." It was true. Cass was obsessed with Amish-made goods. It was one thing she had trouble finding in New York.

"New York City. My, that's a far cry from here."

Having lived in both places, I knew that better than most in both the figurative and literal sense.

He started walking, but I stopped him. "Before we go

look at the Amish-made goods, I was wondering if you could direct me to the right department."

He turned around with the same ready smile. "What department would that be?"

"The one that Isaac Weiss works in. Do you know him?"

Some of the color drained from his face. "Isaac Weiss? Why would you want to find him?"

I considered for half a second mentioning the murder, but I couldn't think of a way it would get me any closer to Isaac. Instead, it might very well get me kicked out of the giant hardware store altogether. "I just have some business to discuss with him," I said, hoping it sounded vague, yet important enough to be pointed in the right direction.

"Miss, you don't want to talk to Isaac Weiss. I promise you don't."

CHAPTER TWENTY

I studied the Amish man in front of me. "What do you mean?"

He looped his thumbs through his suspenders. "There are a whole host of people who can help you find what you need in this store, but don't ask Isaac for help. You will be sorry if you do."

"I'd like to talk to him." I tried to sidestep around him. If this man would not tell me where I could find Isaac, I knew there were a whole host of other people in a store this big whom I could ask.

He stepped into my path. "He's an angry *Englischer*, Miss. You don't want to become tangled up in that."

"I heard that he was Amish," I said, hoping to get a reaction. Dinah had told me that Isaac had left the Amish, but there had to be some reason this man was so insistent that I not look for Isaac.

He swallowed, and his Adam's apple bounced up and down. His jovial expression was long gone. "He's not Amish. He's not like any Amish man I have ever known."

"If you can tell me where to find him, I'll be on my way." I took another step to the side. Maybe he would eventually get the hint.

"I can't do that, miss." With that he walked away.

I frowned as I watched him go. Even though Mueller Hardware was enormous, I was confident that I could find Isaac, assuming he was in the store. I stepped deeper into the retail space and found a young Amish man without a beard stocking birdseed. He glanced at me out of the corner of his eye, far less friendly than the first man I'd met.

"Excuse me?" I gave the best low-maintenance-customer expression I could muster.

He looked at me with a scowl. It seemed to me it was a universal expression with some teenagers, whether they were Amish or not. It was also an expression I had seen on Abel Esh's face at least a hundred times, though he was far from being a teenager anymore. Thinking about Abel brought my thoughts back to Emily and Hannah, which was a good reminder as to why I was here.

"I'm looking for Isaac Weiss. Can you tell me where I might find him?"

"*Ya*," he answered without hesitation. "Isaac works in the machining department on the basement level."

I stared him. "This giant store has a basement?"

"The stairs are over near plumbing fixtures." He turned back to stocking the shelves.

I thanked his back and followed the signs to plumbing fixtures. From there, I spotted the open stairwell.

The hum and thrum of machines welcomed me to the

basement. While the main floor was open and cavernous, the basement level felt closed in, and almost too bright. Despite a lack of natural light, there was enough illumination in the basement to show every last speck of dust in the air.

People outside of Amish Country were surprised the Amish had access to electricity. But it was safe to say that most Amish used electricity in their businesses in order to stay up to code. Some even had it in their homes. The difference being the businesses might be attached to the large public power grid, while the homes were not. More and more Amish homes were powering electric lights and small appliances with solar power. That kept them off the grid and independent from English society. I knew not all Amish agreed with that use. For example, Ruth Yoder, the bishop's wife, had many choice words to say about solar anything.

So the electric lights and machines in the basement didn't surprise me. However, the number of machines was a tad overwhelming with all the saws, drills, and engravers working at the same time.

"Can I help you?" an English man in a plaid shirt asked me. He had dark hair that was graying at the temples and was clean-shaven. "This floor is only for staff and contractors. The shopping area is back upstairs." He pointed at the steps that I'd just come down.

"I didn't know that," I said, but made no motion to leave. "It's pretty noisy down here."

He shrugged. "You get used to it after a while, or your hearing is so damaged that you don't notice it as much."

"What's happening down here?"

"We cut lumber, metal poles, and that sort of thing for a lot of the Amish contractors in Wayne County and

Holmes County. We can do the work much faster here than they can at the job site. For some of them, they'd have to do the cutting by hand. It's not as precise as what we can do here, and it is time-consuming when they just want to get a house or barn up and finished." He shifted his stance. "I can tell you more about it upstairs, but you really shouldn't be on this floor."

Without preamble, I said, "I'm looking for Isaac Weiss."

The man rocked back on his heels. "I'm Isaac. It's not often that someone comes to the store looking for me."

"That surprises me. I got the impression that Rosemary, your wife, came here often, trying to convince you to return to the Amish way."

He stared at me. "Who are you?"

"My name is Bailey, and your daughter is currently at my candy shop."

He looked all around the basement level. Amish and English men who worked in the shop cutting boards and running the machines went about their business. None of them so much as a glanced in our direction.

"We can't talk about Rosemary here," he said in a harsh whisper. "Come with me." He left me standing at the foot of the stairs as he crossed the floor.

I hesitated for a half a second, and then followed him. I told myself that if he tried anything, I would scream. There had to have been a dozen men working nearby, from what I could see. One of them was bound to hear me yell, even over the beeps, clicks, and humming of the machines.

Isaac didn't look back to see if I followed him. He walked to a set of glass double doors that opened automatically onto a long ramp. He went out the doors and marched up the ramp with the determination of an explorer climbing Mount Everest.

At the top of the ramp, he turned right and put his hands on his hips as he waited for me.

I noted that I was a little winded trying to keep up with him, while he breathed normally. I guessed it was time for me go on more walks around the village.

"This is where we load the buggies, wagons, and trucks," he said to my unspoken question about the ramp. "It's not ideal, but the building was made before they added the machining department. This all used to be storage. The owner is hoping to build a second building sometime next year for our department. Being at ground level will make loading a lot easier."

"I would think so."

He folded his arms. "Now, what is this about Rosemary?"

I stared at him. "Don't you know?"

"Don't I know what?"

I bit the inside of my lip. Should I tell him that Rosemary was dead? This wasn't a young child, like Hannah, who needed to be told the news by a professional. No, this was a grown man who clearly wasn't thrilled to be talking about Rosemary.

Another thought struck me. *Maybe he did know because he was the one who'd strangled her.* Considering Rosemary had refused to give him a divorce, it was very possible he could be the killer. I reminded myself that, now that his legal wife was dead, he was free to marry his English girlfriend, wasn't he?

"Where were you on Saturday night?" I asked.

He rocked back on his heels. "Why would you ask me a question like that?" His eyes narrowed. "It's Rosemary, isn't it? She said I did something Saturday night, something illegal. My girlfriend warned me that she would pull something like this when I made it crystal clear to her that I wasn't going back to her or to the Amish."

"How did you make this crystal clear?"

"I showed her the engagement ring that I had bought my girlfriend. I made a point of showing her. I thought when I finally convinced her that I was in love with another woman, she would see that all the time she had invested trying to change my mind over the last few years had been a waste." He stepped up to me and grabbed my arm. "What did she tell you I did? What lies did she tell about me? You can't believe her. No one should believe her. She is a failure. She was a failure as both a wife and a mother." He gripped my arm even harder. "What did she say about me?"

"She didn't say anything!" My breaths came out in gasps, and my arm hurt. I looked down at the doors to the hardware store, but no one came out.

"I don't believe you," he shouted in my face, and I could smell the faint odor of mint gum.

"She didn't tell me anything because Rosemary is dead," I blurted out. As soon as the words left my mouth, I wanted to reach into the air and force them back in again. A lump formed in my chest as the enormity of the mistake I'd made hit me. I didn't mean to present the news so bluntly, but there was no taking it back now.

"What did you say?" The color drained from his face, and much to my relief, he dropped my arm.

I took several large steps away from him and rubbed my forearm where his fingers had dug into my flesh. I shifted my stance. My eyes, looking for any sign of aggression, never left Isaac's face. I felt uncertain around this man and wanted to position myself to bolt if I needed to. From where I stood, I could see my car in the massive parking lot, which was only a third full in the middle of a weekday like this.

"Rosemary. She's dead," I said, being as clear as I possibly could. Now that he knew and I couldn't take my words back, I saw no reason to lie to him.

"Was she in poor health?" he asked in disbelief. "I saw her many times—more times than I wanted to because she was so persistent—she never once mentioned she was ill." His jaw twitched. "I don't understand why she wouldn't tell me something like that. She would have expected me to go back to her and care for her and that deaf girl in her illness."

His vitriol made me shudder. If I didn't think he was such a viable suspect for the murder, I would have believed he had no idea what had happened to the woman who used to be his wife. However, he was a great suspect, and I didn't know him well enough to judge his acting skills. But if he was bluffing now, he deserved an Oscar.

CHAPTER TWENTY-ONE

"She was murdered," I stated.

"What did you say?" He spoke as if his mouth was dry.

"Someone strangled Rosemary in Esh Family Pretzels in Harvest." I waited for a reaction.

He stared at me.

"Does that shop name ring a bell for you?" I glanced back down the ramp leading into the store to see if anyone was coming out.

"Wh-why would she want to go there? That's the last place I thought she'd ever go."

"Why?" I asked.

He didn't answer my question.

"Is it because of Hannah, your daughter?" I pressed.

He took a step back from me. "Hannah is not my daughter. I have no children of my own. That was something Rosemary was unable to give me."

I bit my tongue to keep from snapping at him for blaming Rosemary for his lack of biological children. "You adopted Hannah. That makes her your daughter."

He glared at me. "Rosemary brought that baby home. I had nothing to do with it. I thought it was a mistake from the start. When I learned the child was deaf and dumb, that sealed it for me. I wanted children of my own. I'm not taking on other people's discarded and disabled infants."

I glared at him and recited the different kinds of chocolate in my head three times. Usually, I only had to say them once to calm myself down. Today, saying them three times didn't even make a dent in how angry I was at this ignorant man. All I knew was that there was no way I would let the social worker give Hannah to him. Over my dead body.

"Where were you on Saturday night?" It was time to get to the heart of the reason I was there.

"Why do you want to know?"

I folded my arms.

"Is that when she was killed?" he asked just above a whisper.

I nodded.

"You have no right to ask me that."

I shrugged. "Maybe I don't. But the police do. And trust me, they will ask."

"This is ridiculous. There's no reason that I should have to speak to the police about this. Rosemary and I were not together. We hadn't been for over three years."

"But she moved to Wooster to convince you to come back to the Amish way. You said yourself that you saw her often and she was persistent. She came to your place of work to talk to you. You want to marry your girlfriend, and she wouldn't give you a divorce." I paused. "I would say that any one of those things is a motive. Those motives all together make you look pretty guilty."

He glared at me. "Get out of here. I don't have to talk to you. You're not a cop. If you were, you would have introduced yourself as such, and you haven't."

I didn't correct him, nor to did I try to pretend to be a police office. I knew that if I did, it would get back to Aiden. That would *not* go over well.

"I have to get back to work," he said and stomped down the long ramp to the basement level. The set of double doors closed behind him.

I stood at the top of the ramp. I guessed going back inside the hardware store was a very bad idea.

There was a honk, and a large white van stopped two feet from me. The driver leaned out of the window. "Hey, lady, get out of the way! Can't you see this is a loading dock?"

With a pounding heart, I stumbled away from the ramp. I walked in the direction of the parking lot, unsure whether I'd done the right thing by telling Isaac about Rosemary's murder. Now he would be ready with a story when the police came. I had robbed Aiden and his officers of the chance of seeing Isaac's first reaction to the news. I knew Aiden wouldn't be happy about that.

When I reached my car, I removed my phone from my pocket, intending to text Aiden and tell him my mistake. I sat in the driver's seat of my car and was just about to press SEND when the phone rang. My best friend's face appeared on the screen. In Cass's contact picture, she wore all black, and a wide lock of purple hair hung over her face. That's what she'd looked like the last time I was in New York City to film *Bailey's Amish Sweets*. Cass was direct, sophisticated, and the best chocolatier I knew. When I'd given up the chance to be head chocolatier at JP Chocolates in New York, Cass was given the job. In her position, she had been expanding the shop's offerings and managing chocolate making for huge events in the city, such as Broadway premiers and fashion shows.

JP Chocolates had always been the number one chocolate shop in the city, but now business was exploding. I liked to think that it helped a little bit that *Bailey's Amish Sweets* was partnering with JP Chocolate to make candies the Amish way and sell them in the city.

I answered the call. I'd tell Aiden about my mess-up later.

"When are you coming back to New York? There's no one in the chocolate shop that can make a chocolate Eiffel tower like you can. We have a client who is dying to have one for her wedding. Every attempt we make is terrible. I'd send you pictures of the fails, but they're just too disturbing."

"I'm scheduled to be back in a couple of months."

"A couple of months? That won't work. I need this Eiffel Tower for a week from Saturday. I'm sure Jean Pierre would let me send his private jet to get you. You come here, make the tower, and fly home with a nice check in your pocket. We'd pay you well."

"I can't, Cass, and it's not about the money."

"What's wrong?" Her tone changed. "Is it something more than the dead body? Don't tell me that you and Hot Cop broke up!"

"Aiden and I didn't break up."

"I, for one, am relieved. I like Hot Cop, and I'd hate to

have to break his kneecaps. You know I would if it became necessary."

"Please don't break anyone's kneecap. Ever."

"I'm not sure that's a promise I can make. Tell me what's going on in this murder case. Maybe I can help you solve it, so you can come here and make my Eiffel Tower."

"I don't know if I should be alarmed or happy that you're so matter of fact about my being involved in a murder investigation."

"I'm getting used to it. It's not like this is the first time. It's human nature, really. We have an incredible ability to get used to things and adjust to a new normal. That's not always good, but I think it's part of what allows us to adapt and survive."

"Wow, that was very philosophical."

"I spend a lot of time alone with chocolate. That leads to thinking deep thoughts."

I could practically hear her shrug over the phone, and I found what she said about chocolate to be true.

"This murder investigation is a little more complicated than ones I've dealt with in the past," I said.

"More complicated? How can it be more complicated? You closed down an illegal Amish still last time. I would say that was very complicated."

I quickly told her about Rosemary's death, and about Hannah. I didn't tell her that I suspected—no, more than suspected, I *knew*—that Hannah was Emily's child.

"The poor little girl," Cass said, sounding as serious as I had ever heard her. "Do you need me to come there to help? We make a pretty good team."

I placed one hand on the steering wheel. "What about the bride and the chocolate Eiffel Tower?"

"There will always be another bridezilla and another tall order from an elitist mother of the bride."

"I appreciate that, Cass, but . . ." I trailed off as I watched two men walk to a pickup truck. Two men leaving a hardware store together in Amish country wasn't remarkable. What made it remarkable was one of the men was Isaac Weiss and the other the overtly friendly man whom I'd met at the store entrance.

I slipped down low in my seat, so that the two men couldn't see me, and held the phone close to my ear.

"Bailey, what were you going to say? Don't try to talk me out of coming."

"Wait just a second," I whispered as I peered over the dash. Isaac and the other man stood by the truck and appeared to be deep in conversation.

"Did you just tell me to wait?" Cass sounded offended.

"I see one of the suspects outside the hardware store I was just in, and he's with another man I spoke to. It looks very suspicious," I kept my voice low.

"Why are you whispering? Do you really think they can hear you from where you are?"

"No," I said in my normal voice. "Oh, they just got in the truck and are driving away."

"And what are you doing?"

"Talking to you," I said as I watched the truck pause before turning out of the lot.

"Well, you know what to do. Get moving."

"What's that?"

"Follow them! Have I taught you nothing?"

"You want me to follow them?" I sat up in my seat.

"Of course I do."

That was all I needed to hear. I started my car just as the truck turned out of the lot.

CHAPTER TWENTY-TWO

I turned left onto the road in the same direction the truck had gone.

"Bailey, are you still there?" Cass asked through my car's Bluetooth speaker.

"Yep. I'm following them." I gripped the steering wheel at ten and two, as if I was about to take a driving test.

"Oh, I wish I was there. I would love to be part of a high-speed chase."

"It's not exactly a high-speed chase. I'm going twenty miles per hour." My eyes focused on the license plate, and I committed it to memory. With my right hand, I rifled through my purse on the passenger seat until I came up with a pen and a receipt. I scribbled the license plate number on the receipt, as well as the make and model of the truck. I was dating a sheriff's deputy, after all. I knew what to do.

On the other end of the call, Cass swore as if she'd dropped something on her foot.

"You okay?" I asked with both hands gripping the steering wheel.

"I have to go. The Eiffel Tower bride and her mother are here. They want to talk to me."

"Sounds bad," I said vaguely.

"If you get into a shootout, call me right away," Cass instructed.

"I'm not going to get into a shootout."

"If you do, I had better hear about it. And not a day or two after the fact either." She ended the call.

I supposed that I should be grateful that the pair had not left in an Amish buggy. It was almost impossible to follow an Amish buggy with a car and not be seen.

It was the middle of a weekday in May. The semester was all but over at the College of Wooster. The streets were quiet. I knew that, at any moment, Isaac or the other man was going to notice that I was trailing them.

To my surprise, the truck turned onto the highway heading east. I frowned because that was in the direction of Harvest. However, it was now much easier to follow the truck without being noticed. The highway wasn't busy in the middle of the day, and I was doing my best to stay five or so car lengths back from the other vehicle. It was a good distance, I thought. At least from what I'd learned from the cops and robbers movies my father used to watch when I was a child.

We drove on the highway for close to ten minutes. I was beginning to question the wisdom of following the truck. I should call Aiden and tell him what was going on, and then ask him to run the plate.

Just as I picked up the phone from the console, it rang.

The call was from Swissmen Sweets. I hit the button on the dashboard and answered.

"Bailey, you need to come back to the candy shop." Charlotte was out of breath.

"Why? What's happened?"

"Emily is here. She's really upset, Bailey. She wants to talk to you."

My heart sank. If Emily was at the candy shop, then she had to know about Hannah by now. It must have been a shock. I knew I should have told Emily the day before. I wished that I hadn't promised Aiden I wouldn't.

I grimaced as the truck turned off the highway. I noted the exit number and the sign next to it: Wayne County Racetrack.

I bit my lip, but didn't get off. I continued east toward Harvest.

On the drive to the village, I tried to call Aiden. He didn't pick up, so I resolved to text him what I'd learned from my visit to Wooster when I got back to Harvest. I knew he wouldn't be happy with me for following Isaac and the Amish man, but I was certain that they hadn't seen me. I had information, and I hoped Aiden would acknowledge it as being vital to the case.

I parked in my usual spot on Apple Street, around the corner from the candy shop on Main. I left my car and hurried around the corner. Downtown was relatively quiet. There were just a few people strolling along the sidewalk and peeking into the shop windows to see what the local shopkeepers might have to offer.

I stepped into Swissmen Sweets. The first thing I noticed was there was no one in the front of the shop. That was a big no-no during business hours. We hoped there weren't many shoplifters wandering into Swissmen Sweets, but like every small shop, we had to be careful. It'd become an even more urgent matter with the success of my television show and the dramatic increase in numbers of visitors we were getting at the candy shop.

Thankfully, the only creatures in the front room were Nutmeg and Puff, curled up together on Nutmeg's cat bed.

The back kitchen door swung open, and Charlotte appeared. "Oh, Bailey, I'm so glad it's you. Emily is so upset."

I could imagine.

"Is Hannah all right?" I asked.

She nodded. "She's fine. Cousin Clara took her upstairs to the apartment when Emily became upset."

I frowned. "I hope Hannah doesn't know what's going on."

Charlotte started to say something when the kitchen door behind her began to open. "Please let me through," a soft voice said behind Charlotte.

Charlotte stepped out of the way. Emily stopped when she saw me standing there. "I don't want to talk to you." She threw up the hinged section of the counter that separated the back of the shop from the front. She marched to the front door.

I glanced at Charlotte, and she shook her head.

By the time I turned back to Emily again, she was out the door. I followed her. "Emily, wait!"

She spun around on the sidewalk, and the ribbons from her prayer cap brushed against her cheeks. I marveled again at how lovely she was. It was as if her anger made her even prettier. I'd always thought that whole "beautiful when you're angry" thing was a myth. Or some saying made up by a man determined to distract a woman. Heaven knew, I wasn't pretty when I was mad. I was pretty sure my nostrils flared, and I think one of my eyes twitched. I guessed I resembled a cartoon bull of Looney Tunes fame.

Emily, though, she could lay claim to "attractive anger." She might be the only true example of it on the planet.

"You should have told me, Bailey! You should have told me that my—that that girl was here." She crossed her arms. "I cannot believe you didn't warn me. I thought we were *gut* friends."

"We are friends. I was going to tell you as soon as I could. I certainly wanted to tell you before you saw her, but social services hasn't been here yet to assess Hannah."

"Social services? What are you talking about?"

"Hannah doesn't have a legal guardian, so a social worker has to take her case."

"She's my daughter!"

I held up my hands. "I know, but Aiden said—"

"I do not care what Aiden said. *You* are my friend, and you should have told me. You do not have to wait for this social worker person to tell your friend something."

"I wanted to! And, of course, I planned to! You weren't due in to the shop for a few hours yet. I'd intended to talk to you, tell you everything I'd discovered beforehand. I'd never blindside you like this—you must know that."

Emily appeared to waver for a moment, then squared her shoulders. "Do you have any idea how I felt when I walked into the candy shop and saw her there? I knew instantly she was the child I had lost. When Clara admitted that Hannah had been Rosemary's daughter, I knew it was true. I tried to speak to the child, only to learn that she was deaf. It was like a dream come true and a nightmare all rolled into one."

"Hannah's being deaf doesn't have to be a nightmare. You can learn to sign. Both Aiden and Lois know American Sign Language."

She placed a hand on her pregnant belly and winced.

I took a step forward. "Are you all right? Are you feeling unwell?"

"It shouldn't matter to you how I feel." She took a breath. "I think Esther and Abel were right about you, after all. You can't be trusted. You want to come into our little town and make it more *Englisch.*" Emily walked away.

I deserved her blame. I should have told her right away.

I stood numbly for a few seconds, then chased after Emily again. She stopped when I reached her—whether to avoid making a scene or because she wanted to hear what I had to say, I wasn't sure. "Emily, I am sorry. Aiden asked me not to tell you until Hannah could be evaluated. Child Services is involved."

Tears gathered in her eyes. The anger that had been there seemed to have dissipated. In its place there was a great sadness. "What does that mean? Is this about the social worker?"

I cleared my throat because I was certain she wouldn't like what I said next. "Yes, a social worker from the county is coming to speak with Hannah. She'll tell her about Rosemary and decide where she should go."

She stared at me. "Where she should go? She is my child. There is no question where she should be."

"Do you want her to live with you?"

She opened and closed her mouth. "I have to speak to my husband. It is not my choice. He is the head of the household and is the one to make those decisions."

I bit down hard on my lip to keep myself from saying something that would only widen the rift between us. I knew Amish culture; the husband was truly the head of the household, as Emily said. He was the one who decided what was right and wrong for the family. The wife deferred to her husband. I would make a terrible Amish woman. That being said, I had seen many strong Amish women stand up to their husbands or take charge if the need arose. I knew, however, they wouldn't like that behavior to come to light.

I couldn't imagine my husband ever telling me that I couldn't be with my child. In my book, that was grounds for divorce. Plain and simple. But the Amish rarely divorced, and when they did, it caused turmoil not only in the individual family, but in the entire church district.

A tear slid down her face. "I—I have to go home to my husband."

I took a step in her direction. "I will do whatever I can to help you."

She stared at me. "Then, next time, tell me the truth."

She spun around and walked across the street to a hitching post. I recognized her horse and buggy. I could have followed her and tried to speak to her while she was untethering the horse, but I didn't know what good it would do.

CHAPTER TWENTY-THREE

There was the sound of clapping behind me.

"How many more friendships will you ruin, Bailey King?" an oily voice asked me. I didn't have to turn around to see that it was Emily's older brother, Abel.

I spun around and tried to sidestep him so I could return to my shop. I wanted to check on Hannah to make sure that she was okay. He moved to stay in my path.

I glared at him. "Please, Abel, I need to get back to work."

He cocked his head. "That must be an unusual need for you. It's clear to everyone in this village that you would much rather poke your nose in Amish business, where it doesn't belong, than mind your own store."

"I—" Something in his shirt pocket caught my eye.

"What's that?" I pointed at his chest. There was a glossy piece of paper sticking out of the pocket. Without taking a second to consider what Abel might do, I plucked the brochure out of his shirt. The heading was JOIN US ON THE TRACK. WAYNE COUNTY RACETRACK. Below the headline, there was a picture of a horse pulling an Amish man in a racing cart on a track.

Was it just a coincidence that I'd seen Isaac and the Amish man from the hardware store get off at the exit for the racetrack, and now Abel had a brochure about it in his pocket? It seemed unlikely.

He took the brochure from my hand. "You *Englisch* women are so forward. You can't just take something out of a man's pocket like that."

I pointed at the glossy paper in his hand. "Do you go to that racetrack?"

He stepped back, leaving ample room for me to pass him on the sidewalk and enter my candy shop. However, I'd changed my mind.

"Do you go to the track?" I asked again.

"That's none of your business."

That wasn't exactly the yes or no answer I was looking for, but I supposed that because the brochure was in his pocket, he must have been there. It wouldn't surprise me in the least if Abel went to the track regularly; it seemed that no one in Harvest knew where he spent the majority of his time. It was clear that he did little to no work at Esh Family Pretzels. The shop and, I suspected, the keeping-up of the family's small farm fell on Esther.

"Bailey?" I turned around and saw Aiden coming down the street, accompanied by a Latina woman wearing jeans and a blazer over a colorful blouse. The woman had her hair pulled back into a sleek ponytail high on her head.

"Aiden's calling you. That's my cue to leave." Abel

turned and walked down Main Street in the opposite direction.

Aiden jogged over to me, leaving the woman to catch up.

"Was he bothering you?" he asked in a concerned whisper.

"Not exactly . . ."

The woman joined us and smiled at me.

"Bailey, this is Vanessa Hernandez. She is the county social worker who will be assessing Hannah's case," Aiden said. "Vanessa, this is Bailey. Hannah is staying in her Amish candy shop."

Vanessa appeared harmless to me. However, I knew that Emily—who had been raised to mistrust government in all forms—would not see her that way.

"You were born Amish then?" she asked.

I shook my head. It was a common misconception that I had run into since moving to Holmes County. Everyone assumed that because my grandmother was Amish, I must have run away from the community. That wasn't the case. I had been born English.

"My father left the faith. My grandmother is Amish. I never was."

Vanessa held a navy leather briefcase in her hands. "May I see the child?"

I nodded. "She's upstairs in my grandmother's apartment above the candy shop."

"Then let's go talk to her," Vanessa said.

I glanced at Aiden. "Will Aiden translate for you?"

"I know sign language, too. But I may not be as fluent as Deputy Brody, so I would like him to be there if I struggle to find the right word."

"Of course," Aiden said.

I swallowed and led them to the candy shop. When we stepped inside, Charlotte stared at us.

"Charlotte, this is Vanessa Hernandez. She's the social worker who will speak to Hannah. Are they upstairs?"

Charlotte began to shake. "Cousin Clara is upstairs looking for Hannah."

My heart sank. "Why is she looking for her?"

"We can't find her." Charlotte nervously glanced at Aiden and Vanessa. "Cousin Clara thinks she might be hiding in the apartment."

My grandmother came through the archway leading to the stairs that went up to the apartment.

"She's not upstairs. I looked everywhere, in every closet and under the beds." She wrung her hands together. "She must have slipped out of the apartment when I went to the kitchen to find her something to eat."

"I didn't see her leave," Charlotte said. "But we had a rush of customers a few minutes ago. She could have slipped out when they were coming or going without my noticing."

"We have to find her," I said.

"She hasn't been gone for more than ten minutes," my grandmother said. "She couldn't have gone very far. We will find her."

"Deputy Brody, this is serious," Vanessa said. "You told me this family would be able to care for the girl. Now we have a missing deaf child."

Each of her words hit me like a baseball bat. Everything she said was true. We'd been given the responsibility of watching Hannah, and she'd run away.

"We can discuss that later," Aiden said. "Now we need to find the girl."

"*Maami*, stay here in the shop in case she comes back," I said.

My grandmother bit her lip. I knew she didn't like the idea of being the one who had to wait behind.

Vanessa, Aiden, Charlotte, and I went outside.

"Let's all go in different directions," Aiden said. "Spreading out is our best chance of finding her."

"I'll go to the playground on the other side of the square near the church. If I was a child, that's where I would have gone. She might have seen it when we went to breakfast at the Sunbeam Café this morning." I took off without waiting for an answer or agreement.

I was halfway across the square when an older woman and a young girl walked toward me. It was Lois and Hannah. Lois held Hannah by the hand as if she knew that she had to hold on tight for fear the child might run away.

"Aiden!" I cried over my shoulder and then broke into a run to meet them. When I did, I fell to my knees in front of Hannah. "What on earth were you doing? You gave us such a scare."

Hannah looked at Lois, and Lois quickly signed something to her. I guessed that it was what I had just said.

Lois wrapped her arm around the girl's shoulders. "I think she came over to the Sunbeam because she wanted someone to talk to. I told her as soon as she arrived that I had to take her back to the candy shop."

I looked up at Lois. "Thank you! She was only missing for a few minutes, but it was terrifying."

"I know the feeling," Lois said. "When Darcy was young, I once misplaced her in Disney World. It was terrifying. Turned out she was on the Dumbo ride. How she got on it with no adult, I'll never know. Darcy usually seems meek, but I know from experience that she is meek and wily at the same time."

Aiden, Charlotte, and Vanessa came up behind me. Lois smiled and waved at all of them.

"She's right as rain." Lois squeezed Hannah's shoulder, and then held out her hand to Vanessa. "I don't believe we've met. I'm Lois Henry."

Vanessa shook her hand and introduced herself.

Vanessa knelt in front of Hannah and began to sign. The little girl nodded. Vanessa stood up.

"Deputy Brody, if you will come with me. We can chat with Hannah over in the gazebo." She smiled at the little girl. "I think it will be easier to talk if we're outside."

Aiden nodded, but Hannah grabbed Lois's hand. Then she let go of it and began to sign rapidly.

"She wants to know if I can go with you all, too."

Vanessa pressed her lips together.

"I think that will be all right," Aiden said. "It's clear that Hannah trusts Lois, or she wouldn't have walked over to the Sunbeam to see her. It might help to have Lois there while we tell her the tough news."

Charlotte and I watched while the four of them walked over to the gazebo. What I wouldn't have given to be able to go with them, too. My heart ached for Hannah. She was about to find out that the only mother she had ever known was gone.

Charlotte cleared her throat. "I'm so sorry that Hannah slipped out of the shop without being seen. I know Cousin Clara feels terrible, too."

"It's all right. I'm glad she went to Lois. Lois must be right. It's got to be difficult not to have anyone to speak with."

"What will happen to Hannah now?" Charlotte asked. "Will that woman take her away from her community?"

"I don't know." It was the best answer I had. "I'm sure Aiden will do whatever he can to make sure Hannah goes to the best place for her."

"But is it really up to Aiden? Isn't it that woman Vanessa's decision?"

I bit my lip. Charlotte wasn't English, but she understood enough to know Aiden wasn't the one in control.

CHAPTER TWENTY-FOUR

Charlotte went back to the candy shop to tell my grandmother the good news that Hannah had been found. I knew *Maami* must have felt awful that the child had slipped out of the shop undetected. I told Charlotte to remind *Maami* that it wasn't her fault, but I remained on the square. I knew that if I went back to Swissmen Sweets, I'd be far too distracted to get anything done. I just had to know Hannah's fate. I also realized that Aiden hadn't yet heard that Emily knew Hannah was staying at Swissmen Sweets.

The social worker would have a fight on her hands if she took Hannah away from Emily. That, of course, was assuming Emily's husband granted her permission to keep Hannah.

It was hard to take in. There was so much . . . *hurt*. Emily's. Rosemary's. Hannah's. All innocent—all victims of forces beyond their control. The thought formed a lump in my stomach that rose into my throat. The backs of my eyes burned. There was no way to make it better now for Rosemary, but it was still possible for Emily and Hannah to be happy if the powers that be would allow them to be reunited.

I don't know how long I waited on the square. It could have been thirty minutes, but it felt more like two hours. When I checked my cell phone, I was surprised to see I'd been waiting for just shy of twenty minutes. I debated going back to the candy shop or maybe even stepping a bit closer to the gazebo, so that I could hear the conversation. Honestly, though, I knew that wasn't really an option. Vanessa was here to do her job, and Hannah's fate would be determined by the county. We'd already "lost" Hannah once on my watch. If I appeared to be eavesdropping, that would only hurt my chances of having any connection to the child. Still, I hesitated, because not knowing what was happening was killing me.

A moment later, the four of them came out of the gazebo together. Lois had her arm wrapped protectively around Hannah, who was crying. I felt heartsick. They had told her about Rosemary.

Lois smiled at me. "I'm just going to walk Hannah back over to the candy shop. I'll stay with her for a little bit in case she wants to talk about any of this."

I watched them go. Hannah gripped Lois's waist as if she was a buoy in the middle of the ocean. Perhaps, to the child, she was. I turned to Aiden and the social worker. "What happened? What's the plan for Hannah?"

Vanessa took the lead. "We told her about her mother and said that she would be staying with you for a little bit. The child is clearly traumatized, and I'm reluctant to

move her into a non-Amish home. With her hearing dis-
ability, it would be scary and confusing. Also, you knew
her mother, so I think that will make it a bit easier on
her."

I hadn't known Rosemary. I had spoken to her briefly
at Emily's baby shower. The next time I saw her, she was
dead. I didn't correct Vanessa on that fact, though. "What's
going to happen to her? Not just today, but in the future.
Where will she live?"

Vanessa frowned at me. "I can't answer that yet. I have
only just met the child. There has to be a full assessment.
Also, a person from the county will have to inspect the
candy shop tomorrow to make sure it's up to code."

"Does that mean Hannah is in the foster system?" My
heart sank at the very idea. I knew there were laws to protect children, but going into foster care would be horrible
for the young Amish girl.

"When it comes to Amish children, we handle things a
little differently," Vanessa said. "I have been working in
children's services for the county for five years, and Hannah's the first Amish case I have come across. We find
that the Amish tend to take care of their own. They rarely
come forward when a child needs a placement, and they
do not like my department making visits." She frowned.
"It rarely gets to the point that Amish children are put in
any form of protective custody."

I bit my lip.

"I trust that Hannah's disappearance today was a small
mishap that won't happen again." She gave me a beady-
eyed stare.

"It won't," I assured her. "I know my grandmother is
brokenhearted over it."

"Glad to hear it. If it happens again, I will remove the child without a second thought."

I had no doubt that she would.

"There's something else you should know," I said cautiously. "Hannah's biological mother saw her today. She might very well want to take the child home."

Vanessa frowned and glanced at Aiden. "You told me that the mother didn't know about Hannah."

"I didn't know that she did." Aiden gave me a look.

"I only just found out before the two of you arrived." I didn't add how angry Emily had been at me for keeping this secret. "Emily came into the shop early and saw Hannah. She knew right away that she was her child."

"I see. I'm not sure a shop where people come in and out all day is the right place for a child to live." Vanessa adjusted her grip on her briefcase.

"We are trying to run a business and sell candies. Because of that, the door is open during business hours, and Emily works at the shop. I didn't expect her to be here until late afternoon. My hope was that you would have spoken to Hannah by then." I took a breath. "If Emily wants Hannah back, what would she have to do?"

"The birth mother gave Hannah up for adoption. Why would she want her back?"

"As I understand it, Emily was given no choice at the time."

Vanessa pressed her lips together into a hard line. "Where's the paperwork for the adoption? I'll need to see it."

"There is no paperwork," I said.

"How can that be?"

"You'll have to speak to the people who were involved in the adoption, but Emily insists that she didn't sign anything."

Vanessa rubbed her forehead as if this conversation was giving her a headache. I had no doubt that it was.

"What would Emily have to do if she wanted to claim Hannah?" I asked again.

Vanessa looked at me. Her dark brown eyes appeared tired. I wondered how many tough cases she had worked that week already. I hoped she felt confident that Hannah would be well cared for at Swissmen Sweets for the time being. "There are things that can be done. She could hire an attorney or perhaps a social worker in a private agency who could help her navigate the process of applying for custody."

"Vanessa," Aiden said. "You've worked in Holmes County for a long time. You know that won't work for the Amish."

She frowned at Aiden. "I have, and I don't like the way the Amish think it's their right to hide children from the state."

"They don't hide them."

"They aren't honest about their numbers. They don't have birth certificates, do they? How are we supposed to keep those children safe when we don't know they even exist?" She wrinkled her brow. "It's a practice I have always taken issue with. The county can't protect children we don't know are there."

I wasn't in complete disagreement with her, but I also knew that it went against Amish beliefs to be regulated by the government as much as the government would like to regulate them. They paid taxes and did the bare minimum that was required. As of yet, the state of Ohio, at least, did not require that they have birth certificates. Because the children weren't born in hospitals, it would be difficult to enforce a birth certificate requirement.

Vanessa shook her head. "I need to get back to the office. Deputy Brody, you have my number. If the birth mother wants to make a case for taking the child, call me. The goal of my department is always reunification with family." She glanced at me. "If it can be proven that your friend Emily is, in fact, Hannah's biological mother, then it is possible she would be granted custody of the child, as long as there are no other claims. I'm told the adoptive father is still alive and the adoptive mother is deceased."

Does she know that Rosemary isn't just dead, but has been murdered? I wondered. *If she knew it was murder, would she still leave Hannah here in Harvest with us, so close to the scene of the crime?* I shook off these thoughts and said, "The adoptive father is still alive, but he doesn't want anything to do with Hannah," I said.

Vanessa frowned at me. "How would you know that?"

I swallowed and glanced at Aiden. "I spoke with him today."

The only reaction from Aiden was the tightening of his jaw, but it was enough to let me know that I was in a whole heap of trouble.

"I'll need to speak to him as well. Deputy Brody, I assume you'll arrange that?"

Aiden nodded.

"Very good," she said and started in the direction of a beige sedan. Just before she reached it, she turned around. "I will do my very best to make sure Hannah is cared for. Trust me, Miss King. I take my job seriously." She climbed into the car.

I didn't quite know what to make of her last comment.

When the car drove away, Aiden folded his arms. "Bailey."

I held up a hand. "Before you start your lecture, let me tell you what I learned."

He groaned.

I gave him the briefest possible summary of my visit to Mueller Hardware and my conversation with Isaac. "He didn't know that his wife had died. I thought you must have told him already, or I wouldn't have let it out."

"We were planning to tell him, but we have had trouble finding him."

I wrinkled my brow. "I just walked into the hardware store and asked to see him. An employee gave me directions."

Aiden frowned. "That may be because you are not a sheriff's deputy. When we went to the hardware store, we were told that Isaac wasn't there. The Amish owner asked us to leave. I was waiting for a warrant to force the issue." He rubbed the back of his neck. "I also have deputies stationed at his home in Wooster, with the permission of the Wooster police, waiting for him to return. As of yet, he has not come back to the house."

I nodded.

"I, not you, should have been the one to tell him about his wife. They were still legally married, so he is technically the next of kin. It would have been helpful if you'd told me as soon as you found him so that we could have made the first contact." He frowned. "Now he will be prepared when I or another one of my deputies finally catch up with him, which will be soon. We now have the warrant to make Mueller Hardware tell us his location."

I swallowed hard because I knew everything he said was true. "Maybe this will make up for it just a little." I removed the receipt on which I had scribbled the make, model, and license plate of Isaac's truck. "This is Isaac's truck."

He looked at the piece of paper and smiled. "Thank you, and you're right that this is his truck. We already got his license plate from his driver's license."

"Oh." I felt my face grow hot. "Of course, you did."

"It was quick thinking to grab it." He smiled at me again.

"Well, I might be able to share at least one thing you don't yet know." I quickly told him about the Amish man I'd met, the one who'd gotten in Isaac's truck. "I just find it very suspicious that they left together, especially after the Amish man told me that I shouldn't have anything to do with Isaac. I think the two of them might have gone to the racetrack."

Aiden squinted at me. "Might have gone?"

"They got off at that exit. I didn't follow them to see if the track was their destination because Charlotte called to tell me Emily was at the candy shop."

"So you don't know for sure that they were heading for the racetrack."

"Call it a hunch."

He scowled. I had a feeling Aiden wasn't very keen on my hunches at the moment.

After a beat, he said, "It's a lead. I'll put Deputy Little on it. Maybe he can find a connection."

"At the very least, I know that's where Dinah's son, Mason, works. He agreed with his mother that they could not keep Hannah. It's so strange to me."

"Why's that?" Aiden asked.

"Because they are Amish, and Dinah was Rosemary's cousin, even if a distant one. It's ingrained in the Amish to take care of their own, and that's especially true with children."

"You said Dinah refused because she couldn't communicate with Hannah."

"That's what she said, and it seemed to be true. She didn't sign at all while Charlotte and I were at the bakery, and she was shocked with the little bit I knew."

"It is out of character for the Amish. I will give you that."

"There's another thing that bothers me about all this."

"Just one?" he asked with a raised brow.

"More than one, but the issue I'm thinking about at the moment is Hannah's adoption. Was it an illegal adoption?" I asked. "It seemed to me that Vanessa viewed it as illegal."

"In the English world it is. You can't take a child away from a mother unless the mother relinquishes maternal rights, or unless the court, for whatever reason—drugs, abuse; sadly the list goes on—deems her to be unfit. Emily was young at the time, but it was still her legal right to decide what became of her child."

My face fell. "I don't think Esther presented it to her in that way."

"I'm sure she didn't. Esther is Amish, too, and giving her the benefit of the doubt, she might not have even known. However, the English family that let Emily stay with them when she was pregnant should have known better."

"Perhaps they weren't involved in the adoption."

"It's hard for me to believe that they would be unaware of what was happening if Emily was in the same house. A young girl, in the late stages of pregnancy . . .

But we'll find out one way or another. I don't have the time or manpower to run over to Indiana to talk to them. I'll call in a favor with the sheriff's office there. There are Amish communities in both of our counties, and we've been in contact before when issues come up that cross state lines."

I wanted to ask him what those issues were, but I knew I was already walking on thin ice after telling Isaac about Rosemary's death. It was best not to push Aiden at the moment.

I folded my arms as another thought hit me. "So wanting to keep the adoption secret would be a motive for murder."

"A very good motive, I think," Aiden said. "I suppose the question is who would resort to murder to protect this secret?"

A few names came to my mind.

CHAPTER TWENTY-FIVE

I'd become involved in this case because Emily had asked me to clear her sister's name. Now it seemed to me that Esther had the greatest motive to silence Rosemary. Rosemary had wanted Hannah to know and meet her biological mother. If what Dinah had said was true, Rosemary might have even wanted Emily to take the child back because Emily was married to a loving husband. A loving husband—something Rosemary had lost when she'd tried to save her marriage by adopting Hannah in the first place. The Amish firmly believed children needed both a mother and father to care for them, except in very extreme cases. Rosemary, despite her love for Hannah, had possibly felt she wasn't enough. Her culture told her she couldn't raise a child alone.

I wished that she was still alive so I could tell her how ridiculous that notion was. Rosemary had learned and taught her daughter American Sign Language. She had done—from what I knew—everything she could to give Hannah a normal life.

If anyone was to blame for the dissolution of that family, it was Isaac. However, which would have been more detrimental to Hannah—no father or a father who thought she was "less than" because she was deaf? I didn't have the answer to that.

After Aiden left, I went back into the candy shop. *Maami* held Hannah on her lap, and together they were looking at one of the picture books Lois had given us. Hannah rested her head on my grandmother's shoulder. Hannah's blond hair was in two braids, and she wore a lavender dress that complemented my grandmother's navy one. They looked as if they belonged on one of the postcards sold in the county gift shops. The only problem with the scene was the tears rolling down Hannah's face.

Maami looked up from the book. "What did the social worker decide? Lois said that Hannah will be with us for at least another night."

I nodded. "It looks that way, and it could be longer, too." I pressed my lips together. "Hannah seemed to be taken with Jethro. I was thinking maybe we could walk over to the church to visit him."

Maami smiled. "I think that's a fine idea, but I have to admit, I'm a little bit surprised. I would have thought that you'd be running off to solve the murder."

"I want to, but it seems that the next step in the investigation is going to happen in Indiana, where Hannah was born. I'm certainly not going to go all the way out there." I glanced out the window. "I should talk to Emily and Esther again. Emily to smooth things over, and Esther to find out what she knows. But, honestly, I just want to make sure that Hannah is feeling a bit better first. I don't want her to feel the need to run away from the candy shop again."

"I didn't mean to let her slip out." Tears gathered in my grandmother's eyes, and she hugged the girl close.

"I know, *Maami*. Emily's unexpected arrival must have been a shock to all of you."

She nodded. "It was. I thought that she knew Hannah was here with us, so I brought her right out to see her. Bailey, I have never seen someone's face go as white as Emily's did when she saw the child. It was like milk. Even her lips lost their color. When I saw that, I realized what a terrible mistake I had made."

"Hannah went to Lois. We should be grateful for that," I said, and then I waved to Hannah.

She looked up at me.

I stuck my hand under my chin and waved my fingers up and down at the knuckles. It was the sign for "pig." I had looked it up on my phone before coming back to the candy shop. Hannah's face lit up, and she made the sign back to me.

It seemed to me Jethro was going to be called to save the day yet again. He was a remarkable little pig.

Hannah and I stepped out of the shop. I glanced in the direction of Esh Family Pretzels, and the thin curtain moved. It could have been a draft, or it could have been Esther trying to see what was happening. My money was on Esther. I wasn't looking forward to having another conversation with her. I knew Esther was keeping some-thing from me, but what? If she didn't tell me or Aiden what was going on, there was a very good chance she could find herself in jail.

I held onto Hannah's hand as we crossed the street

onto the square. There were several Amish men there, setting up booths and chairs for the coming weekend's event. Margot Rawlings, who planned village events, had e-mailed me the May and June schedule for the square, but I had to admit that I hadn't worked up the courage to open the e-mail. Knowing Margot, it held more work for Swissmen Sweets.

That Margot was a wily one. I don't know how she managed it, but I found myself roped into all of her events. I sighed. I had better look at the schedule soon, or I might be blindsided again by one of her ideas.

We crossed Church Street and stopped in front of the large white church, where Juliet was the pastor's wife. After a long courtship, she had finally married Reverend Brook last summer. It had been the wedding of the year for the little village of Harvest.

I had not called ahead to see if Jethro was at the church. Maybe I should have. I had made an assumption because Juliet could almost always be found at the church, and Jethro—if not pawned off on me—was always with Juliet.

We found Juliet right away, working with a group of ladies planting flowers around the church. Juliet waved to me. "Bailey, dear, it's so good to see you. How are you holding up after that terrible discovery you made Saturday night?"

I wasn't surprised that Juliet had heard about the murder. It had been a few days, and gossip traveled fast in Harvest. By buggy or by cell phone, the news about what was happening in our little Amish village always got out.

The other ladies of the church waved to us and went back to work.

Juliet removed her garden gloves. "And this must be Hannah," she said, waving at the young girl.

Hannah held onto my hand a little more tightly. "You know about Hannah?" I asked, but, again, I wasn't surprised that she knew. Harvest's rumor mill was fierce.

"The reverend and I had lunch at the Sunbeam Café, and Lois told me all about her. She thought rightly that I would want to know." She studied Hannah. "Poor girl, her mother murdered, and no one to care for her. My goodness, doesn't she look like someone we know? I just can't place her at the moment."

Time to change the subject. I certainly didn't want Juliet to make the connection between Emily and Hannah. At least not yet.

I glanced around. "Hannah was really taken by Jethro, so I thought I'd bring her over for a visit. Where is he?"

Juliet pressed her gloves against the blue and yellow polka-dotted blouse she wore tucked into her jeans. Juliet, who almost always wore dresses, was not a jeans woman. I guessed this was her gardening garb. It would be difficult to plant anything in an A-line skirt, which was her preference.

"Well," she said in her soft, Carolina drawl. "I'm not surprised for a moment that she and Jethro have a connection. Personally, I think it's impossible to feel low when Jethro is around." She started walking around the side of the church. "He's over here eating his lunch."

Jethro was lying under the split-rail fence that separated the church property from the public playground. He had his belly pressed up against the grass with a half-eaten cabbage between his two front hooves.

Hannah pulled her hand from mine, ran over to the

pig, and sat on the grass beside him. She broke off a piece of cabbage and fed Jethro. The black and white polka-dotted pig looked up at her adoringly. Apparently, he had been hoping that someone would come along and hand-feed him. Leaning over to eat was far too much work for the little bacon bundle.

I raised my brow at Juliet. "Cabbage?" Typically Juliet fed him dog food, fruit, and even table scraps. I had never seen him eat cabbage.

"I know. He was quite put out that this is his lunch, but it's for his own good. You know pigs only get as large as you feed them. If I were to keep feeding Jethro like I was, I might not be able to carry him around." She sighed. "Besides, I spoke with his agent, and she said that Jethro has to lose a few pounds if he has any hopes of getting a sponsorship."

I winced. Hollywood was harsh if it was even asking pigs to lose weight. "How's Jethro's career coming?"

"Eloise, Jethro's agent, has been a godsend. She really is the first person I've spoken to who sees Jethro's full potential in the same way I do." She gave me a look.

I knew better than to respond. I had doubted Jethro's—or should I say Juliet's—dreams of the pig becoming a star. However, he was proving me wrong. The little pig had appeared on several episodes of my television show. Those episodes were the most highly rated and the most difficult to shoot because Jethro ate half the ingredients and knocked the other half off the counter. He didn't have the best kitchen etiquette.

"I'm happy for you and Jethro."

Juliet smiled. "Thank you. It's been a dream of ours for a long time."

I was sure.

"Thank goodness I caught you, Bailey King!" Margot Rawlings called from behind us. "Why do I have to run all over this village to track you down? You should be in your shop." She held a clipboard in her hands and drummed her fingers on top of it.

"I'm sorry, Margot," I said. "I didn't know you were looking for me. You could have called or texted." I shifted my stance so that I blocked her view of Hannah. I did not want to talk to Margot, of all people, about the little girl.

"I did." She sniffed.

"Oh." I looked at my phone, and there were two missed calls from Margot. A voice mail no doubt accompanied one of them; I'd bet the candy shop on it.

"Just assume I am always looking for you," she huffed. "Honestly, I think nothing in this village would get done if it weren't for me pushing it through." She narrowed her eyes at me. "I trust that you read the e-mail I sent you with the schedule. So you know what will be happening on the square Friday evening."

Internally, I swore. I knew I should have read the e-mail! I glanced at Juliet for help. For once, she picked up on what I needed. "Margot, of course Bailey read the e-mail that said there would be a brass band concert on the square Saturday. I'm sure she has already made a list of the desserts to sell at the event."

Oh! I cleared my throat. "Yes, that's right. We're all set."

Margot narrowed her eyes and looked from Juliet to me and back again. "What's the name of the band that will be performing?"

Ugh, sometimes talking to Margot—as much as I liked her—was testing. This was most certainly a test.

"You know, I can't remember myself," Juliet said. "What was the name of the band again?"

"Butler's Brass," Margot said in a way that told me she still believed Juliet and I were up to something.

"They are going to be the first of our Friday night concert series. I booked a new band for every Friday night through August. I'm counting on the local businesses to help support this effort. Harvest is not known for its nightlife, but this series of concerts will change that."

"You want Harvest to have nightlife?" I asked.

"Not in the way you are thinking as someone from the city." Margot put her hands on her hips with such force, the tiny curls on the top of her head bounced in place. "But I do want visitors to stay downtown in the summer, so that we drum up business for the local shopkeepers. This place, like all the towns in this county, rolls up the sidewalk at four or five o'clock. How are you supposed to expand business if hours are so limited? I'm going to change that."

I couldn't argue with her there, but I suspected she would get some pushback from the Amish in Harvest, namely Ruth Yoder. Pushback was something Margot was used to. In fact, I think she reveled in it at times.

"Whatever you need, Swissmen Sweets will be able to pull it off." As I said this, I hoped she wouldn't ask for a giant candy statue, as she had in the past. That would be near to impossible to pull off in a couple of days. Maybe I should have put a condition on my statement.

"Good," Margot said with finality. "We'll have a booth set up for you to sell your candies and sweets. I think treats from Swissmen Sweets will be just the thing to accompany the band." Margot clapped her hands. "That should do it." She pointed at me. "Read the e-mail that you have ignored up to this point. There is important information there about summer activities in Harvest. I would hate to have to remind you each time something is going on."

Busted.

Margot turned back to me before walking away. "I hope you are making this little mess with the murder go away, Bailey. That's what we expect you to do."

I didn't bother to respond.

Margot marched off.

"Margot is a good person to have on your side if you want to get something done in the village, but don't cross her," Juliet said, as if she knew this from experience.

Jethro finished off the last of the cabbage.

"I should get back to the garden," Juliet said. "The ladies want to get all the annuals in today. It'll be so nice when the members come to church on Sunday. There's just something about spring flowers that lifts your soul."

"I agree, and I'm glad that you have so much help this year to get it done."

She smiled. "I've been working hard to get the women of the church more involved. Reverend Brook says I have made a real difference. Maybe you and Hannah could keep an eye on Jethro for a little while until we finish the garden. As you know, it's hard to watch him and work at the same time."

Hannah wrapped her thin arms around the pig's neck and gave him a great big hug. Jethro just went along with it.

"Sure, we can take him to the playground," I offered.

"Oh, he would love that." She blew a kiss to me. "Thank you, Bailey. You are going to be the best mother."

My eyebrows went up. As usual, Juliet had made a great leap—from watching a young girl and a pig, to me being a mother.

Hannah, Jethro, and I walked to the playground. It was the middle of a weekday, and school wasn't out yet, so we had the whole place to ourselves. Hannah went straight for the swings. She hopped on one and began pumping her legs. I smiled. The swings had been my favorite at the playground, too. While other little girls would do flips and tricks on the monkey bars, I always went back to the swings. I loved to see how high I could go, trying to reach that point where I was higher than the bar. It was both thrilling and scary.

I waved at Hannah and pointed behind her. When she swung back toward me, I gave her a small push. She laughed, and her laughter sounded like the tinkling of wind chimes. When she swung back again, I pushed harder the second time. Each time she came back, I pushed a little harder.

Jethro sat on his hind legs a few feet away from the swing set. He cocked his head as if he was coming to some sort of decision. Then he wiggled his back end and dashed under the swing while Hannah was high in the air. Hannah squealed in delight. I gave her another strong push, and Jethro bolted back the other way.

I laughed, too. I felt the tension of the last few days falling away with every push of the swing.

And then the comfort was gone. At the edge of the playground, an Amish man stood watching us, with a scowl on his face. It was Abel Esh. Did he have any idea it was his niece on the swing? Did he care? If he didn't care, why was he standing there watching us?

I had so many questions when it came to Abel. Most

importantly, what was his connection with the racetrack in Wayne County?

However, I wasn't going to confront him when Hannah was with me. Abel was nothing if not unpredictable. There was no telling what he would do. Hannah had been through enough.

As I pushed the swing, Jethro ran back and forth, while Hannah giggled in delight and Abel walked away.

After Hannah and I returned Jethro to Juliet, I looked up the sign for "store" on my phone and signed it to Hannah. Holding her hand, we walked the two blocks to Harvest Market. Harvest Market was more than a food market; it was more of a general store. There were a few things on my list to buy for Hannah. Inside the market, I handed her a basket, and we picked out a toothbrush, a plain Amish nightdress, slippers, soap, fruit snacks, chips, and crackers. By the time I reached the cash register, our basket was too heavy for Hannah to carry, and I carried it to the checkout counter.

"Oh, Bailey King, I see you have quite a load there," the jovial owner said as he rang us up on the old-fashioned cash register. He leaned over the counter. "And who is this charming girl? My, she's a beauty. You look so much like Emily Keim. How odd!"

I swallowed and realized my mistake, the same mistake I'd made this morning by taking Hannah to the Sunbeam Café. The more people who saw Hannah, the more likely someone would tie her to Emily. If the local grocer could do it, anyone in the village could.

I quickly thanked him and paid for our purchases, then ushered Hannah out the door. I didn't know how much longer we could keep the secret as to who Hannah truly was.

CHAPTER TWENTY-SIX

Thursday morning, I went in early to Swissmen Sweets and checked on Hannah. I found myself feeling anxious about the child all the time. I wondered if she was all right and if she had everything she needed. Most of all, I worried about her mental state. Because of her lack of hearing, it was difficult for her to describe what she was thinking and feeling.

When I walked into Swissmen Sweets, Lois was sitting in the front of the shop. She and Hannah were talking.

Lois waved at me. "Bailey, so good to see you. I just popped over before the breakfast rush to see how Hannah is doing."

I waved at Hannah and then looked at Lois. "Is she okay?"

Lois smiled. "She's coping. She's a resilient little

thing. Most children are. I was just telling her about a trip that Millie and I made recently to the Akron Zoo. She would like to go."

I smiled. "That would be a good outing once everything is settled."

"Bailey," *Maami* said as she came through the kitchen's swinging door. "What are you going to do today?"

"I'm thinking of going back to Wooster, if you and Charlotte can handle everything here. I know it's a tall order with Hannah here as well."

"Hannah can come stay with me at the café," Lois offered. "I'll give her a piece of lemon pie; then she and I can talk on my breaks. It will be great fun for both Darcy and me. I've loved using my sign language again, but Hannah says I'm a little rusty." She signed this last sentence for Hannah's benefit.

Hannah laughed and shook her head no.

I glanced at my grandmother. "I can go, too, and spend the day in the café with Hannah," *Maami* said. "After what happened yesterday, I don't want to let her out of my sight."

Lois nodded. "That would be fine with me. The more the merrier. But what about your shop?"

"Charlotte can manage it," my grandmother said. "I believe we are all in agreement that Hannah is the most important concern we have now."

Lois and I nodded.

Lois clapped her hands. "Then it's settled. I'll just tell Hannah."

She began to rapidly sign to Hannah.

Hannah nodded and stood up. She was ready to go. Knowing that Hannah was in good hands with Lois and *Maami* for a few hours, I felt free to drive to Wooster. I really wanted to go to the Keim Christmas tree farm and make things right with Emily, though. However, I knew, from past experience, that Emily needed to process what she had learned before I attempted to make amends.

It tore me apart thinking about Emily that morning. I knew she was hurting. She felt betrayed, and rightfully so. She had been treated poorly by so many people in her life. It made my stomach twist into a knot to think that I might be another person on that list.

As much as it pained me, I would wait to speak to Emily. I'd go to the racetrack first.

The Wayne County Racetrack came up right away on my phone. The drive to Wooster was uneventful. I slowed the car as I as drove through the main part of town and passed Dinah's bakery. It was still early, and there was a CLOSED sign on the door. I frowned. Bakeries, in my experience, typically opened very early so that people could buy their morning muffins and pastries. It was well into breakfast time now. The CLOSED sign made me wonder if the shop was always closed at this time or if it was shut because of the murder.

The racetrack's hours were much different from a bakery's, and I wondered if I had come too early to the track as well. I wasn't a gambler, nor did I have any reason to spend time at the track, so I wasn't really sure what reason I could give for going there. My GPS directed me out of town and back onto the highway.

I got off at the same exit I had seen Isaac use the day before, and then I followed the signs until I came to the track.

I turned into the parking lot as a siren whirled and flashing lights came on behind me. I glanced at my speedometer. I hadn't been speeding. I parked in the closest parking place, and a Holmes County Sheriff's Department SUV pulled up next to me.

I rolled my window down, and Deputy Little did the same on his car.

"Little, you have no jurisdiction here to give me a ticket."

"I didn't beep my siren at you to give you a ticket. I only wanted to get your attention."

I climbed out of my car and tucked my keys and cell phone in my pockets. "You have it."

Deputy Little got out of his vehicle as well. "What are you doing here? Does Deputy Brody know you're here?"

"Does he know that you're here?" I countered.

"Yes," the young deputy said. "He told me to come here."

"To see if this place had a connection to the murder."

He pressed his lips together.

"Come on, Little, you don't have to be closed-mouthed with me about this. I was the one who brought the track to Aiden's attention."

"Fine," he said. "Yes, that's why I'm here, but I don't think you should have come. You should go home. Deputy Brody would not like it."

He was right about that, but I still wasn't leaving. I reminded myself I wasn't just there to solve the murder, I was there for Hannah. That was motivation enough not to yield. "I'm not going home."

The deputy put a hand on his handcuffs.

I pointed at him. "Don't you act like you're going to handcuff me."

He dropped his hand from the cuffs at his side. "I wouldn't."

Likely story.

"So we're here for the same reason. We want to know what this place has to do with Rosemary. It's come up a couple of times in my investigation."

"Your investigation," he said with a sigh. He sounded almost exactly like Aiden.

"We might be able to cover more ground if we do it together."

Deputy Little's brows knit together. "I suppose that is true. It's a big place." He frowned. "If we don't do this together, you're going in there anyway, right?"

"Yep," I said. "I mean, unless you arrest me to prevent it. Please don't do that."

Deputy Little rubbed his forehead as if I was giving him a massive headache. I felt bad about that, but at the same time, I had to investigate for Hannah.

"All right," Deputy Little said. "We can both go in, but not together. I think it would be better if those at the racetrack don't realize we know each other."

"Fine by me."

"And when we come out, you tell me what you learned," he said, sounding as cop-like as I had ever heard him. Deputy Little had grown up a lot over the last several months.

"What about you tell me what you know?" I asked even though I could guess his answer.

"I can't do that. Police business."

It was the answer I had expected, but I couldn't argue when Deputy Little was letting me go inside the racetrack for a look around.

"Deal," I said.

He cocked his head. "I feel like you agreed to that too quickly."

Deputy Little and I had parked some distance from the

front entrance of the racetrack. The large, dusty graveled parking lot reminded me of the giant one outside the Holmes County Fairgrounds. I imagined the lot would be mostly full on the weekend. At the moment, there were a few pickup trucks and a dozen or so Amish buggies.

Until I'd moved to Holmes County, I didn't know that the Amish participated in any kind of racing. Horse racing was synonymous with gambling, and gambling didn't seem to be a very Amish activity to me.

But this racetrack wasn't exclusively Amish. It included Amish harness racing and English thoroughbred riders. If the race schedule that was nailed to the worn wooden wall by the entrance was any indication, it was a busy place, and the Amish races only happened twice a week. The rest of the time, the track was dedicated to everything from dressage to horse racing to lessons. It was an intricate schedule worthy of super planner Margot.

I wondered if Amish horse racing involved gambling.

To my surprise, no one stopped me when I walked into the track area. Ahead of me, I could see the racetrack, with a green grass circle in the middle of the dirt ring. A curved split-rail fence ran around the outside of the track. The top of the fence was capped with worn two-by-fours. I imagined that, on race day, dozens of men, and maybe a few women, would be leaning over those rails cheering on their favorite racer.

To my right was a large enclosed stable. I stepped inside, and horses poked their noses over the stalls as I walked by. The stable smelled like manure, hay, and leather. The combination of scents was oddly comforting. Racing carts were lined up at one end of the barn, and horse tack seemed to hang from every available nail in the massive building, which was easily twice the size of any barn I had ever been inside.

One very friendly horse bumped my shoulder with his broad nose. I stopped and patted his cheek. He was all white except for an outline of black around his eyes. It made him look as if he was wearing eyeliner. He nuzzled my palm with his horsey lips. "If you're looking for carrots, I don't have any. If I come again, I'll bring you some, I promise."

He blew hot, pungent breath in my face, and I yelped.

Then the horse lowered his head as if inviting me to scratch him between the ears. I obliged.

"You are a pretty one, aren't you?" I asked the horse. "I really should have thought this through better and brought some carrots. If you want to make friends with horses, you need carrots, am I right?"

"That's Cooper," a voice said behind me, and I jumped.

When I spun around, I found Dinah's son, Mason, behind me.

"He's the best harness racing horse on the track," Mason said. "I'd never bet against Cooper. Are you waiting for lessons or something?" He looked me up and down.

I was wearing jeans and a checkered blouse, but on my feet, I wore sneakers. I didn't think they were made for horse riding. Not that I knew—I had never been much for horse riding. The shoes were for running, though I wasn't much of a runner either, now that I thought of it.

"I hope you brought your boots," he said, confirming my hunch that a real rider wouldn't ride in sneakers.

"I'm not here for a lesson," I said. "But I am curious

about Amish horse racing. I didn't know the Amish did that."

He studied me and then said, "The Amish have been racing horses for a very long time. Street buggy racing is common among the young men. I don't like that kind of racing. It's dangerous, and it's just Amish youth competing to see who is the coolest guy."

I raised my brow. That was the first time I had ever heard "Amish" and "cool" in the same sentence.

"I prefer harness racing. That's what we do here." He pointed to several two-wheel carts at the end of the large barn.

I nodded. "Are those bicycle wheels on those carts?"

"They are," he said, sounding pleased that I'd noticed. "They are faster and better equipped for racing than buggy wheels. We hitch horses like Cooper to those, and the driver sits in the seat, guiding the horse with his reins and urging the horse to run faster with a whip."

I winced at the thought of the whip.

"A lot of *Englischers* are squeamish about the whip, but a *gut* driver doesn't hit the horse with it. He cracks it above the horse. The sound is loud enough to make the horse run faster. It's intense, and the horses are fast. Much faster than buggy horses. They are pulling less weight, and they are trained to run." He paused. "The cart is called a sulky. Some people call it a bike or even a spider. At the start of a race, typically a truck leads the pack to pace the horses until the speed picks up. Then the truck leaves the track, and the horses go all out. It's thrilling." His eyes lit up. It was clear to me that Mason Stoltzfus desperately missed racing himself.

"Are there races today?"

He shook his head. "Not official ones. Just practice runs. Saturday is always race day during the season. You should come back then and place a bet."

"I might do that," I said.

He frowned at me as if he was trying place where he had seen me before.

"Cooper is a sweetheart." I patted the white horse again. "I was never one of those horse-crazy girls, but I think I could be if all horses were like him."

"I think most people would say that." He stepped forward, dragging his bad leg behind him. "Do I know you?"

"I'm Bailey King. I was at your mother's bakery a couple of days ago. She asked me to take Hannah with me when I left."

He bristled. "Then what are you doing here?"

"Ummm." That was a more difficult question to answer. Should I tell him that I thought a murder suspect had come to the racetrack the day before? That didn't seem like the best idea I'd ever had.

Instead, I took this as a golden opportunity. "I was hoping I could talk to you about Hannah."

The friendly rapport we'd had when talking about Cooper the horse was gone.

"I don't know anything about Hannah. She was the daughter of my mother's cousin. That's it. It wasn't like I ever spoke to the girl. She's deaf," he said in a way that made it seem like an insult.

I continued to scratch Cooper's nose to keep myself calm. I wished people would stop acting as if Hannah's deafness was some kind of contagious disease.

"When was it that Rosemary and Hannah came to Wooster?" I asked.

He frowned at me. "I don't know. Two or three years

ago. Rosemary came here as a desperate woman. Did my mother tell you that? She drove her husband so crazy that he turned *Englisch* and ran away from her. And she never gave up. She kept pestering him over and over again. I could see her doing it."

"Why was that?"

He studied me as if he was gauging whether or not he should give me an answer. "She was so nervous. The woman wouldn't sit still. The only time she seemed to be calm at all was when she was with Hannah. My mother allowed her to work in the bakery, but she was no real help. You would not believe the number of mistakes Rosemary made that my mother then had to clean up, which made me even angrier that she would . . ."

"She would what?" I asked, sensing the answer to this question was important.

"It doesn't matter. You asked me what I know about Hannah. Next to nothing. I would see her when Rosemary brought her to the shop. All I ever saw her do was sit on the floor and play with her books and toys. She was deaf, harmless, and easily forgettable."

I balled my fists at my sides again. "And what about Rosemary? How well did you know her?"

He shrugged. "She worked at my mother's bakery." He paused. "When I was hurt and had to spend so much time at the hospital and then in rehab for my leg, she was a good cousin to my mother. Even though she was nervous, dropped things, and made mistakes, she ran the bakery while my mother cared for me. I think that's the reason why my mother never had the nerve to fire her." He paused. "And now she won't have to."

He didn't say "because she's dead," but I was sure he was thinking it.

CHAPTER TWENTY-SEVEN

I watched Mason shuffle away and felt a twinge of empathy for him as he dragged his foot behind him. I wondered if there were surgeries and options for him to improve his quality of life. Did he not take those opportunities because he was Amish or because of a lack of money? Because of their religious beliefs, the Amish were exempt from buying health insurance, which was required for the rest of the country.

Instead of health insurance, they relied on their districts to pool money and support anyone who was sick or in the hospital. They took up collections for those in need and saved money, whenever they could, for those times when it would be needed. I wondered if those funds sometimes became strained, as they covered so many families; perhaps, for that reason, the Amish were less likely to have intensive treatments. Or maybe the leg injury didn't measure up against other medical emergencies in the community. There had to be times that a district must put one person's medical bills above another's. Most districts were made up of forty-some families, and families were large, so there were a lot of people who needed to be taken care of. If only two of those members were seriously sick or injured, the cost could be astronomical without insurance.

After my grandfather had died, his hospital bills had been steep. The district gave my grandmother what they could to help. It wasn't enough, and I quietly paid the remainder of the bills. I never told my grandmother I'd done that, and I never would. I wanted her to believe that her community had come through for her. I knew firsthand that not every district could cover hospital bills for every member.

I wondered if Mason would have been able to race again if he'd had the money to pay for surgeries to correct his limp.

I will admit I felt sorry for him, but I couldn't forget how he'd spoken to his mother in the bakery. Even so, it was clear to me that he was hurting. Perhaps I should give him the benefit of the doubt. Obviously his dearest ambition was to be a harness racing driver, and an injury had stolen his dream. Now he worked in the stable every day and watched as other Amish young men did what he wanted to do most. Would he be happier if he found another line of work?

Cooper bumped my shoulder again, and I scratched him on the nose. "You're a sweet guy. I promise I will be back with carrots."

He blew his hot breath in my face again, and I didn't even care.

A rumble of voices shook me from my thoughts. I turned toward the racetrack. A group of men, both Amish and English, were clustered on the fence near the starting line, which was about thirty yards away from me. I walked up to the fence and leaned on it. I watched as four Amish men in plain clothes and helmets guided their horses and harness racing carts into a line.

When all four horses had formed a straight line across the track, someone fired a gun, and they were off. I felt a rush of wind as the horses and their drivers passed me. As they flew around the curve on the far side of the track, I noticed that a cart in the middle of the pack began to wobble. It rocked violently back and forth, while the other three carts held firm. The driver pulled hard on the reins to steer his cart and horse out of the way of the other drivers.

The other carts rushed past just as the left wheel of the wobbling cart popped off and went crashing into the fence. It bounced off the fence and careened down the track in the opposite direction.

The cart with only one wheel now lay on its side. The driver cried for help. There were shouts in both Pennsylvania Dutch and English as men jumped over the rail and ran onto the track. The other drivers pulled up their horses. The race was over without being completed.

I followed the men onto the other side of the track and wasn't the least bit surprised when I spotted Deputy Little among them.

From where I stood now, I could see that the cart had fallen on the driver's arm. He groaned in pain. One man untethered the horse from the cart. The horse appeared to be fine. The other men lifted the cart off the fallen man's arm.

The driver screamed when the cart was moved.

"It looks like a bad break," one Amish man said. "We will have to take you to the clinic to have your arm set."

"But I need to train for the race this weekend," the young driver said through the pain. From the look on his face, leaving the track appeared to be a worse fate than the injured arm.

"Son, you are not going to be in the race this weekend. Your arm is broken. Let's hope it's a clean break so that you can get back on the track as soon as possible."

The young driver looked as if he might cry, but he stopped himself. I knew Amish men were trained to be stoic and not show their feelings. I hoped, for his sake, that he would let himself cry in private at least.

An English woman ran onto the track. She was petite and wore jeans, a Western shirt, and cowboy boots. "What's going on?"

"There's been an accident."

She threw up her hands. "Another one. We can't have this happening time and time again. It's bad PR, and as the track's publicist, that's a big problem for me."

"Calm down, Jill," the Amish man said. "It's just an accident."

"Tell that to the Ohio State Racing Commission. We could lose our license if this keeps up."

The man hushed her and ushered her off the track.

I watched them go and walked back to the betting window. As I did, I saw Mason leaning over the rail, watching as the other men helped the driver off the track with a strange expression on his face. It was an odd mix of satisfaction and disgust. I also realized that he had not climbed or leaped over the fence; with his twisted leg, he most likely could not. Was that why he had that disgusted ex-

pression on his face? Was he disgusted with himself that
he could not help?

After the driver was taken away, a wagon pulled onto
the dusty track. The men slowly moved the damaged cart
onto the wagon.

When the cart was safely on the wagon, one of the
men ripped his black felt hat from his head and threw it
into the dirt. "This was no accident. It's the fifth time something like this has happened on the track. I am telling you,
someone is causing this! There can't be so many mishaps
without a reason."

To my surprise, the Amish man speaking was the same
one I'd seen at the hardware store. The same man who'd
told me that I wouldn't want to speak to Isaac Weiss. His
jovial demeanor was gone.

I stepped away from the rail and behind a nearby stable post. I didn't want him to see me, but from my look-
out, I could still hear the men as long as they didn't drop
their discussion down to a whisper. It turned out they
were yelling, so that wasn't a problem.

"Amos, you need to calm yourself," another Amish
man said to the one from the hardware store.

Good, I finally have a name for him. That will help.

"I do not need to calm myself. I need people to stop
messing with my track. Jill is right. This looks bad."

I frowned. His track? I thought he worked at the hardware store. Had I been wrong? When I thought back to
the hardware store, I remembered that the workers had
been wearing name tags. This man had not. Then why
had he asked me if I needed help? I frowned.

"We are lucky that the horse wasn't hurt. That animal
is worth hundreds of thousands of dollars, and Michael
was our best driver at the stables. We need him to finish

on top," Amos went on. He picked his hat up from the track and hit it against his thigh to knock the dust off. "This can't continue. And I will make sure it doesn't. Now I have to go calm Jill down again." He stomped off the track and right in my direction.

I slipped farther behind the post so that he wouldn't see me and pressed my back up against it. For a moment, I had an absurd feeling that I was in a James Bond movie, but instead of being in the French Rivera, I was in Amish Country.

When he was gone, the Amish man he'd been yelling at said to two of the younger men, "Take care of the horse, and make sure he's not hurt. We can't have any more mishaps. We can't lose another animal. If we do, the state will start sniffing around."

I raised my brow as I heard this. Had there been an accident in which a horse had been killed? It seemed to me that there were serious problems at the Wayne County Racetrack, and I was very surprised to learn that the place was owned by an Amish man—if, in fact, Amos's claim was true.

"Bailey—" Deputy Little walked over to me. "I thought that was you hiding behind that post like an international spy. What are you doing back there?"

I stepped out from behind the post. Most of the men were gone, and the horses were being guided back to the stables.

I shook my head. "Deputy Little, I'm so glad to see you. There is something strange about this accident. From what I overheard, this isn't first time something like this has happened. From what those men said, it's the fifth time. Also, Mason Stoltzfus was in an accident like this over a year ago and was seriously hurt."

"Should I recognize that name?" the deputy asked.

"He's Dinah's son. Dinah who put Hannah in my care."

"Oh! Where is he?" He glanced around.

I looked around. I didn't see him in the group of Amish men walking near the track.

"He must have taken off shortly after the accident." I told him about what Amos had said.

Deputy Little rocked back on his heels. "If something strange is going on here with racing accidents, I can't really do anything about it. We're in a different county. It would be up to the Wayne County Sheriff's Department or the Wooster police to step in. If it has to do with gambling, it might even be a place where BCI would take the lead. I have no jurisdiction."

I blew out a frustrated breath and supposed that I resembled Cooper, the horse, quite a bit at that moment. I understood what Deputy Little was saying, but someone had to look into the accident at the racetrack. If not him, he should pass the information along to those who could.

As if he read my mind, he said, "I'll give the Wayne County Sheriff's Department a call and let them decide who has jurisdiction. It might be BCI actually."

His mention of BCI reminded me of Aiden's job offer. I put that to the back of my mind. What I needed to concentrate on now was solving this murder and making sure that Hannah was okay.

"If you have a case that leads you out of your county, you can still investigate outside your jurisdiction as long as you give the department in charge a heads up. It's just common courtesy." He squinted into the sun. "We should probably leave, so I can touch base with the Wayne County sheriff's office."

"Deputy Little, I'm telling you that something strange is happening here."

He sighed. "And I believe you, but we have to follow protocol. If we don't, any arrest made will have a hole that will be big enough for the criminal to waltz right through, and then sue the department for defamation of character."

My shoulders sagged. "All right," I said, even though I hated the idea of leaving the racetrack with so many unanswered questions. More importantly, I didn't know how it was all connected to Rosemary's murder. Had she ever come to the racetrack? It seemed unlikely. I had seen Mason, whom I had expected, and Amos, whom I had not expected, at the track. There was no sign of Isaac. I kicked myself for not asking Mason about him when I'd had the chance.

Deputy Little started toward the exit. I knew he expected me to follow him. I did.

As I looked over my shoulder at the track one more time, a tall, blond Amish man walked across the entrance. I blinked. I could be wrong, but the man looked like Abel Esh. I jogged back through the entrance, but when I got there, the man was gone.

Deputy Little came back through the entrance after me. "Bailey."

"I'm coming," I said, taking one last look around.

If it had truly been Abel, it was the second time I had seen him in Wayne County. That was no coincidence.

CHAPTER TWENTY-EIGHT

In the parking lot, Deputy Little shifted his feet, and to my surprise, he didn't climb into his SUV and leave.

"Is everything okay, Little?"

He licked his lips. "Has Charlotte spoken to you lately?"

"I talk to Charlotte every day," I said.

"Yes, I know that. She's not said anything *new* to you?" He searched my face.

New?

My brow wrinkled. I had a feeling I knew where this was going. Over the last few months, I'd notice that Deputy Little and Charlotte had become more than friends. Each seemed to go out of their way to see or talk to the other. I had my suspicions as to what was going on, but Charlotte hadn't told me yet how she felt about the deputy. It was her place to come to me. That didn't mean

I wasn't curious. I was also proud of myself for not interrogating her about it. Sometimes it was very difficult to keep all the questions in my head to myself.

The deputy had brought the issue up, so I believed it was fair to ask of few of him. "Little, be straight with me. What's going on between you and Charlotte?"

He swallowed, and his Adam's apple bobbed up and down. "If Charlotte didn't tell you, then I shouldn't either." There was an air of disappointment in his voice.

"Then why did you ask me? You could have asked Charlotte whether she spoke to me."

He wouldn't look at me. "She keeps telling me that she will speak to you and Clara."

I raised my brow. If Deputy Little wanted Charlotte to talk about their relationship with my grandmother and me, this was more serious than I'd thought. I mentally kicked myself for not asking Charlotte about it sooner. I had the best intention of respecting her privacy, but now I was terribly curious.

"I guess I know what's happening," I said. "No one can miss how you look at each other."

He didn't say anything.

"Charlotte is more than my cousin. She's like a little sister to me. I just want to know that you won't do anything to hurt her. That your intentions are pure."

"I—I would never hurt her. Hurting Charlotte is the last thing I would ever want to do. I l—care about her more than I can even believe. I want us to be together, even get married someday. But that's not something we can do now."

My eyes widened. I had not expected him to come out and say it like that. Unfortunately, there was still a giant problem standing in their way. I doubted that I needed to point it out to him, but the words still came out. "How could you ever marry? She's Amish."

He nodded. "She has to make a decision, and I'm not going to ask her to choose between her culture and me. That would be cruel. I don't want to be Amish. I've already told her that."

I wasn't surprised to hear it. If Deputy Little joined the Amish church, not only would he have to live a plain life, he would have to give up his job as a deputy. Over the last year, Deputy Little had grown a lot in his job. He was coming into his own and proving himself to be a good officer. I knew that, after all the hard work he'd put in, he'd be loath to give that up. I didn't blame him.

There was nothing I could tell him that he didn't already know. Charlotte had to make the final decision.

"Please don't tell her I spoke to you about this." His cheeks and ears flushed red.

I promised I wouldn't, and then I watched as he got into his car and drove away.

I climbed into my car, too. The deputy might have asked me to leave the racetrack, but he hadn't said anything about leaving the county.

I was still thinking over my conversation with Mason and his remark about Rosemary being nervous. When I'd seen her at the baby shower, she had been tense, but I would not say nervous. Tension made sense to me. She was speaking to Emily for the first time, and she was in a strange place in the middle of a baby shower. Anyone in that situation would be nervous.

I parked in front of the Dutch Muffin, in the same spot where I had parked just a few days ago. It was hard to believe that Hannah had only been at Swissmen Sweets for a couple of days. When I'd first driven through Wooster, the bakery had been closed, but I was now relieved to find it open.

As I went through the door into the bakery, a bell in the shape of a strawberry chimed.

"Be with you in a moment," Dinah called through the open kitchen door.

Just as it had the first time I'd been in the bakery, my stomach rumbled when I saw all the delicious pastries and breads. There was a lemon pie with five inches of perfectly peaked meringue on the top. I knew that both Emily and Hannah would love that pie.

"What are you doing back here?" Dinah asked, out of breath as she slid a tray of fresh-baked dinner rolls onto a rack to cool.

I straightened up from where I had been studying the pie. "I wanted to speak to you about Hannah."

She removed her plastic gloves and wiped her hands on the edge of her apron. Both her apron and her dress were dusted with flour. Her graying hair sprang out of her Amish bun, and her glasses sat askew on her nose. She fixed her glasses, but managed to leave a giant flour thumbprint on them in the process.

"You seem to be a little out of sorts. Do you need help in the bakery?" I asked.

She peered down her nose at me. "I don't—" She sniffed the air.

I smelled smoke. "Is something burning?"

"Oh, the cupcakes." She grabbed a dish towel from the counter and ran into the kitchen. I followed her. The work-space was about half the size of the kitchen at Swissmen Sweets. She opened the convection oven door and a cloud of smoke came out. Grabbing the cupcake pan with the towel, she dropped it on a trivet on the granite countertop. "They're burnt."

I opened the back door to let the smoke out, picked up a towel, and began fanning the air.

Dinah fell onto a stool by the counter. "I'll have to make them over again. I don't have time for that." She expelled a deep breath. "They are for a little boy's birthday party tonight. His mother was going to pick them up at three."

I glanced at my phone. "It's only early afternoon now. You have enough time."

"No, I don't." She moved her glasses again and put a dot of flour on the other lens. "He wants each cupcake decorated with a shark. Four different kinds of sharks. I don't have time to do the decorations if I begin again."

"I'll help you. I once carved a shark out of chocolate for an aquarium opening. I don't think I'll have any trouble crafting them from icing."

She sniffled. "I would hate to ask you to do that, especially when I was so rude to you when you arrived."

"It's no matter. You're in a bind, and I can help. It's the Amish way to offer help when you can."

"But you're not Amish." She gripped the end of her apron.

"I'm not, but my grandmother is, so I know how the Amish operate."

The strawberry bell on the door jingled, and she looked anxiously back at the open kitchen door.

"Just tell me where the recipe is, and go. I know my way around a kitchen. I'll find what I need."

After calling to the customer in the front of the store that she would be with them in a minute, she hastily removed a recipe card from a wooden box on the counter.

The bell on the bakery door chimed again.

"I have to go."

I studied the recipe. It was written in faded block letters, and there was a smudge of chocolate on the corner of the card. It was a beloved recipe and had been used many times before. It was a straightforward chocolate cupcake. There was no recipe for icing, but any chocolatier worth her salt could make icing. I thought a white chocolate icing dyed blue and gray for the various sharks would be just the thing.

It took me a few minutes to understand how Dinah's kitchen was organized, but when I did, I got right to work on the cupcake batter. Judging by the burnt cupcake pans, there were twenty-four cupcakes ordered. It was a relatively small order, but I knew I had to get the cupcakes in the oven quickly so they could cool before I iced them.

There was something calming about working in the kitchen, even though it wasn't my own, and I hummed to myself as I mixed up the batter and then poured it into the cupcake pan. In the convection oven, the baking would take seven to eight minutes. So I got right to work double-boiling white chocolate for the frosting.

As I worked, my brain traveled back to the murder. There were a number of suspects, but in my mind, at least, there was no clear winner. I knew, from an outsider's view, that Esther Esh was the very best candidate. She had the means, motive, and opportunity. She also wasn't the most forthcoming of witnesses. I think her reluctance to speak to the police, or to me, would cause her trouble in the end.

Abel Esh was a suspect for the same reason. I was inclined to believe that he was more capable of murder than Esther was.

Also on my list was Gideon Glick, the accountant and Hannah's biological father. I doubted that he would want the circumstances of Hannah's birth to come to light. However, Emily had said he hadn't known about her pregnancy. He was only told that she went to Indiana to get away from him because her siblings saw him as a bad influence.

Then there was Isaac Weiss. He had the strongest motive, in my eyes. Now that his legal wife was dead, he could marry his girlfriend, and Rosemary would no longer show up unannounced at his job or other places.

Lastly, there were the lesser suspects. I glanced at the kitchen door as I pulled the cupcakes out of the oven and set them on a wire rack to cool. Dinah might have been tired of having Rosemary and Hannah around her bakery. I wrinkled my nose. That wasn't much of a motive. She clearly needed and missed Rosemary's help. No matter how she might have felt about Hannah, she needed another pair of hands to keep the bakery running smoothly.

Then there was Dinah's son, Mason. He didn't seem to care one way or another that Rosemary was dead. If what he'd said was true, he hadn't bothered to get to know her in the last two years she'd worked for his mother.

The final person on my list was Emily. She had motive. She certainly seemed to want her daughter back. It was a strong motive, especially now that I knew Hannah's adoption had not been legal. At least it wasn't legal in the eyes of the English authorities. Even as a teenager, Emily might have chosen to keep the child if she'd been allowed to consider it. That choice was never given to her.

I stirred the icing, spooned each color into white icing bags, and began to ice blue and gray sharks on the cupcakes. I made them cartoon sharks. It was for a child's party, after all, and I took care to make each shark look just a little bit different. I hoped the parents at the party wouldn't by upset by the different sharks and the kids wouldn't fight over not getting one shark cupcake over another.

I put the final touches on the last funny-faced shark and sat back on my stool. I smiled at the sharks and grabbed two white bakery boxes. It was the first time in a long time that I'd been able to make up something as I went along. In the last few months, my chocolate and candy making had been so regimented. At the candy shop, I had to make the things that sold the best. And on the television show, all my recipes had to be approved by the network's test kitchen and the producers to make sure they were simple enough for the average home cook.

It was nice to create—to just help someone out and go into it without any preconceived notions of what the treat would look like at the end.

I found bakery boxes on a shelf and lovingly tucked the cupcakes inside. I glanced at my phone for the time. It was a quarter to three. Perfect timing.

I was about to go to the front of the shop and tell Dinah the good news when I heard a frustrated male voice say, "I just need a little money. Don't you understand?"

"I'm sorry," Dinah replied. "I have nothing to give you. The bakery is struggling, and it will continue to struggle if I can't find someone to replace Rosemary."

"I'm your son."

There was a bang, and I went through the kitchen door. Dinah stood at the far end of the counter from her son, holding her apron.

"Is everything okay?" I asked, looking from Dinah to Mason.

"What are you doing here?" Mason demanded. "Are you following me?"

"How can I be following you, if I was here first?"

"What do you mean?" Dinah asked Mason.

"She came to the racetrack and spoke to me there, and now she's here in your kitchen." He narrowed his eyes at his mother. "Did you send her to talk to me?"

"*Nee*, why would I do that?" Dinah grabbed the end of her apron and held it tight.

"Then what is she doing here?" he demanded.

"Son, she's only offering help. With Rosemary gone, my workload has doubled. I haven't found someone to replace her yet. I have told you that I need help."

"How hard can that be?" he asked. "There are plenty of Amish women in the district who would be happy for the work."

She played with the edge of her apron. I was starting to notice that as a nervous habit. The same went for fiddling with her glasses. "*Ya*, but it has to be the right fit. Rosemary has only been gone for a few days. I just have to sit down and take a breath before deciding what to do."

"There is nothing to be decided. Hire the help. You can afford it now, can't you, because you are making a point of not helping me?" He asked this last question with a curl to his lip. "All that money you make here has to go somewhere."

Dinah removed her glasses with shaky hands. "I—I can't help you."

He glared at her. "You choose not to help me. There is a difference."

CHAPTER TWENTY-NINE

"Mason," Dinah said in a soft voice, "this is not the time."

He glared at his mother.

The door to the shop opened, and a woman and a young boy who was wearing a Little League uniform walked inside.

The woman held the boy's hand. "Dinah, Brandon is so excited. He has been telling all his friends about his shark cupcakes. I think he's more excited about them than any of the gifts he might get."

"I like the gifts, too," Brandon piped up.

"Let me go grab the cupcakes." I went into the kitchen and carefully picked up the two white bakery boxes in which I had snuggly nestled the cupcakes. I carried the boxes to the front of the shop and set them on the counter.

I opened each box. Brandon's mom picked him up so he could have a look inside.

"Oh my goodness. These are so different, but even better than the picture you drew me. The boys will love them."

"Can I see?" Brandon jumped up and down.

His mother picked up her son. "I love that each one has a different face."

"I didn't—" Dinah began to deny having made the cupcakes.

"The Dutch Muffin did a great job, didn't they?" I asked. Out of the corner of my eye, I saw Mason slip into the kitchen.

The customer set her son back on the floor and removed her wallet from her purse. "They did the very best job," his mother agreed. "I'll come back here for every one of our family parties. I know the kids and the parents will love these cupcakes."

Dinah blushed. "*Danki*, you are too kind."

I smiled at Dinah. "I'll close up the boxes, and you can ring her out."

She nodded and went to the end of the counter.

Brandon watched me as I tied up the boxes. "I love white chocolate," Brandon said. "I love all chocolate."

I grinned. This was a kid after my own heart.

While Brandon and his mother were happily chatting with Dinah, I poked my head into the kitchen. As I suspected, Mason was gone.

I turned back around and found that Brandon and his mother had left. Dinah gave me a shy smile. "Bailey, I can't thank you enough for what you did for me. Those shark cupcakes were so much better than I could ever have done."

I shook my head. "Your cupcakes would have been just as good. I used your recipe, so they would have tasted the same."

She frowned as if she wasn't so sure about that.

"Now that I have helped you, maybe you can help me, too."

She removed her glasses and cleaned the flour off the lens, using a tea towel. "I don't know how I can."

"You put Hannah in my care, but all you told me about her is that she's deaf and Rosemary's daughter."

"I don't know any more. I don't know sign language, so I didn't communicate with her. I don't have much to tell you."

"What did Rosemary tell you of the adoption?"

"Very little. It wasn't until recently that she told me the child's birth mother lived in Ohio. I had no idea she had plans to go to Harvest to speak with her. That was out of character for Rosemary."

"Because she was a nervous person?" I asked.

"How did you know that?"

"Mason told me when I was at the racetrack earlier today."

She swallowed. "*Ya*, Rosemary was a generally anxious person. You might have noticed that I am, too. It's something that runs in our family, but with *Gott*'s help we can calm our nerves." She looked down at her trembling hands and grabbed her apron again. It seemed that if she had something to do with her hands, she could calm herself. "At least that's what the bishop tells me whenever I go to him for counseling. He tells me I need to lean on *Gott* and pray more."

I frowned. I was sure that Dinah's bishop was giving sound advice, as far as it went, but she was so on edge at the moment, she was shaking. I wondered if medicine wouldn't be the best answer for her. The Amish used English medicine all the time, everything from simple surgeries to chemotherapy. They saw those medicines as essential. But medicine for mental health would be another thing entirely. They wouldn't see antidepressants as an answer for someone like Dinah, when they believed that prayer should be enough. They also wouldn't think much of counseling outside of speaking to the church bishop and elders. I thought that counseling of any kind would be of benefit to her, and trained medical professionals would be able to provide the best results.

Just as I had wondered at the track if surgery would help Mason with his leg, I wondered if Dinah's culture and Amish district were holding her back from getting all the help she needed.

"I had nothing to do with the adoption," Dinah went on. "It happened in Indiana years ago. I was here. I didn't even know Hannah was adopted for a very long time. I assumed she was Rosemary's child. She always introduced her as her daughter, or her and Isaac's daughter. She liked the latter better. She would have done anything to put her family back together and return to Indiana." She set the tea towel on the counter. "She was not happy here. I could tell that the longer she was here, the worse she felt."

"Did she ever consider going back home?"

"I think so, but she was determined that Isaac go with her. It was only recently that she spoke of that not happening. I'm sure it had something to do with the *Englisch* girlfriend."

The English girlfriend. I needed to find her. She was another suspect.

"Do you know the girlfriend's name?"

She shook head. "I don't."

I guessed it was something that Deputy Little or Aiden could find out when they spoke to Isaac. It made me wonder if Deputy Little had been off to find Isaac when he'd left the racetrack. That would make sense to me.

"Can you tell me about when Rosemary moved to Wooster?"

She paused and seemed to consider this. "It was two years ago, or close to it. Hannah wasn't quite four, and she will be six in June. At first, I let them live with me, but it wasn't a good fit." She pressed her lips together. "I like things to be a particular way, and that's hard with a small child around. Even harder with a small child that you can't speak to. Rosemary knew I was unhappy and, with the help of the church, found a place to rent. As it turned out, there was a room for rent over the candle shop next door. It was the perfect place for her. It was close to the shop, and the cost was low. After that, we settled into working together. She was a *gut* employee. Really, the only difficulty I had with her was that she went on and on with Isaac. She was so in love with him, you see. She couldn't understand why he would leave her the way he did." She swallowed. "It became far worse when she learned about the *Englisch* girlfriend."

"How?" I asked.

She sighed. "All she would talk to me about was the other woman. She believed the girlfriend stole him from her. It was constant. I finally had to ask her to stop talking about it. I couldn't bear hearing about it any longer."

"But you still didn't know the woman's name."

"*Nee*, she only ever called her *that woman*. She would say *that woman* this and *that woman* that. She never called her by name, and honestly, I didn't ask. I didn't ask about any of it." She picked up the tea towel for a second time and fiddled with it.

"What's the name of the person she rented the room from?"

"Stella Boxer. She will be right next door now. She's always at the shop. I think she's at her candle shop even more than I am at my bakery, and it feels like I only leave the bakery to sleep."

I knew the feeling. I also knew I was being nudged toward the door. Dinah wanted me to leave. That was clear. I had helped her with the shark cupcakes, but now because of my many questions, the goodwill I'd earned was long gone.

I left the Dutch Muffin a few minutes later with the lemon meringue pie that I had been eyeing for Hannah. I told Dinah that I wanted to buy it, but she gave it to me after the work I had done.

I set the pie carefully in my car before heading to my next destination: Stella's Candles.

CHAPTER THIRTY

When I stepped into the shop, a woman in a long caftan and feathered earrings floated toward me. Her earrings caught my eye because I also had a penchant for long, dangly earrings. At the moment, I was wearing a silver geometric pair that Cass had gotten me for my birthday. Cass only shopped in the best boutiques in New York, so I was terrified to think how much they'd cost her. Not that she would have told me.

The woman caught me staring. "You were expecting an Amish person, weren't you? I suppose that makes sense because most people in Amish Country associate candles with Plain folks."

"No, I'm sorry, I was just admiring your earrings," I admitted.

"Oh, these?" She put a hand to her ear, and the giant ruby ring on her finger caught the light. "These are one of my favorite pairs. They were made especially for me by a Navajo chief when I was on a spirit quest in New Mexico."

That statement alone proved to me she wasn't Amish, if I'd been in doubt from her appearance, which I wasn't.

"What can I do for you? I'm sensing a lot of questions. Maybe a candle for calming. I have one called Water of Peace that would do wonders for you. Think it will help you to stop asking so many questions. You have an inquisitive air about you. It's a good trait, but one that can also get you in a bind at times."

How well I knew that.

"Why would I want to stop asking questions?" I asked, which I knew, of course, was a question.

"One never wants to stop asking questions." As she moved, her caftan fanned out around her legs, and I noticed her feet were bare. "But it's good to give the mind a rest now and then and slow it down."

"I'm not actually here for a candle to calm me down. I'm here about a—a friend of mine. She rented a room from you. Rosemary Weiss."

Her hand flew to her face. "Poor Rosemary. I could not believe it when I heard what happened. To be strangled in a pretzel shop of all places. I'm not sure I can ever eat a pretzel again, and I dearly love a soft pretzel. To be strangled with dough!" She shuddered.

"She wasn't strangled with pretzel dough."

"Hmm, that's what I heard. Usually my information is accurate."

I wasn't going to argue with her over how Rosemary had died, but if there was a rumor that pretzel dough was involved, that wouldn't be good for Esther's business.

"When was the last time you saw Rosemary?" I asked.

She tapped a long midnight-blue fingernail against her

cheek. "I suppose it was a week ago. It wasn't unusual for whole weeks to go by without my seeing her. Both Rosemary and Hannah were as quiet as church mice. There were many times when I was working in the shop and had no idea they were upstairs. Only when they came down and I saw them walk by the window did I know." She smiled. "They really were the best tenants. I'm hoping to rent to Amish again when the room is ready to be opened up. They are wonderfully neat, no fuss, and they don't cause a jump in my utility bills. We got along fine. She didn't agree with all my ideas, but I didn't agree with hers either. I never did understand why the Amish make themselves wear such dreary clothes. The world is forlorn and drab enough as it is. It doesn't mean that your wardrobe must be."

"What do you mean when you say, 'when the room opens up?'" I asked.

"Well, I do want to wait a couple of weeks out of respect for Rosemary. She was a sweet woman, and I want the room to have time to breathe before I foist a new person on it. You have to let a person's essence escape after such a tragic death, or any death actually."

I wrinkled my brow.

"Also, there is the issue that Rosemary's things are still in the room. They belong to Hannah now, I would think. I have asked her cousin, Dinah, to come and clear out the space. She hasn't yet. I think she needs just as much time to breathe as the room does."

"Did anyone come to see Rosemary? Recently? Or ever?"

"She only had a visitor once. I would say it was about a month ago. What surprised me was that the woman was English, not Amish. Rosemary was very Amish in her beliefs, and she kept all the rules. For one, she wouldn't use any of my energy candles, even though I offered them to her for free. She said it went against her teaching. I always say, to each her own, so I didn't pressure her about it."

"Who was the woman?" I knew this was important.

"She said that her name was Jill Penn, and she had been told at the bakery where Rosemary lived. She very much wanted to talk with her. Rosemary and Hannah weren't home at the time, and I was glad for that. That Jill woman gave off negative vibes. When I asked why she wanted to see Rosemary, she said that she was Isaac's fiancée. That was news to me because it was my understanding that Rosemary and Isaac were still legally married."

Fiancée, not girlfriend? It was a notable distinction, and it also proved that Isaac very much wanted to be married. Just not to his Amish wife.

"I told Jill that I would give Rosemary the message. Sadly, Rosemary came home from the market just then. She and Hannah were carrying their groceries up the sidewalk. Jill saw them, so she ran outside, and what a scene that was. It was right in front of the bakery's front door. I'm sure every shopkeeper on the block heard it. Jill wasn't controlling her volume."

"What did she say?"

"She told Rosemary that she had to sign a paper, and Rosemary refused. Jill was furious because Rosemary wouldn't do what she asked. Jill said that she would report Rosemary to the authorities for being an unfit mother.

"Rosemary had been renting a room from me for nearly two years, and I had only seen her be lovely and sweet to Hannah. That was the point when I decided to put an end to it. Hannah was right there. She might not have been able to hear their conversation, but she's an intuitive child. She could pick up on the energy and hostility. No child should be subjected to such venom. I told the woman to leave. After a few unkind words, she finally did." She brushed her hands together as if she had just taken out the trash. "When she was gone, I told Rosemary if she needed a character witness, she could always count on me."

"When was this?" I asked.

"Goodness, I would say it was about a month ago. After that encounter, Rosemary was different."

"Different how?"

"Her energy was off. She was always a bit tense. There was always a nervousness about her. I begged her to take some of my calming candles, but she still refused. I lit some here in the shop, hoping that would help. I think it did because the last time I saw her, her mood had changed again."

"What do you mean?"

"She was still sad, but I felt determination coming off her. It was as if she finally knew what was the right thing to do." Her earrings brushed her shoulders.

"Right thing to do about what?"

She shrugged. "I didn't press. I believe in letting people tell their stories at their own speed."

I couldn't be more different from her; I was always pestering people for information, especially in the middle of a murder investigation.

Could Rosemary's decision have been to speak with Emily about Hannah? I didn't know what else it could have been, but when it came to Rosemary Weiss and her last movements, there was so much I didn't know. There was so much that Aiden didn't know either. Finding out where she had been between her conversation with Emily at the baby shower and Esther's discovery of her body in the pretzel shop just might lead me to the killer.

If I was right in my assumption that she'd wanted Hannah and Emily to be reunited, I was more determined than

ever to make sure Hannah ended up in the right place, and I
was more certain that was with Emily. Rosemary's wish was
that Hannah be reunited with her birth mother. The only
issue was what Daniel, Emily's husband, would have to say
about that. A decision had to be made soon. We couldn't let
this young girl be unsettled for too long. And for what? Em-
barrassment? Shame? Hannah wasn't responsible for any of
it. I realized one part of Stella's story didn't sit well with me.

Dinah had just told me that she didn't know who
Isaac's girlfriend was, while Stella claimed that Dinah
had told Jill where Rosemary lived. Why would Dinah lie
to me? My stomach turned. I had thought that Dinah and
I had a good rapport. I'd made her shark cupcakes. That
had to be worth something, but she'd still lied to me
about knowing who Isaac's English girlfriend—no, his
English fiancée—was. "Dinah said she didn't know who
Isaac's fiancée was," I said.

She cocked her head, and her earrings waved back and
forth. "That's odd. I'm pretty sure that she did. Jill works at
the racetrack with Dinah's son. I would have guessed that
she knew her." She shrugged. "Who can say? I don't judge!"

I gasped. Could the Jill I'd seen at the racetrack be the
same person? It seemed unlikely there would be two Jills
connected with the racetrack.

"What became of that sweet little girl?" Stella asked.
"I have been worried about her. I went over to see Dinah
about her yesterday, but she wouldn't tell me where the
child had gone."

"She's with an Amish family now," I was careful not
to tell her she was with my own family. I had misjudged
Dinah, and it was possible, as quirky and likable as this
woman might seem, I might have misjudged her as well.
I didn't trust my own judgment at the moment.

"That is a relief. When the police came, I asked about her, and they said she was safe. That relieved me, too, but they didn't tell me she was with an Amish family. For Hannah, I think that is best. She is a sweet girl."

"Would you mind if I went up to the apartment and took a look around? Maybe there will be some things that Hannah would want, and I can take them to her. I know the family she's staying with."

"Knock yourself out. You can take everything, for all I care. It doesn't seem that Dinah is in a rush to take care of it." She floated to the window. Her caftan swirled around her as she pointed to the side of the building. "The outside stairs to the room are just on the other side of the building here. It used to be a storage area, but I turned it into a studio apartment. When you go up, the door should be unlocked. I was up there earlier, looking around. There isn't much to steal, so I didn't see any point in locking the door. I hoped if I left it unlocked, Dinah would go up and clean out the room." She wrinkled her nose. "Dinah refuses to come into my shop. She finds my candles suspicious." She shrugged. "I don't argue with her about it. As I said, everyone has their own beliefs. Don't step on mine, and I won't step on yours."

I thanked Stella and went out the door. On the sidewalk, I paused, wondering if I should go to the apartment first or confront Dinah about why she'd lied to me.

In the end, the CLOSED sign on the bakery door made the decision for me.

Outside the candle shop, there was an external staircase attached to the brick building. At the top of the staircase was a bright blue door. It was such a striking color; I knew that it had to be Stella's choice, not Rosemary's.

More notable than the color, the door was wide open.

CHAPTER THIRTY-ONE

I bit my lip. Stella said that she'd left the door unlocked. Could the wind have blown it open? Or was someone in there? There was only one way to find out.

The stairs leading up to the apartment were sturdy and didn't so much as creak when I stepped on them. At the landing, I peered through the open door. The room was tiny, and I could see every corner, except the area behind the beaded curtain that led into what I assumed was the bathroom. Tucked in the corner of the room was a small kitchenette that wasn't much bigger than the bathroom vanity at my house.

One double bed sat against the wall. A sturdy cardboard box served as a nightstand. There were pegs on the walls to hang clothes. Other than the beaded curtain, the room very clearly belonged to an Amish person. There were few possessions.

I stepped inside and threw back the curtain, hoping to scare anyone who might be lurking there. I was right. It was the bathroom, and it was empty.

I let out a breath, feeling relieved. The wind must have opened the door, or maybe the police hadn't latched it all the way after they'd been here.

I looked under the bed and found a square brown suitcase that looked as if it was right out of a Paddington Bear book I'd read as a child. I grabbed the handle and opened it on the bed. I began putting what I thought Hannah would like into the case.

Any toy or book I found went inside. I followed that with two child-size dresses and a prayer cap. There was a teddy bear on the bed, too. Tears gathered in my eyes as I picked up these things. Poor Hannah. Her life had been shattered by Rosemary's death, and what would happen to her was still unknown. I prayed that Emily and Daniel would ask to take the child. However, even if they did, there was no guarantee that the county would award the little girl to them. Then what? Would she go to an Amish or English home? Would she be sent to a home that knew sign language?

I decided to include Rosemary's lone dress, too. I didn't know if seeing it would make Hannah sadder, but I thought that she should be the one to decide what happened to it.

I opened the nightstand drawer, hoping to find a letter or note with Rosemary's handwriting on it. That could also be precious to Hannah someday.

There was nothing with writing on it in the drawer. However, I found a small photograph of Rosemary holding a baby. The picture was encased in a silver frame with daisies etched around the edges. The baby had to be Hannah. How rare this photo must be. The Amish were staunch believers in not taking pictures of themselves or other Amish people. They claimed that it went against God's commandment not to create graven images.

Rosemary had been strict in following Amish beliefs, so much so that she refused to divorce her husband when he left her, but she'd kept this photograph. It was meaningful to her and also would be meaningful to Hannah someday.

I circled the room again. There was nothing more to be found or to take. All of Hannah and Rosemary's possessions were in that little Paddington Bear suitcase.

With the suitcase in my trunk, I drove back to Harvest.

In the village, Margot Rawlings wielded her megaphone as a weapon while she directed the Amish men on the square, telling them how she wanted the concert set up. A person would think she was angry from the sharp tone of her voice. However, I had learned that was just how Margot spoke when in organizer mode. It was as good time as any for me to sneak into Swissmen Sweets undetected. I didn't want to come under Margot's steely gaze when she was shouting orders.

Inside the candy shop, I let out a breath. It was always a small victory when I snuck by Margot without being seen.

I was surprised to see Deputy Little and Charlotte standing across from each other, gazing into each other's eyes. When they heard me enter, they jumped apart as if they'd been caught doing something wrong, even though they hadn't been touching.

I eyed them.

"What's going on?" I asked, even though I had a few guesses.

Deputy Little swallowed. His Adam's apple bobbed up and down. "I'm here with Deputy Brody. He's upstairs with the social worker, Emily Keim, and her husband."

I blinked. "Emily is here?"

Charlotte nodded. Her cheeks were still flushed. "She came to get Hannah."

A smile broke out on my face. This was the news I was most hoping to hear. "Do you think I can go up?" I was eager to hear whether the social worker would grant Emily custody of Hannah.

"Ummm," Deputy Little said, seeming unsure.

I didn't wait long enough for him to decide, but went quietly up the stairs from the candy shop into my grand-mother's two-bedroom apartment. When I reached the top floor, I heard voices coming from the end of the hall-way. As I expected, they had gathered in my grand-mother's sitting room at the end of the hallway. It wasn't a very large room, and I guessed that it was a tight fit with that many people inside.

Through the door, I heard Vanessa say, "I am happy to hear that you are interested in Hannah. I am reluctant to place her in foster care in an English home. I think the cultural shock would be difficult for her. What I'm going to do is ask a judge if she can stay here with Clara King until her placement is finalized. If that's all right with you, Clara? There will be some paperwork and classes that you will need to take to be a foster guardian for the child. We can make a request to expedite things."

"We love having Hannah here. We would be happy to keep her, and we can do what is needed to make that hap-pen."

My heart swelled with pride as I listened to my grand-mother speak.

"Why can't I take my daughter home today?" Emily asked.

I heard the tears in her voice. My chest tightened. Emily would not understand all the steps that would have to be taken for Hannah to move to the Christmas tree farm.

I peeked through the crack in the door. I saw Vanessa perched on the arm of my grandmother's rocking chair. *Maami* sat in the armchair holding Hannah in her lap, and Daniel and Emily sat side by side on the love seat.

Aiden stood in the corner of the room with his arms crossed. He glanced in the direction of the cracked door and shook his head. He knew I was there.

Vanessa took a moment, it appeared, to gather her thoughts. "I know you want this to go more quickly, but there are steps we have to take. With your permission, we'll do a maternity test first."

Emily looked at Aiden.

"She means they'll take a sample of your blood and test it to prove you are Hannah's mother," Aiden said.

Vanessa nodded. "If that comes back showing conclu-sively you are Hannah's biological mother, we will do a series of home visits to make sure your family is ready to welcome a child."

Daniel stood up. "I do not like the way you are ques-tioning my wife's ability to be a mother or implying that my farm is unfit for a child."

Emily put a hand on her husband's arm. "Daniel, please. I know Hannah is my daughter. I have waited nearly six years to see her again. I can wait a few more days." She looked at Vanessa. "*Danki* for agreeing to meet us like this."

"Thank you for giving me the opportunity." Vanessa stood and smoothed the front of her jacket. "Because you are Amish, there are some exceptions we will make when it comes to the home visit. For one, it will not be necessary for your home to be up to code as far as electricity goes and other modern conveniences that we would examine more closely in a non-Amish home." She smiled at Emily and Daniel. "Trust that whatever happens, I will not let Hannah go to the wrong home."

I hoped that was a promise she could keep. As she came to the door, I hopped away.

"Hello," I said with a bright smile as I was caught in the act of snooping.

Vanessa eyed me as she passed by. "Miss King." She nodded to me and went down the hallway.

Aiden walked by me, too. "I'll stop by your place tonight. We have to talk," he said under his breath.

"About what? The murderer?"

He shook his head. "We'll talk tonight. I need to collect Little and return to the station. We are drowning in the paperwork caused by this case."

I frowned at his back as he followed Vanessa down the stairs. Then I turned and stepped into the sitting room. Tears rolled down Emily's cheeks. "I knew it would not be easy to get her back, but I did not know that we wouldn't be able to take her home today."

Daniel held her hand. "Maybe not today, but we will take Hannah home. Until then, you know that she is safe and cared for by Clara."

Emily wiped the tears from her eyes. "*Ya*. Clara, thank you so much for taking care of my daughter."

"I can't imagine anything I would want to do more."

She hugged Hannah close and smiled at me. "Bailey, you are back. You were gone for quite some time."

"I know. Everything took longer than expected. I overheard some of the conversation. I'm glad Vanessa is giving you a chance to keep Hannah."

More tears rolled down Emily's cheeks. She could only manage one word. "*Danki.*"

Then the child wriggled off *Maami's* lap and sat on the other side of Emily. She leaned her head on Emily's arm. Emily wrapped her arms around Hannah and cried. Anyone who saw them next to each other would know that they were mother and daughter. I was certain Vanessa had seen it, too.

CHAPTER THIRTY-TWO

After Emily and Daniel left Swissmen Sweets, we locked up for the night. I stayed and had dinner with Hannah, Charlotte, and *Maami*. I was surprised that *Maami* and Charlotte now knew more signs than I did.

Charlotte must have noticed my expression because she said, "Lois came over while you were gone and taught us thirty of the most common signs."

"She brought us a children's book of American Sign Language, too," *Maami* said. "Hannah has been having great fun looking at the book and showing us the signs. We've turned it into a bit of a game."

"That's great. When I'm here tomorrow, I want to be a part of the game, too." I pointed at myself and then signed the word for "game" for Hannah's benefit.

Hannah grinned and nodded.

After dinner, I left the candy shop feeling more optimistic about Hannah's future than I had since I'd brought her to Swissmen Sweets. I knew that Aiden wanted to speak to me about something—was it the job offer?—but he wouldn't be at my home until late. This gave me enough time to pop in on Esther.

The pretzel shop was closed, but before Aiden had left the candy shop, he'd told me the Sheriff's Department had released the premises back to Esther on Monday afternoon. She was free to go into the shop now, clean it, and get it ready for business. But she had yet to reopen the doors. What could the delay be?

I knew Esther. She would be in the shop making sure everything was sparkling clean and ready for opening. I peeked through the front windows. The lights were off. I tried the door, but it was locked.

I went into the alley between our two buildings. Light shone from the back window. I went to the door and knocked.

"Abel, it's unlocked!" Esther called from inside.

I turned the knob and went in. I found Esther on her hands and knees, scrubbing the floor. I had always thought Esh Family Pretzel was a clean shop, but now it positively sparkled. She sat back on her legs.

"What are you doing here?" She pointed her scrub brush at me.

"You were expecting Abel?"

"I'm always expecting Abel. This is his shop, too, even if he doesn't treat it as such. What are you doing here, Bailey King? I have much work to do and don't have time for your questions."

"You need to make the time. I want to talk to you about Rosemary."

She stood up, dropped her scrub brush in the bucket,

and dusted off her skirts. The hem of her skirt was damp from kneeling on the floor. "I have nothing more to say."

I barreled ahead. "When Rosemary made contact with you in her search for Emily, why did you intervene? You and Emily haven't spoken in well over a year. Everyone in the district and the village knows the two of you are estranged. Anything that Emily does or did no longer has any bearing on you."

She narrowed her eyes. "Do you think I wanted it to come out that my sister had a baby out of wedlock? That she sinned? That I wasn't the sister to her I should have been when our parents died? That I failed? You say it has no bearing on me, but that's where you are wrong." She choked on the last words.

"Why do you think you failed?" I asked.

"Because I should have warned her, told her what could happen if she fell in love with a disrespectful young man like Gideon Glick. I should have stopped her from being courted so young. I didn't expect her to be so stupid. I thought she would know the difference between right and wrong." She brushed back a strand of blond hair that had fallen out of her Amish bun.

I realized something for the first time. "How old were you when your parents died?"

She glared at me. "Seventeen."

"A lot fell on your shoulders at seventeen. You had to care for the family farm, run this shop, and care for your younger sister. My guess is Abel wasn't much help, and you had to do it all on your own. You blame yourself for Emily's pregnancy because you still believe, after all this time, that you could have stopped it if you'd tried harder."

She glared at me fiercely, but slowly, almost as if it

was happening muscle by muscle, her face began to crumple, and she cried. These weren't the sweet, silent tears that Emily shed, but gut-wrenching sobs that rocked her entire body.

Her knees began to bend, but before she could collapse on the still wet and soapy floor at her feet, I grabbed a chair that had been set against the wall and tucked it under her. She fell onto the chair with a wail.

I patted her shoulder and made soothing sounds like *Maami* did when I'd cried as a child. Eventually, Esther calmed down. "I'm sorry. I've never done that before." She wiped her eyes with the end of her apron.

"I think that's been pent up for the last six years."

She took a sharp breath.

"Tell me about the adoption."

She frowned, and for a moment, I thought she wasn't going to tell me. "There is an *Englisch* family in Indiana who were friends of our parents. My father knew the husband through work. They both were in construction. When I learned of Emily's condition, I asked if she could live with them to hide the pregnancy and told them she would give the baby up for adoption. They agreed."

"Were they involved in the adoption?" I asked, thinking that, if they were, they could be in some serious trouble.

She shook her head. "*Nee*, I did not want to involve them. An Amish midwife delivered the baby and told me of an Amish couple who desperately wanted a child but couldn't have one. I knew that Emily could not keep the baby. If she did, her shame would come out. The childless woman happened to be the Amish woman who came to our *Englisch* friends' home once a week to clean. She knew Emily was going to have a child that she could not keep. She seemed kind, from what I saw of her. I felt she would be a *gut* fit."

I swallowed. Esther had observed Rosemary for a few days and then decided the fate of Emily's child? I didn't think she'd had nearly enough information to make that sort of decision.

"I know what you are thinking," she went on. "But we could not care for the child. I could barely manage the responsibilities I had already. I told the midwife to take the baby and give it to the couple. I thought that would be the end of it. I never thought the midwife would tell the new mother anything about us. I never thought she would tell her where we lived.

"I had not thought of that day for years, and then, out of the blue, I received the letter from Rosemary, claiming she was the adoptive mother of Emily's daughter and asking Emily if she wanted to meet Hannah. I couldn't allow that! It would open old wounds." She cleared her throat and sat straighter in her chair. "So I wrote her a note, telling her to stay away. She came to the baby shower, so the note did not work at all."

"Did you speak to her at the shower?"

She nodded. "I did. I asked her to meet me that night at the pretzel shop. I was going to tell her in no uncertain terms that Emily had no interest in the child. She was starting a new family with her new husband. She didn't want a mistake back in her life."

I bristled when she referred to Hannah as a mistake and clenched my jaw to think that she'd tried to take Emily's chance to meet her daughter away from her.

"When I got to the shop that night to meet with her, the back door was open, and Rosemary was already dead. I then ran to Swissmen Sweets, and you know the rest."

"And where was Abel in all this?"

She blinked at me as if I'd shaken her out of her memories. "Why do you think any of this has to do with Abel?"

"Does it?"

"*Nee*, Abel is never here enough to do anything."

"Because he's at the racetrack?" I asked on a hunch.

She turned pale, and I realized that I wasn't far off the mark. "I saw Abel earlier, and he had a brochure for the Wayne County Racetrack. Why would he have that?" I asked.

She frowned at me. "I don't know, but what does this have to do with Emily or Rosemary?"

"I just find it interesting because Mason, the son of Rosemary's cousin, works there. It just seems to be popping up a lot in relation to the case."

Her frown deepened.

She stood up and picked up her scrub brush from the floor. "I need to get back to cleaning." She got on her hands and knees and began again to scrub the clean floor. "I need this place to be spotless so that we can open tomorrow. There will be much traffic with the concert Margot has planned on the square."

"What can you tell me about Abel and the track?"

"*Nix*. Nothing. Now leave." She would not look at me. She ran the stiff bristles of her brush aggressively back and forth over the floor.

I hesitated in the doorway for a moment, wanting to offer to help, but I knew that she would only find that an insult, implying she was not able to do it on her own. And Esther thought she had to do everything on her own.

CHAPTER THIRTY-THREE

Later that night, Puff and I were watching a movie on the small love seat in my living room. Actually, I wasn't watching the TV at all. Puff was. My white rabbit seemed captivated by the shootout scene on the screen, so I left it on. I was watching the door, waiting for Aiden to arrive.

When the movie ended, I was about to give up and go to bed. This was not the first time Aiden had said he was going to drop by but didn't. It seemed his job was always pulling him away. I was thinking about going to bed, but felt too tired to climb the stairs to my bedroom on the second floor. The stress of the week had finally caught up with me.

Before I could make up my mind, there was a knock on the front door. I jumped off the love seat, and the large white rabbit hopped away from me, looking offended.

There would be payback later. I would have to remember to get all my shoes off the floor. She liked to chew the toes off.

I peered through the peephole and gave a sigh of relief when I saw Aiden. I opened the door. "Finally!"

He laughed. "I don't know if I should be happy or offended by that greeting."

"Go with happy." I suppressed a yawn.

He chuckled, removed his shoes, and sat on the love seat. I curled up next to him, and Puff settled on his foot like a chicken sitting on her precious eggs. My white rabbit had a terrible crush on Aiden. It was clear that I wasn't the only one who didn't want to see him go.

Aiden smiled down at the rabbit. "She sure is clingy."

"She likes you." I kissed his cheek. "I do, too."

"Well, that's a relief." He sighed.

"Is something wrong? What's going on? You said you didn't want to talk about the murder." I scooted away from him so I could see his face better.

"I have a few things to say about the case, but I don't think you are going to like them." He sighed. "Little told me about your outing to the racetrack. You shouldn't have been there."

"It's open to the public."

He rolled his eyes.

"I do have one question about the murder," I said.

"Just one."

I shook my finger at him. "Don't you roll your eyes at me again, Aiden Brody," I teased.

He held up his hands as if in surrender.

"Did you ever find Rosemary's reading glasses?"

He shook his head. "But based on the description, the coroner thinks that the chain you described was what was used to strangle Rosemary. Had you not told me that, I think we would still be wondering what the murder weapon was."

I put a hand to my throat at the very idea. "So it was a murder of convenience?"

"Possibly." He bent over to pet Puff. She sighed happily. The rabbit was really in love. I didn't know what she would do if Aiden was gone for six months for BCI training. To be honest, I didn't know what I would do either.

"So what's up? Not murder, but . . ."

He licked his lips nervously, and then he cracked his knuckles. My eyes went wide. He wasn't going to ask me to marry him, was he? After the talk we'd had the other night about his job offer, I thought a proposal was off the table if he took the BCI job. Was I wrong? Maybe he would throw caution to the wind, and we'd figure it all out after we were engaged. A long engagement wouldn't be a horrible thing, would it?

My pulse began to race as he bit his lower lip. I sat up a little straighter in my seat. I touched my hair. It was tidy in a knot on the top of my head. But I wasn't ready.

He leaned forward.

Oh my God. He was going to reach into his pocket for a ring.

"Bailey, you know this was a very hard decision."

My brow wrinkled. That wasn't the best way to start. Maybe it would get better. He was nervous.

"I . . ."

Here it comes.

"I—I took that job at BCI."

I blinked at him. "What?"

He turned to me, confused. "What do you mean, what? I told you about the job offer I got."

I shook my head, trying to reset my brain. "Umm, yeah, of course I remember." Disappointment flooded my body. This talk was about the job offer. Of course, it was about the job offer. How could I think it was anything else? My face felt hot.

"What's wrong? Did you not want me to take the job?"

I swallowed. I couldn't let him know why I was really upset. I couldn't let him know that I was disappointed because I'd stupidly thought he was going to propose. "Yes, I want you to take the job." I forced a smile. "That's wonderful news. I'll miss you when you're away for training, but I want you to be happy. I know you aren't happy working under the sheriff."

"Oh-kay," he said. "You're acting strange."

"I guess I'm tired. I've been really worried about Hannah. I hope the judge lets Emily have her."

"I do, too. It might take some time. Child services and custody are complicated, and there are many hoops that will have to be jumped through."

I frowned. I hoped child services would understand that Hannah was Amish and not English, so some things might be a little different. Vanessa, the social worker, had said they would change the rules a bit because Hannah was Amish.

"Anyway," Aiden said as he gently removed his foot from under Puff's body. "I wanted to tell you. I'm turning in my resignation to the department tomorrow. I have to give them one month's notice. Hopefully that will be enough time for them to find and train a new deputy. My hope is that Little is promoted in my place. He's come a long way."

I nodded vaguely. I was still reeling from the proposal scare. Or was it from the proposal disappointment?

He stood and kissed me on the top of my head. "You do look tired. We can talk about it more tomorrow. I just wanted you to know before word got around town."

"Thank you for that." I got up and followed him to the door. Normally, I would have asked him to stay, but tonight, I just wanted to be alone.

At the front door, I watched until his taillights disappeared down the street. When I closed the door, I leaned against it. It felt odd knowing that Aiden was going to leave the Sheriff's Department. He had been a deputy for over a decade. From the outside, it appeared that he loved his job.

But over the last year, I had seen how he'd become increasingly frustrated with the sheriff and his policies. He hated the fact that he had to do what the sheriff decreed, even when he didn't agree with it.

The problem was I wasn't sure he'd be that much happier at BCI. There would be even more bureaucratic tape to cut through, but it would be different. Different might be just what he needed. Of all people, I should have understood. When I was working for Jean Pierre at JP Chocolates in New York, I had found myself in a rut, too. It wasn't until I was forced to make a choice between New York and Ohio that I realized that leaving the grind of the city was what I needed the most. I shouldn't have been surprised that Aiden was at a similar career crossroads.

But that didn't change the fact that I'd wanted him to propose tonight instead of telling me about his new job.

CHAPTER THIRTY-FOUR

The next afternoon, Margot was in fine form on the square.

"Don't put the music stands by the food vendors! Put them in the gazebo where the band will be," she shouted into the bullhorn.

Charlotte winced where she stood next to me in the booth we were setting up for Swissmen Sweets. "Why hasn't anyone figured out a way to get that bullhorn away from her?"

I set a tray of lemon drop bags on the table. We had made them in honor of Hannah and Emily. "I think she sleeps with it like a teddy bear, so they can't pry it out of her clutches."

Charlotte barked a laugh, but then she suddenly stopped laughing.

I glanced over at her to see what had caused the sudden

change in mood, and then I noticed Deputy Little walking around the square chatting with villagers as he went. Ahhh.

"You okay?" I asked as innocently as I could manage.

She fumbled with the boxes of fudge in her hands. "I'm okay," she squeaked. "Why wouldn't I be okay?" She set the boxes on the table in a line. Appeared to be unhappy with the line and straightened it.

"Because you look like you saw a ghost."

"I'm Amish," she sniffed. "There are no such things as ghosts."

I looked away so that she couldn't see my smile. I didn't for a moment want Charlotte to think I was making fun of her. However, it was obvious what, or should I say who, had caused her nervousness all of sudden. "Because you saw your crush, then?"

Her face flushed red. "What are you talking about?"

I raised my brow as she set out a basket of individually wrapped pieces of caramel on the table. "Deputy Little."

"Luke—I mean Deputy Little is just my *gut* friend."

I eyed her. "Is that so?"

Her pale cheek turned bright pink. "Don't the *Englisch* believe that men and women can be friends?"

"Yes," I said. "They do. However, you just called Deputy Little *Luke*, and I think that was telling. I don't think anyone calls him by his Christian name . . . maybe not even his parents."

"That's silly." She opened a package of napkins and put them in a holder on the table.

"Is it? Because when Deputy Little talked to me about you, he was very serious. He said that you were more than friends."

The napkins fell from her hands onto the grass.

"Oh no." She gathered the napkins up again. She set

them on the table and looked at me with her bright green eyes. "Did he really say that?"

I nodded.

She let out a breath. "Then it's up to me. I know I have to make a choice between the Amish world and the *Englisch* one. It's just so hard. I want to be in both places."

I nodded. "I'm sorry to tease you about it. It's a very big and difficult decision, and the last thing I want to do is put more pressure on you. You need to be careful, Charlotte, and be sure this is what you really want. You will be giving up quite a lot to be with Little."

"I know that," she said. "But my family already gave up on me. All I have for family now are you and Cousin Clara. You would not give up on me."

"Of course, we wouldn't, but I mean your culture. Being part of the Amish community, being a member of an Amish district."

"I know this," she said as she opened a new package of napkins to replace the ones that had fallen in the grass. "I have been thinking about all of this for so long now. It's time to make a choice."

"And what do you choose?"

"I know what I have to do." She held the fresh napkins, crinkling them just as badly as the ones she had dropped on the ground.

"What's that?"

She grinned at me. "I want to tell Luke first."

And I knew the choice she had made. I told myself not to worry about Charlotte's decision. She had been struggling to make up her mind about being baptized into the Amish church for years, for longer than she'd known Deputy Little, longer even than she'd known me. Just the same, she was like a little sister to me, and I could not help but worry about her. I thought I always would.

I pushed those thoughts aside as best I could and tried to focus on yet another event on the village square. As usual, Margot had been able to scare up a decent crowd. Over an hour before the concert was to begin, villagers and visitors alike sat on blankets all around the square. By the time the concert began, there was overflow seating on the church lawn. Everyone seemed to be enjoying the music. Swissmen Sweets' booth was busy as people bought sweet treats for their families. About midway through the concert, the booth's traffic began to slow down.

"What are you doing here?" a woman asked me.

I looked up from my task of setting more chocolate Jethro bars on the table. They had been a big seller that evening for us. Leslie Marin, the accountant, stood in front of me, next to the handsomest man I had ever seen. He had lush dark hair and striking, blue-green eyes. His jaw was strong, and he was tall and lean.

Next to me, Charlotte let out a gasp. I guessed that she noted his good looks, too.

"I asked you a question," Leslie said. "What are you doing here?" She looked at the man. "Gideon, this is the woman I told you about who was looking for an accountant." To me, she said, "*This* is your small business?"

So this was Gideon Glick, Emily's former suitor and Hannah's biological father. Considering how handsome he was, I could see how Emily had been swept away by him when she was young.

I cleared my throat. "Yes, I own Swissmen Sweets with my grandmother." I picked up a plate of chocolate-covered caramels and held it out to her. "Care for a sample?"

"No, I don't want a sample. You said nothing about working at Swissmen Sweets when you came to our office," Leslie snapped.

I set the tray back down.

"If you had told Leslie what your business was," Gideon said, "I would have known it had to do with Emily. I heard she was working here when I first moved back to the county. Where is Emily?"

I didn't say anything, feeling grateful Emily had the evening off from the candy shop.

"We came here to find Emily Esh," Gideon said. "She has to answer to me."

"She's not here," I said.

"Then where is she?" he demanded. "I need to talk to her."

There was no way I was answering that question.

He leaned over the table. "Tell me where she is. Because of her, a sheriff's deputy paid me a visit. He told me I have a child."

"Do you have any idea how hard it was for me to hear about Emily and this child?" Leslie asked. "Don't you care how you are hurting people?"

I cared about how Hannah could be hurt. Gideon and Leslie's feelings were much lower on my list.

Charlotte hopped back from the table. I wanted to do the same, but I held my ground. "I think you need to take a step back."

"Tell me!" Gideon demanded.

"If you don't back off, I will scream." I glared at him.

He rocked back on his heels.

"She should have told me that I had a child," Gideon hissed. "She will see me in court!" He and Leslie stomped away.

I caught my breath. "I think Hannah's future just got way more complicated."

"No kidding," Charlotte said.

The brass band played on.

A half hour later, *Maami* brought Hannah over, and I handed the little girl a bag of lemon drops with a wink. I was so grateful that Hannah had not been in the booth when Gideon had stopped by.

"Charlotte and Bailey, go enjoy the concert and walk around," *Maami* said. "Hannah and I can take care of the booth."

She didn't have to tell Charlotte twice. My cousin hurried away from the booth. I guessed it was to tell Deputy Little her decision.

I thanked *Maami* and wandered around the square. On the other side, Esther worked in the pretzel booth all alone. I headed in that direction with the intent of giving Esther a hand, or trying to. There was a good chance that she would turn me away.

Before I reached the booth, Abel walked up to her. I stopped a few feet away and pretended to be listening to the concert.

"I need help tomorrow at the shop," Esther said. "There are supplies that need to be picked up from our wholesaler. I have not had time to get them."

"Have them delivered," Abel said.

"I can't afford delivery right now, especially because the shop was closed for so many days."

He leaned on the post holding up the tent over her table. "You are too tight with your wallet, Esther."

"Being tight with my wallet is how I have kept the business afloat all these years and kept our family together."

"You didn't do such a *gut* job keeping it together when it came to Emily," he scoffed.

She gasped and then closed her eyes as if she was centering herself or, more likely, reminding herself she needed Abel's help. "Please pick up the supplies tomorrow. It's very important. We must have a *gut* weekend, or I am worried that we won't be able to pay our bills."

"That's your problem, *schwescder*," he said to his sister.

"It is our problem. If you would not squander what money I give you, we would not be in this position."

He narrowed his eyes at her. "I can't pick up the supplies tomorrow. Pay an Amish driver to do it. I have plans at the racetrack all day. Saturday is a big race day."

"You can't go to the track every Saturday. I need help. You are wasting money and time when you could be helping me." She sounded desperate.

"You're going to have to find help somewhere else because I can and will go to the track as often as I like, just as I have always done." He loomed over her. "I am your *bruder*, and because you have no husband or *daed*, I am in charge of our family."

"Bailey King suspects you, you know," she hissed.

I jumped when I heard my name. I clapped a hand over my mouth, afraid that I'd made a sound that would alert them to my presence. When they didn't react, I lowered my hand and let out a breath.

"Of what in particular?" Abel asked. "She seems to *know* quite a bit about everything that happens in this village. She suspects me of a great many things as well."

"Something about killing Rosemary. She thinks it's related to the track, too."

I clapped two hands over my mouth this time. Was I

about to hear Abel confess to the murder? I ducked behind a tree trunk so I could still hear them.

"Do *you* think I had something to do with it?" He laughed.

She didn't answer.

My eyes were wide. Could it be that Esther believed her brother was in fact the killer?

"I do a lot of things. Killing is not one of them. I no longer care if people find out about Emily's mistake and that deaf child. She is no longer a member of our family as far as I am concerned."

I dropped my hands from my face and balled them into fists at my sides.

"Bailey said that Rosemary's cousin works at the track, and she connected you to the track as well. She will put the blame on you. I'm telling you to be careful."

He stepped back, so that he was standing a few feet away from her now. The brass band continued to play in the background as brother and sister fought and I watched.

"He does work at the racetrack," Abel said. "His name is Mason. I know him, but just because I go to a place where a relative of Rosemary happens to work doesn't mean I killed anyone."

"I'm telling you to be careful, *bruder*. You know if Bailey is watching you, Deputy Brody is, too. She is the bug in his ear."

I didn't hear what he replied because someone grabbed my arm and pulled me away from the tree.

I raised my hand to smack my would-be attacker away, but then I realized it was Charlotte. A very excited Charlotte, actually.

"Bailey!" Charlotte squeezed my arm for all she was

worth. "I told Luke that I have decided to leave the Amish way, not just for him, but for myself. There is so much more of this world I want to explore, and a lot of it I can't reach and still be Amish. I'm at peace with my decision. I know it's the right thing for me. I didn't realize what a toll the uncertainty was taking on me. I feel free!"

I hugged her. "I know that *Maami* will be surprised, but she will understand."

"I know she will. I think everyone in the community has believed I would jump the fence for a long time."

She held out her left hand to me. "And that's not all. Luke and I are getting married. He proposed the moment after I told him I was leaving the Amish. He said that he just couldn't wait any longer."

There was a small diamond on her ring finger, and it sparkled in the sunlight. "It's beautiful," I whispered.

She jumped up and down. "I need to calm down, and I have to talk to the bishop about my choice before too many people find out. It's the right thing to do. His wife, Ruth Yoder, is certainly going to have a lot to say about it, but I don't care." She hugged me again. "Bailey, I don't know if I have ever been this excited before."

For Charlotte, that was saying something.

"I'm so happy for you." I hugged her back, feeling all the love and excitement possible for Charlotte and for Deputy Little, but still feeling a twinge of envy, wishing that I had an engagement to celebrate, too.

Over her shoulder, I glanced at the pretzel booth. Esther was hard at work again. Alone. Abel was gone.

CHAPTER THIRTY-FIVE

Saturday morning, I went to the candy shop well before dawn and did all the pre-opening work I could. When Charlotte and *Maami* came into the kitchen at four that morning, most of the prep work was done. Charlotte was still wearing Amish clothes, I noted. I didn't know if she had yet told my grandmother about her decision to leave the Amish and marry Deputy Little, so I didn't say anything. I guessed that she hadn't yet because her engagement ring was absent from her finger.

Maami rubbed her eyes. "Bailey, why are you here so early?"

"I wanted to make sure you two are set for the day. I'm going to head over to the Wayne County Racetrack again."

"More sleuthing," Charlotte said knowingly.

"Something about that place doesn't add up." I carried the silicone chocolate molds I had just filled to the freezer.

"I'm sure there's some connection between the track and Rosemary's murder. It's worth another look."

My grandmother studied me. "Does Aiden know your plans?"

"No," I admitted. I had called Aiden the night before and told him about my encounter with Gideon Glick, and the argument that I had overheard between Esther and Abel. He'd agreed that going to the racetrack the next day was a good idea. However, he'd said that he and Deputy Little would go to the racetrack. I was to stay in Harvest and make candy. He should have known it wasn't going to work like that.

My grandmother sighed. "Just be careful when you go."

"Always," I said.

Charlotte and *Maami* shared a look.

The Wayne County Racetrack was far more crowded on a Saturday than it had been on the weekday when Deputy Little and I had been there. The gravel parking lot was packed with cars, trucks, and Amish buggies and wagons. I parked far away from the main entrance, and crossing the massive parking lot turned into a game of chicken as more and more people arrived at the track. According to the track's website, the first five races of the day were Amish harness racing. I hoped that meant I would find Abel at the rail.

Earlier in the week, I had been able to waltz into the track area with no one noticing, but today there was a line to purchase tickets to watch the race. I stood at the end of the line, which ran all the way back to the grassy edge of the parking lot. I fidgeted and scanned the faces of the people around me. I felt exposed.

The line shuffled forward. When I finally made it to the entrance, I handed over my five dollars and had the back of my hand stamped with a stamp shaped like a tractor.

Once I was inside the track area, I didn't know how I was going to find Abel, Amos, or Mason in this crush of people. The open space between the stable to my right and the track itself was filled with collapsible bleachers. I felt the carrot in my pocket that I had brought for Cooper. Even if this trip was a complete waste, I could give the horse his promised treat.

A booming announcer's voice came over the loudspeaker. "All right, everyone, are you ready for the next race?"

A roar went up from the several hundred spectators on the bleachers and at the rail. Cheers came from the gambling booth behind me, where both English and Amish placed bets. It wasn't the Kentucky Derby exactly. There were no mint juleps or outlandish hats, but the excitement in the air was palpable.

A truck pulled onto the dirt track. On the back of it was mounted a wide gate the width of the track. It stopped just ahead of the starting line. As the truck idled, stable hands held the bridles of the six horses and directed them to their places at the starting line. Behind the horses walked the six harness drivers. They didn't wear expensive silks. The Amish men wore button-down shirts and jeans, just as they would wear to work on their farms. The only difference in the outfits was that their black felt hats had been replaced by riding helmets. Mason was one of the stable hands. He was easy to pick out because of his limp. He scowled as he held the horse while the young driver climbed into the sulky and took the reins. The horse Mason held was my friend, Cooper.

"I can't hear you!" the announcer shouted. "Are you ready for the next race? I know our track owner here, Mr. Amos Miller, is ready to get this started."

I looked in the direction of the open-air booth near the starting line of the track. Jill Penn and Amos were inside the booth with the announcer. Both waved to the crowd.

The roar was twice as loud this time.

"Good! The horses are primed, and the sulkies are rigged. We have the finest Amish harness racers in the country for you today. It should be a race to remember!" He paused. "Abel Esh, I hope you've placed your bets. If anyone can get a sneak peek at Abel's bets, let me know. He almost always wins."

The response from the crowd this time was mixed. There were cheers, but a good number of boos as well.

Then I spotted Abel. He was at the rail and waved to the crowd. It seemed that in this little microcosm, he was some sort of celebrity, and he basked in the cheers and the jeers directed at him.

All the riders and horses were in position now. A large Amish man stood on a platform near the starting line. He held a gun in his hand and shot it in the air. The truck roared to life and sped down the track. The horses ran after it. At the second curve on the other side of the track from me, the truck turned off onto a road, but the horses and drivers stayed on the track to make their four complete circles to finish the race.

The screams and cries of the crowd were deafening, and I wanted to cover my ears to block out the noise.

The announcer cried, "Grandma's Beard is in the lead,

followed by Luck Would Have It. No! Christmas Cookies
is overtaking Grandma's Beard. Grandma's Beard is giving it all he has, but he can't keep up. It's Christmas
Cookies for the win!"

Abel held his fist triumphantly in the air. I was certain
the horse he'd placed his money on had won, and I suspected that somehow he'd influenced that outcome.

A man next to me tossed his bet on the ground with an
angry shout. After he left, I picked up the bet to see what
it looked like. It was just a handwritten slip that read,
"$100 on #4." The number four horse, Luck Would Have
it, had come in last.

The horses walked around the track one time to cool
down and then the stable hands were back on the track,
holding the horses' bridles while the drivers climbed out
of the sulkies. The winning driver waved to the crowd.

My eyes were on Mason. He led Cooper off the track.
I followed Mason, but it took me some time to weave
through the crush of people. Visitors were hurriedly plac-
ing bets at the booth, buying snacks from the concession
areas, while staff wove through the crowd, using long,
pointed sticks to pick up trash tossed carelessly in the
dirt. Most of the trash on the ground was discarded betting tickets like the one I had picked up.

Abel was walking around the outside of the track just
three people away from me. I could see him because he
was a head taller than most people, laughing and pounding men on the back. He was a like a politician making
the rounds. I ducked behind a group of spectators so that
he couldn't see me.

A man in boots and a cowboy hat that seemed out of
place in Ohio said, "Abel, you always win. You always
seem to know where to place your bets."

"I always have a security deposit when I gamble," he said with a laugh.

The crowd closed around him, and I couldn't see him anymore. This was probably not the best time to talk to him about Rosemary or about his gambling.

I backed into the stable and bumped into someone. "I'm so sorry."

"Bailey."

I looked up and found Aiden standing behind me.

He frowned at me. "What are you doing here?"

"Oh! Aiden! Hi," I squeaked.

"I told you that I would check out the racetrack." He was wearing street clothes. He wasn't in his Sheriff's Department uniform. Instead he wore jeans with a flannel shirt over a T-shirt. I knew the flannel shirt was to hide his gun. Was his undercover garb the reason I hadn't picked him out in the crowd? Was Deputy Little dressed like a civilian, too?

"I know that," I said. "But you must have known I would want to see this through."

He sighed. "All right, but I'm the one who will speak to Abel just as soon as I can get close enough to him." He squinted in the sun. "He is a bit of a celebrity around here."

"He wins a lot of races."

"I got that impression."

I lowered my voice. "I don't think he wins by completely legal means."

Aiden's cell phone rang. He looked at the screen. "It's the sheriff. I have to take this, and I have only one bar here. I have to go closer to the parking lot for better reception."

"Go ahead," I said.

"You're not coming with me?" He searched my face.

"Right. I'll be in the stable. I'm going to visit Cooper."

"Cooper?" Aiden asked.

"He's the horse I made friends with the last time I was here."

"Of course you made friends with an animal while you were here." He shook his head. "Don't go far, please." He pushed his way through the crowd toward the entrance with his phone up against his ear.

I stepped inside the stable and let out a sigh of relief. It was much quieter inside the building. Stable hands led the horses for the next race out of the building, but Mason wasn't among them. I knew he had been there, though, because Cooper was back in his stall.

Cooper hung his head over his pen. I scratched him on the nose. "You remember me, don't you? I didn't forget you either." I reached into my coat pocket and pulled out a carrot. "I brought you a treat."

The horse ate the carrot out of my hand and then laid his cheek in my palm. I murmured to him for a few minutes. None of the staff stopped me. Then I heard over the loudspeaker the call for the next race. When I looked around, I was alone with the few horses left in the building. I wondered what the sheriff was saying to Aiden that was taking so long. I knew it couldn't be anything good. Sheriff Marshall must be livid that Aiden was leaving the department.

"You're not in this race, Cooper?"

He nuzzled my hand.

"I suppose I should have brought two carrots."

"I thought I saw you wandering around the track earlier," an oily yet familiar voice said. Abel sauntered into the stable. "When I saw Deputy Aiden at the front gate, I knew you were here."

I spun around. "Shouldn't you be at the track? A new race is about to start. You are poised to win again."

He grinned. "I almost always win."

"How often do you win your bets here?" I rested my hand on the top of Cooper's stall, close to the latch that kept it closed.

He scowled. "What do you mean?"

"You said you don't *always* win. I was wondering what the percentage of losses is." I paused. "Do you sometimes choose not to bet on the right horse because you don't want to look overly suspicious?"

He narrowed his eyes at me. "What are you getting at?"

I shrugged as if it was no big deal. "Just that if you won every race, people would be on to you. They'd realize that you were the one who was causing the accidents on the track to bend the odds in your favor. It's interesting the accidents have only affected the Amish horse races."

He chuckled. "That's a great theory."

"I don't think it's a theory. It's fact. I should have known you were connected to this place when I saw you and Amos together at the hardware store. My guess is he is the one you're paying to do his dirty work. As the owner of the track, he would have full access to every corner of the property, wouldn't he?"

Across from me, a stall door flew open, and Mason came out, holding a pitchfork as if he was going to run Abel through with it. "I knew you were behind it!"

I screamed, but with the race fully underway and the crowd so loud outside, I doubted that anyone heard me.

Abel held up his hands. "What's going on here?"

"I'm going to take from you what you took from me: your life." Mason shook.

"I didn't kill anyone. You're the one who did that," Abel said. "I saw you there that night. You left the pretzel shop just before I peeked inside and saw Rosemary's dead body. You're a murderer."

Mason licked his lips. "I didn't have any choice. I needed the medicine. I can't function without my medicine. I needed money for it."

"Oh, Mason, are you addicted to prescription pills?" I asked. It made sense in light of his desperate requests for money from his mother.

He held the pitchfork a little higher. "I need those pills. They make me feel normal! It's almost impossible to feel normal in my crippled state."

"How were you going to get money by killing Rosemary?" I asked quietly. Out of the corner of my eye, I noticed Abel edging to the back of the stable, searching for an escape route. I didn't want him to get away. He was partly to blame in all of this.

"Jill," Mason said.

I stared. "Isaac's girlfriend Jill?"

"She offered me money to kill Rosemary so that she and Rosemary's husband could get married. I took it. I had no choice." He took three steps closer to Abel, aiming the pitchfork prongs at the other man's throat. "And now I learn that you purposely caused the accident that ruined my entire life, so that you could win a stupid bet. You destroyed me for money."

Abel glared at him. "And you killed an innocent woman for money. We aren't all that different really."

I wished that someone would come into the stable. Why was this race taking so long? It had to be over soon, and then it would be quiet enough for someone to hear our shouts.

I fiddled with the latch on Cooper's stall as an idea formed. Neither Abel nor Mason noticed. I felt Cooper's nose on my hand.

"Can you help me out, buddy?" I whispered.

I opened the stall and jumped back. Cooper ran out and charged Mason.

Mason, who was already unsteady on his feet from his injury, fell over and dropped the pitchfork. I scooped it up and pointed it at Abel just as Mason had been doing. "You're not going to weasel your way out of this like you always do. I'll make sure of it this time."

He glared at me. "You will be surprised what I can get out of, Bailey King."

"Bailey," Aiden called.

I turned around and found Aiden and a whole host of spectators at the stable doors. An Amish man held Cooper by the bridle. I was relieved to see the horse was all right.

"Bailey?" Aiden asked. "What's with the pitchfork?"

"Deputy," I said, "I have made a citizen's arrest, but this isn't even a start on the number of people you will need to handcuff."

On the dirty stable floor, Mason bent over his injured leg and wept.

EPILOGUE

When I first moved to Ohio, an Amish neighbor said to me, "Don't like the weather? Wait an hour, and it will change." A month after the fateful visit to the race-track, it was a rare perfect spring day.

The day was made even more special because it was homecoming day for Hannah. Emily and Daniel had gone through all the necessary steps, and the county had awarded them custody of Hannah as Emily's biological daughter. There had been fear that Gideon Glick and his wife, Leslie Marin, would come forward and ask for custody, but in the end, Gideon agreed that Hannah would be better off with Emily and Daniel. Having grown up Amish, he said he knew that taking a child out of that environment would be difficult. The Keim family were celebrating with an early sixth birthday party for Hannah on the Christmas tree farm. Emily told me that she'd invited

Gideon and his wife to the party, but as far as I could see, they were not in attendance. I didn't know if that was good news or sad.

Charlotte stood at the cake table speaking to my grandmother. *Maami* was dressed in plain clothes, as she always was, but Charlotte wore a long denim skirt and a flower-printed blouse. She didn't wear a prayer cap, and her long red hair was gathered in a single red braid down her back. She was just dipping her toe into the world of English clothes, but having made her choice, she had an air of peace about her I had never seen before. Deputy Little smiled at Charlotte from across the lawn. The way he watched her made me miss Aiden more. He had left the day before to begin his six months of training to be a BCI agent. There was no more talk of marriage before he left. I wondered what the future held for us.

His last duties as a deputy for the Holmes County Sheriff's Department were buttoning up Rosemary Weiss's murder case, which included an astounding number of arrests. Mason was arrested for Rosemary's murder. Abel and Amos were arrested for gambling crimes and attempted murder related to the accidents they'd caused at the racetrack. Jill Penn was arrested for a contract killing, and from what I heard, it looked as if her marriage to Isaac Weiss was off. He had wanted to marry her, but murder didn't seem to sit well with him. All of those arrested were awaiting trial. However, I had heard that Abel and Amos were likely to be released on bail any day now.

Juliet, Reverend Brook, and Jethro were also at the party. Juliet held on to her husband's arm and happily chatted with Bishop Yoder and his wife, Ruth. Jethro pranced around the grounds with a white, polka-dotted bow around his neck as if he thought the party was for him. In fact, I was sure the little pig thought it was. It would be a great shock to Jethro to learn he was not always the center of attention.

However, at this party, the center of attention was Hannah. Emily glowed as she watched Hannah play with the other Amish children from the district. She cradled the new baby in her arms and looked up at me. "I can't believe I have another girl, and I'm so very glad. I know that Daniel wanted a son, but I wanted a sister for Hannah." She looked down at the baby. "Olive and Hannah will be the best of friends. I want for them what I didn't have with my own sister."

Another buggy pulled into the driveway. It seemed that every Amish person in the district was coming to Hannah's party. Emily's eyes went wide, and she stood up. "That's Esther's buggy," she whispered.

A moment later, Esther climbed out of the buggy. She tethered her horse to a tree, because all the hitching posts were taken, and walked over to us.

Emily held tiny Olive close to her chest. "Esther, I am glad you came, but what are you doing here?"

Even though she was trying to hide her awkwardness, Esther stiffened as she glanced around the farm. "I came to meet my nieces."

Emily's face broke into the most beautiful smile, and with her new baby in her left arm, she held out her right hand to her sister. "Let me introduce you."

Esther took her hand and let Emily walk her over to Hannah.

Grandma Leah walked over to me, leaning on her cane, and watched the scene unfold as Esther waved to Hannah.

Lois hurried over and started to translate Emily's words

into sign language for Hannah. Her red-purple hair gleamed in the sunlight.

"The Lord's words say that *Gott* will work for the *gut* of those who love him," Grandma Leah said. "That means *gut* things will come out of everything. Even bad things. Not that we wish for bad things. Our hope is to make as few mistakes as possible and live a righteous life, but we will all fall short of the glory of *Gott*. When we do, he will be there to catch us and guide us back onto the right path. How Hannah came into the world may not be the way we would have liked, but she's here now and deserves to be cared for. She's a child of *Gott*, too."

Tears sprang to my eyes as Hannah wrapped her small arms around Esther in a hug. "She is a very special child of God, I would say."

Then the sisters, both young and old, sat on a blanket together. Hannah sat cross-legged on the blanket and held out her arms to Emily. Emily gently set the baby in her arms. Hannah looked up at me with the most radiant smile I had ever seen. Then I glanced at her mother and saw the matching smile.

Maami's Easy At-Home Lemon Drops

Ingredients
Baking spray
1½ tablespoons lemon juice
1 teaspoon lemon extract
2 cups sugar
½ cup light corn syrup
½ cup water
3 or 4 drops lemon food coloring
Confectioner's sugar
Candy thermometer

Directions
Spray a cookie sheet and kitchen scissors with baking spray.

Mix the lemon juice and lemon extract in a bowl.

Combine the sugar, corn syrup, and water in a saucepan over medium heat. Stir until the sugar is dissolved. When the sugar has dissolved, stop, place a candy thermometer in the saucepan, and keep the mixture on the burner until it reaches 300°F.

When the mixture hits the correct temperature, remove it from the heat and let it rest for 1 minute.

Add the lemon juice, lemon extract, and food coloring to the sugar mixture, and stir.

Working quickly, pour the mixture onto the cookie sheet.

When the mixture is just cool enough to handle but still soft, pull off pieces and roll them into ropes. Use the kitchen scissors to cut the ropes immediately into drops.

Roll the still-warm lemon drops in confectioner's sugar. Enjoy!

Please read on for an excerpt from *Marriage Can Be Mischief*, the next Amish Matchmaker Mystery by Amanda Flower.

CHAPTER ONE

Lois Henry pulled at her multi-colored, geometric-patterned blouse. "It's so hot this evening, I feel like I'm baking bread inside my shirt. When will this concert be over? Is it running long, or is that just me, because I'm perspiring like Jethro the pig in the noonday sun?" She fanned her red face with the concert program.

I patted away the dew on my forehead. "Pigs don't actually sweat," I said. "That's why they wallow in mud and water on hot days to cool down."

"I didn't say it for an animal husbandry lesson," she said. "Did you see what this humidity is doing to my hair?"

I turned on the lawn chair to have a better look at her. The chair, which, according to Lois, was "vintage" and "a steal" at the local flea market, felt like it could go at any second. I stopped twisting.

Lois's typically upright, red-purple, spiky hair dropped to the left side of her head. I didn't say it, but it reminded me of a grassy field that had been bent over in the wind. "Your hair looks different from normal." I felt this was the nicest way to put it.

"It's going to take me an hour to set my hair again after this. People really don't know what it takes to look like I do."

I certainly didn't. Lois's appearance and mine could not be more different if we tried. Although we were the same age, nearing the end of our sixties, and had grown up on the same county road, our upbringings had been very different. I grew up Amish, and Lois grew up *Englisch*. Even so, we were and remained the best of friends.

However, I knew that, to many people, we appeared to be an odd pair. I wore a plain dress, sensible black tennis shoes, and a prayer cap. My long white hair was tied back in an Amish bun. Lois wore brightly colored clothes, chunky costume jewelry, and heavy makeup, and she had that striking haircut.

She leaned across the arm of her chair, and the seat made a dangerous creaking sound. "Did I sweat my eyebrows off?"

I shook my head "*Nee*, they are still there." I did not add that they were looking a tad more wobbly than usual. It was certainly due to the trickle of sweat running down her forehead. I had to agree with Lois that, on such a hot night, the concert should have been over an hour ago. We weren't the only ones who thought so; several couples and families had gotten up and left.

Lois shifted her folding lawn chair, and I found myself wincing at the creak and rattle the chair made. I didn't want her to be hurt if the chair gave way and Lois hit the ground. We were still on the grass square in the middle of the village of Harvest, but any time you fall at our age, it can leave a mark.

"Careful, Lois, that chair is not as sturdy as you think it is," I warned.

She bounced up and down in the chair. "Don't be silly. It's as sturdy as they come. They don't make chairs like this anymore." With her final bounce, there was a loud crack, and Lois and the chair went down.

I jumped out of my seat. "Lois, are you all right?"

The children playing the instruments in the concert froze and stopped playing. The band leader had his arms frozen in the air. Lois waved from the grass. "Keep playing—I'm fine."

Several people from nearby blankets and chairs ran over to us. Two *Englisch* men helped Lois to her feet.

"Are you hurt?" I asked.

"Nothing more than a bruised ego, and that stopped really bothering me twenty years ago." She smiled. "If I became upset every time I fell over, I would be in a perpetual state of nerves." She smiled at everyone who'd rushed over to help. "Thank you, you're all too kind. Now run back to your seats, so the concert can continue."

After they were out of earshot, Lois said, "Because we need to move this concert along. It's going on forever." Lois rubbed the side of her leg. "I spoke too soon about not being hurt."

"What's wrong? Should we find a doctor or nurse?"

"No, no, it's nothing as serious as all that. I just banged up my knee."

"Let me at least give you some ice for the knee, and

here—" I moved my chair next to her. "Sit in this until I get back."

My chair was as unstable as hers had been, but it had to be better than standing if her knee was bothering her. "Stay there. I will find the ice."

She rubbed her knee. "We can only hope that, by the time you return, this concert will be over. I don't know how much more of this I can take."

"All right," I said. "Please stay there, and I will find some ice."

On the far side of the square there was a small concession booth. I thought I would start there. If I didn't have any luck, then I would run across the street to the Sunbeam Café and grab a cup of ice from Lois's granddaughter, Darcy Woodin. But I didn't want to scare Darcy until I knew how badly Lois was hurt.

"Excuse me," I said to a man waiting in line. "Can I just ask for some ice? My friend fell out of her chair and bumped her knee."

The *Englischer* stepped aside. "I saw her go down. It looked like a nasty tumble."

The girl inside the food trailer handed me a cup of ice and a fistful of paper towels.

I smiled at her. "*Danki*, this is so kind of you."

"I'd hurry to get back to your friend if I were you. Margot Rawlings is headed this way, and she has her eyes right on you," the girl said.

I looked over my shoulder and found that she was right. I thanked her again.

"Millie Fisher, can I have a word with you?" Margot called. Her voice had an amazing ability to carry over the struggling notes of the middle school band.

I sighed and stopped in the middle of the grass. Margot walked up to me and put her hands on her hips. Margot was an *Englisch* woman who was just a few years younger than I was. I had known her most of my life. Although she was *Englisch* like Lois, their appearances were very different. Margot wore her hair short like Lois, but it was a pile of soft curls, which she had a habit of patting and pulling at when she was frustrated. She also had a much simpler wardrobe of jeans and plain T-shirts. She was a no-nonsense woman who was doing everything within her power to make sure that Harvest, Ohio, became the number one tourist destination in Amish Country.

The concert that night was one of her events. Throughout the summer, she had been hosting a concert on the village square every Friday evening at seven. I had heard from Lois that Margot thought it would bring people back into the village in the evening. Typically everything in Harvest closed at five or six, even in the summer. The concerts were popular, and tonight's had drawn a nice crowd.

Margot tapped her sneaker-clad foot in the grass. "What is this I hear about Lois Henry falling out of her chair?"

I held up the cup of ice. "She's not seriously hurt. We're taking care of it."

"What happened?" she asked.

"Lois found the chairs at the flea market for what she calls a steal. I think they were past their prime when she got them. I'm very careful when I sit on them, and I try not to breathe while sitting there."

Margot shook her head, and her curls hopped in place. I would never say it to her, but her signature curls always reminded me a little bit of baby bunnies hopping up and down on the top of her head. I didn't think that was an observation she would appreciate.

"Lois and her flea market finds. Her house is just one big warehouse."

I made no comment because Lois was my friend, but at the same time, I agreed with Margot. Lois had an addiction to things, furniture in particular. She loved to collect it, but she really didn't have anywhere to put the acquisitions in her two-bedroom rental house on the edge of downtown. On the other hand, she lived alone, her collection wasn't hurting anyone, and it made her happy. It wasn't as if she was a hoarder. Lois was a collector.

Also, she was one of the most giving people I knew. If a friend came to her and she heard that they needed a piece of furniture, she wouldn't think twice about giving it to them, no matter what it had cost her to buy it.

Margot looked over her shoulder at Lois. "It's not the village's fault that she had a defective chair."

"I don't believe she was blaming anyone for the accident."

"Hmm."

"And if you are so concerned about Lois, why not go speak to her? She's sitting right over there. I was taking her this ice, which is melting quickly in the heat."

"Well, I am glad she's all right. I will check on Lois later. You know that when there is an event on the square, I'm very busy. I always have to run from one thing to the next."

I pressed my lips together to keep myself from saying something I would regret. I still thought she might ask *Lois* how Lois was doing.

"But I am glad I caught you alone. I very much wanted a word with you in private."

I shook the ice in the cup and listened for the rattle. I just wanted to know it had not all completely melted away. I had no idea what Margot would want with me. As an Amish person, I could not be on any of her village committees, and I did not offer goods or services that could be part of the programming on the square. I was a quilter by trade and a matchmaker by inclination. I subsisted by making and selling quilts for local shops and custom orders, and I helped the young Amish men and women in the county to find their matches. I have had this gift since I was a small child. I knew in my heart when two people were right for each other. I knew when two people were wrong for each other, too.

I did not charge for the matchmaking. It was a gift from *Gott*, and I knew it was not meant to be a business venture, but an adventure in true love.

"What can I help you with, Margot? I hope you're not planning to ask me to join any of your committees."

"When was the last time you saw Uriah Schrock?"

"Uriah?" I asked. That was not what I'd expected her to ask. I thought for a moment. As a child, I had gone to the Amish schoolhouse with Uriah. When we were young, he had been sweet on me, but I only had eyes for Kip Fisher. Kip and I were married young and had many wonderful years together, but then he passed away when he was only forty-seven.

Today Uriah was the groundskeeper of the village square, and that made Margot his boss. If anyone should know where he was, it would be Margot.

"Yes, he was supposed to be here today for setup as always, but he never showed. I called the shed phone at the farm where he's been renting a room, and there was no answer."

My stomach dropped. That wasn't like Uriah at all. He was typically a very responsible man. He would not ignore his work.

"I just wondered if he said anything to you about going back to Indiana. I know the two of you are special friends." She narrowed her eyes at me when she said that last part.

I pressed my lips together and willed myself not to blush. I was far too old for blushing. I did not like the idea that people in the village were saying that Uriah and I were "special friends." I wasn't sure what that meant, but I surely did not like the sound of it. Special or not, he was my friend, and it worried me that he had not shown up for work or told Margot where he was. That was not like him at all.

"Where is he renting a room?" I asked, realizing for the first time that I didn't know where Uriah had been living since he'd returned to Ohio. Had I never asked him?

"He's renting from the Stollers. They are a young couple who live a couple of miles from here on an alpaca farm."

"Alpacas?" I asked. "I didn't know anyone was raising them."

"It became very popular in Ohio while you were away from the county."

Ten years after my husband died, I moved to Michigan for a decade to care for my ailing sister, Harriet. Only after she passed away did I return to Ohio.

I nodded, feeling a little surprised Uriah had never

mentioned that he lived on an alpaca farm. I would think that would be an interesting bit of information to share.

"So have you seen Uriah?" Margot started tapping her foot again. Apparently, it was taking me too long to give her a straight answer.

"*Nee*, I have not seen him in a few days. I expected to find him at the concert tonight."

I did not admit to her that I had been looking for him when I first arrived. Every time Lois and I came to the concert, Uriah made a point of stopping by our chairs and saying hello. Months ago, Uriah had asked me to go on a buggy ride with him. I had been so taken aback by the courting request that I declined. Some days, I wished I had the nerve to tell him I'd changed my mind.

Margot tugged on her curls, and like some miracle, every time she let them go they bounced perfectly back into place. "It's very poor form that he didn't tell me he wouldn't be here tonight. I had to scramble and tell everyone where to put the chairs and where the band should set up. In the past, I have always relied on Uriah to do that sort of thing. You don't think he found himself in some kind of trouble, do you?"

I folded my hands and held them tightly. "Trouble? What do you mean when you say trouble?"

"Could he have gotten lost or hurt? He's just not the type not to show up at work without a word. I expect that sort of behavior from the high schooler we hire during the summer to help out with the grounds, but not from someone like Uriah."

"*Nee*, it does seem odd." My worry grew. "There must be some sort of explanation. Maybe his buggy broke down."

"Maybe," Margot said. "I'd be lying if I didn't say that I'm even more concerned, knowing you haven't heard from him. I thought if anyone in the village would know where he is, it would be you. He's been saying recently that he thought he would move back to Indiana at the end of the summer. He would not leave without telling me first, though."

My chest tightened. "I did not know. When did he say that?"

"A week or two ago," she said, as if the exact date did not matter. "It was always his plan to go back. All his children and grandchildren are in Indiana. What could be keeping him here?"

"Nothing, I suppose." My voice trailed off.

"He said he would let me know when." Margot stopped tapping her foot. "So that I had plenty of time to find a replacement caretaker for the village square. That doesn't sound like someone who would just blow off work."

She was right, it didn't. "He would have told you when he was leaving. I'm sure it's something else." I hoped he would have told me, too, but I didn't say that.

She stood up. "Well, if you hear from him, let me know. Whatever his reason for not being here tonight, it had better be good. I will not be amused if he doesn't have a solid excuse."

I swallowed hard and watched her walk away. At the time, neither of us knew how *gut* his excuse was going to be.